DEATH by Diploma

CHALKBOARD OUTLINES BOOK ONE

KELLEY KAYE

RED ADEPT PUBLISHING
Unlocking New Worlds

Death by Diploma
Chalkboard Outlines™: Book 1
Copyright © 2016 by Kelley Kaye. All rights reserved.
First Print Edition: February 2016

ISBN-10: 1940215625
ISBN-13: 978-1-940215-62-4

Red Adept Publishing, LLC
104 Bugenfield Court
Garner, NC 27529
http://RedAdeptPublishing.com/

Cover and Formatting: Streetlight Graphics

No part of this book may be reproduced, scanned, or distributed in any printed or electronic form without permission. Please do not participate in or encourage piracy of copyrighted materials in violation of the author's rights. Thank you for respecting the hard work of this author.

This is a work of fiction. Names, characters, places, and incidents either are the product of the author's imagination or are used fictitiously, and any resemblance to locales, events, business establishments, or actual persons—living or dead—is entirely coincidental.

For my father, Donald W. Bowles. You're the one who started all this... :)
I miss you so much, Daddy!

You shall not know by what strange accident
I chanced on this letter.

—*The Merchant of Venice V.I.278–9*

PROLOGUE

Wednesday, August 26

Dearest Mickey,

Please, please write me back. Oh, I'm so worried these letters aren't finding their way to you. Our love deserves a chance to flourish. I know you think so too. You might want to give me one of your favorite quotes: "Don't cry because it's over, smile because it happened," but you don't really feel that way. I don't believe we're over, not yet.

Never forget how much I love you—let the colors remind you. Your Airborne Raquel Welch is thinking of you.

Love,
Marlena

MELVIN McMANUS RAN HIS FINGERS over the letter again. The paper was worn until almost transparent, and the care with which he folded it and inserted it back into its envelope made it seem as though he held a priceless jewel. He picked up his silver flask and stared at it. His left hand started to raise the flask to his lips, but then he flung it against the wall of the narrow room. He stood.

Melvin closed the small hidden doorway and routed the pipe maze to get to the basement. He stumbled through the basement door and lurched up the stairs, his bulky form weaving as if he weren't sure of finding the next step. Covering his mouth to muffle a hacking cough, Melvin stopped and listened. He really shouldn't be there after midnight—his shift only went from three to ten. But sometimes the work took much longer than that, because he hoped the care he took with the building might help the students stop taking this important time in their lives for granted. Many of them did take it for granted, though, and might end up like Melvin, navigating the world without any education or any real options. Those students didn't make any kind of connection between now and later.

He opened the door at the top of the stairs and continued through the gymnasium and into the hallway. The brown tile on the commons floor gleamed, and he thought of Adam and when he'd found the poor kid splayed out on the now-shiny floor. Melvin had been thrown out into the world so young, he'd never had to deal with schoolyard bullies as Adam had. Poor kid. Melvin ran a hand through his sparse gray hair, pondering.

As Melvin paced through the commons, steadying himself briefly against some lockers and again on a wall painted with a fierce-looking blue cat, he stopped to look at the sign above the main office: "Wildcats: Producing Proud and Productive Future Citizens." He'd seen that sign many times, but tonight, it made him long to become, finally, the future citizen he wished to be. He didn't know how much longer he could stand the waiting, even with his helpful hideout in the basement. He knew he was close, though—close to achieving his goal. Edward had said as much last week, and the closer Melvin got, the less he drank and the better he felt. He allowed the moment of anticipation to swell, forgot about the Wildcats sign, and almost ran back to the basement for the letters.

He sighed, an explosive whoosh that flattened his belly and whispered his nose hairs. *Almost there, almost there.* He looked at his hands, dirty and greasy from work but still strong. He thought of those hands in his younger years, how she'd kissed each of his fingertips as if they were precious. He remembered what those hands had felt like when they held her, and the dirt fell away like magic.

A muffled thump startled him out of his reverie. *Crap.* Melvin knew he was a little tipsy, not done with his work, and in the wrong part of the building to boot. He walked nonchalantly in the other direction, but he heard the thump again, followed by a tinkling noise like breaking glass. *Damn.* Maybe he should look. It could be a cat or other animal, and he'd hate to trap one in the school for the whole night.

He peeked through the windows of the main office and looked at the front desk, where the computer monitor flashed and he saw someone sitting. Melvin checked his watch: half past midnight. Oh, he hoped it wasn't who he thought, but he had to check. After unlocking the doors, he curved around the front counter to approach the left desk and stiffened when he saw who it was.

"Oh, I can see you didn't listen!" he exclaimed. "We have to make this stop. That's it; I don't care what happens. I'm gonna..."

Melvin heard a whoosh followed by a crack, and he felt his body fall as it slammed hard onto the shiny brown tiles.

Love goes toward love as schoolboys from their books
But love from love, toward school with heavy looks.

—*Romeo and Juliet II.2.176–8*

CHAPTER 1

Monday, August 24

EMMA LOVETT WALKED ONTO THE campus of Thomas Jefferson High School, in Pinewood, Colorado, at seven thirty in the morning. She looked at a wide expanse of the courtyard. Lovely. In all four corners, nubby split-log benches enclosed small gardens of pastel flowers, their soft scents floating through the morning air.

The center of the yard was divided into two sections, each marked off by cement benches encircling a monstrous and splendid old tree—walnut, she thought. Maybe oak. No, oak trees would leave little acorns all over the benches, and one would be unable to sit there without getting hard nuggets up one's butt. That would be an interesting excuse—no, teacher, my homework isn't done because I have hemorrhoids.

She smiled at the image and let out a breath she hadn't realized she'd been holding. Whew—no allowing nerves to get the best of her! They're just kids, for Pete's sake. She hadn't signed on to fly the space shuttle, only to teach some kids how to diagram sentences and recognize iambic pentameter. Okay, that latter part could be hard. No, stop—she could do this. She rubbed her freckled nose, which already felt oily.

Emma gingerly touched the long brown hair hanging about her shoulders and smoothed her flowered skirt. Maybe she should have dressed more like the teachers she'd had growing up in Holly Hills—colorless dresses and a bun so tight it pulled one's face back toward one's ears. She took another deep breath and shook her head. No, this was her new life, and she was determined to be herself, act like herself, look like herself. Lifting her chin, she strolled toward the center of the courtyard as if she'd been doing this all her life.

A knot of boys stood in the corner where the cement yard met the tall brick wall of the school. As soon as they spied Emma, they let out a string of catcalls and wolf whistles that would do a construction worker proud. She was tempted to run for cover, but she called on her Southern upbringing and walked directly toward the pubescent crew.

"Good mornin', boys. How're y'all doing?"

The boys mumbled, embarrassed, clearly uncomfortable interacting with adults.

Only one, a medium-sized kid with a shock of bleached-blond hair, managed a red-faced, "Fine."

Emma continued, "I want to talk to you about the whole catcall thing. It's really awful. There are so many better ways to tell a nice girl you think she's pretty."

"Like what?" said a tall one in the back corner. He had pieces of metal poking out of several spots on his face and a T-shirt that read "Chicks hate me."

Instead of lecturing him on the dangers of infection from all the piercings, she launched into her maiden attempt at molding the young minds of the world. "Well, a sincere compliment, for starters—about her dress, her hair. Maybe a nice note that explains why you like her. And that should be aspects of her *personality* you like, guys! Ah don't know—flowers and chocolate are my personal favorites." With this sage advice, and without waiting for a response, she started for the blue steel double doors leading into the commons.

As Emma walked into the school building, she took another deep breath, inhaling the metallic smell of lockers that mingled with refrigerated air and floor wax. Not a pleasant combination, but so rife with nostalgia it might as well have been a donut shop. She'd only been to the district office for an interview on Friday—late hiring here—so this was her first time at the school. She'd had education classes at college before she arrived, and her student teaching had been an odd experience at an alternative school held in an office building in Holly Hills, so this was technically the first time she'd be teaching at a real school. Hoo-ee, that sounded so scary! It was all right though. She was so excited to start this part of her life, independent and making a difference, she felt as though she could do anything.

One of the boys from the group she had just spoken to ran up beside her. Up close, she noticed that his black hair had a distinctive streak of white, making him look sort of like a skunk, though she knew better than to point that out to him.

"What if... what happens if she says she doesn't like me?"

The question and the yearning behind it sounded a lot more like what she knew was true about teenaged boys. They wanted love but had no inkling of what to do if they found it.

"The right one won't ever say that," Emma promised, a smile building on her face.

For a moment, the boy looked as though he wanted to say something else. Instead, he bolted back toward the doors that separated him from his friends.

Well, that had gone okay—her first official teacher/student exchange. No one had flipped her off, and she hadn't assigned any detention. Did detention still exist? She thought it must, although with her general lack of preparation to be here, how would she know? She turned back toward the interior commons, ready to find her classroom.

The interior commons was as open as the courtyard, with high ceilings and tall windows framing double doors on both ends. Rows of skinny royal-blue lockers lined the walls on either side, with a renegade door here and there between sets of lockers; two in the back were labeled Gym. The right and left walls of the commons had doors labeled Main Office and Athletic Office, respectively. Hallways extended from all four corners of the space, giving the effect of a giant H. On the map, anyway. Which wouldn't keep her from getting lost. Visualize the H—how would that help? She wondered if getting lost on the first day would be an omen. *No, I don't believe in omens. That rabbit's foot in my purse is there only because petting soft things calms my nerves. Really.*

She skimmed across gleaming brown tiles toward the gym, turned right at the far corner, and walked down the hall. Her map gave the room numbers: 100, 102, 103... and 104 was hers. She walked into the room and gazed around, dry mouthed. The desks stood at attention, and an empty wooden bookshelf begged for literary redemption. The teacher's desk—*my desk*—squatted in the right-hand corner facing the student chairs, and she tiptoed forward, reverently touching everything she passed.

This room alone made the journey of the past few years—leaving her jerk of a husband, going back to school, moving thousands of miles away from home, getting a scary new job—worth it. Upon reaching the big desk—*my desk!*—Emma settled into the rickety wooden teacher chair, spread her arms wide for the "this is my throne" ritual—hands clasped behind her head, eyes closed—and heaved an enormous sigh of contentment.

A knock at her open door made her eyes pop open.

"Hellooo? Hi there!" The hand that had knocked was attached to a man. Probably in his sixties, with thinning gray hair and watery blue eyes, he wore a gray jumpsuit. "I'm Melvin, the janitor for this side of the building."

Emma jumped from her chair and hopped over to shake his hand. "Hello, Melvin. So nice to meet you! You're the first adult I've seen here today. Are y'all gonna be greeting me every mornin'?"

He ducked his head. "Wow. I like your accent. It matches the flowers in yer skirt." He colored, as if the comparison embarrassed him. He continued past Emma, eyes roaming across the corners of the room and lighting on the garbage can next to the desk. "Nah, I won't be here every mornin'. My shift goes from three to ten every night, but at the start of the school year, first week or so, I like to make the trip in early, just to make sure school's goin' off right." He smiled and peeked into the garbage can, double-checking it.

Emma spread her arms, figuratively embracing the room. "Melvin, it looks great! Not a speck of dust or dirt to be found, and I am rarin' to make some use of it educatin' the youth of our future. I'm so happy you take such pride in your work. Maybe it'll rub off on the students."

He smiled again and shrugged. "You know what I always say? 'What's the point of doing anything if yer not gonna do it right?'"

Tears sprang to Emma's eyes. She quickly turned away from Melvin and ran a hand over the desk, pretending to care how clean it was. "My dad said that too."

"Your dad's a smart man," said Melvin. "Have a great first day! I'm sure I'll see you again all this week." He tipped an imaginary hat and shuffled from the classroom.

Emma's eyes followed his bulky form as he lumbered away. "He was," she said to the air. "The smartest."

In preparation for her first day, Emma pulled some supplies from her bag, including a college-ruled notebook with spanking-clean pages ready to be defaced by a fountain pen. Melvin reminding her of her dad had sent her off on a memory tour, and the new notebook had her thinking of her best friend, Hannah. Friends since birth practically, she and Hannah had always started the new school year with a beautiful new notebook. They always christened them with their names in oh-so-neat handwriting, some years with hearts and flourishes, some without. The ritual was symbolic of starting a new year with all its expectations. *Oh, Hannah, if you could see me now. I'm a teacher!*

She looked at the students' names on her roll sheets: American Lit, two classes of Sophomore Lit, and Speech. Emma's plan for the first day was simply to teach her students some get-to-know-each-other name games, and she wanted to write names down as the students played. She felt learning their names as quickly as possible was essential for connecting with them.

As she wrote her name—Ms. Lovett, no flourishes—on the notebook cover, the most un-teacher-like woman Emma had ever seen appeared in the doorway, hands raised up on either side of the frame. She stood at least five feet eleven inches tall, with blond bobbed hair dropping to a sleek angle along her chin. Perfect makeup emphasized her smooth fair skin and almond-shaped blue eyes. A slim red suit coat was buttoned over her black top and calf-length black skirt, her long legs ending with pumps that definitely sported a stiletto heel. Her of-course-she'd-worn-braces smile bathed the whole room in its sparkling light. She looked almost exactly like Hannah would have if she'd ever paid more than twelve dollars for a haircut and worn anything but jeans and Keds. They both had the same self-assurance though. Emma could already tell she would like this woman.

"Hey there," the woman said languidly, without Emma's Southern drawl. Her smile widened. "I'm here for your indoctrination."

The grin was so contagious Emma couldn't help but grin back. "You are? Well." She threw her own arms up in a V and struck a queenly pose. "I'm feeling real 'indoctrinable' at this particular moment. Teach me your ways, O Wise One."

The woman came over to the desk and plopped down on the corner with a grace that belied the word "plopped." "That's it! I just was curious to see if you knew what the word 'indoctrinate' meant. You're in!" She stuck out her hand. "I'm Leslie Parker, head of the English department, defender of the second-semester word, and crusader against PDAs in the hallways."

Emma returned the greeting. "I'm Emma Lovett, one of your new departmentees. Is that a word, 'departmentee'? Now... the meaning of 'second-semester' word is patently unmistakable. Conspicuously evident. Alarmingly discernible. But PDAs? I thought those were electronic organizers, like a pre-Blackberry datebook."

Leslie laughed and shook Emma's hand. Emma shook back vigorously—no shrinking Southern violet, she.

"No, here at TJ High, PDA stands for public display of affection. You've never seen anything that makes you *really* want to hurl until you've seen two sixteen-year-olds playing tonsil tag in the middle of a crowded hallway."

"Oh. Yuck." *She even sounds like Hannah, although Hannah would have called it "tonsil hockey." I love this woman already!* "But a crusade? Shouldn't you be more worried about—oh, I don't know—stamping out ignorance?"

"That's classroom work. Hallway work's important too." Leslie paced, bobbed hair swaying as she shook her fists. "I did it, yes. During my junior and senior year, I was routinely impaled against my locker by the tongue of one Timothy Andrews. I followed my fool tongue, married the bastard four years later, and *here* I am! A divorced, bitter old maid at the age of thirty-seven. No, ignorance is bliss, but PDAs can never be unlearned and must be stopped!" Leslie took a huge breath and seemed to step down from an invisible soapbox.

"So how do you stop them?" Emma asked.

Leslie made a dismissive gesture. "Oh, well, I usually bonk 'em upside the head as I walk by."

The image made Emma laugh. "My friend Hannah hates when

people neck in public too. Does that stop it, thunkin' them upside the head?"

"Oh, I don't know." Leslie sighed. "I keep hoping if I do it often enough, they'll get tired of biting their tongues and just stop." She started toward the door and held it open for Emma to follow.

"I thought I saw a chunk of tongue lying in the hall as I came in. Ick."

"But worth it if I can stop one poor impressionable girl from following her face. Your friend Hannah, a fan of discretion even at a young age, sounds like the original Southern woman. A debutante, perhaps?"

Emma's laugh was almost a yelp. "I don't think Holly Hills, South Carolina, is much for debutantes. Wooden shacks maybe, and Hannah's more inclined to wear overalls than ball gowns. But she feels the same way as you. Said that fun stuff should be only for the ones havin' the fun."

"Ah, smart girl. So, Emma Lovett, are you ready for the fifty-cent tour of Thomas Jefferson High, our lovely institute of erudition?" Leslie waved her through the door.

Emma smoothed her blouse and ran her fingers through her hair. "I'm ready. Erudite me!" She giggled. "I must really be nervous, because all I can think about is how dirty that sounded."

"Oh, Emma Lovett, I think I'm going to like you. I'll erudite you. 'They that thrive well take counsel of their friends.'"

"Shakespeare. *Venus and Adonis.*" *I'll never tell her that's one of maybe two Shakespeare pieces I know, and that's only because of the Adonis part.*

"Oh, Emma Lovett, I take it back. I *know* I'm going to like you!"

The two women walked down the hallway toward the heart of the building, comparing "second-semester" vocabulary words and keeping an eye out for any PDA.

CHAPTER 2

THERE WERE VERY FEW KIDS in the commons, and apparently none of them felt the urge to make out at such an early hour, so Leslie kept her hands to herself while leading Emma toward the office. A large blue feline bared its teeth at them from its position on the wall by the gym. A sign about proud and productive Wildcats hung over the entrance to the office, and Leslie jumped and hit it with her hand as they walked through the door. How she landed on those heels was a mystery to Emma.

"What'd you do that for?"

"When you first learned to drive, did you ever hit the car roof when you drove through a yellow light?" Leslie asked.

"Well, sure. Actually, we kissed our hand first then hit the roof. It was supposed to keep you from being in an accident the next time you ran a yellow." Emma's face colored. "Ah do it still, if you want the truth."

"Well, I hit the sign to keep from being in an accident when entering the office."

"Oh my. What kind of accident can you get into here?"

Leslie wiggled her eyebrows like Groucho Marx. "Oh, I dunno. You can get buried in junk mail. Anger a secretary. Be forced to communicate with a coach—that's my personal horror. C'mon, I'll show you the teachers' lounge."

They walked around a long white rectangular counter. Behind it were two big triangular desks covered with office paraphernalia: phones, computers, trays overflowing with paper and mail. The one on the right, closest to the counter, had the long side facing front, apparently for kids to approach. The chairs were in back, on either side of the point. The left desk had the point in front with chairs on either side, computers and phones arranged there. File cabinets lined the long side, and Emma saw two stairs just beyond them. The ceiling was lower here than in the commons. The office chairs that bumped up to the desks looked a lot more comfortable than the one Emma had in her room, but... it was her very own room!

The two women continued on around the counter. At the rear side of the office, two steps led up to a large open area full of round tables and chairs, with three long couches against the back walls. The walls were covered in papers: sign-up lists for chaperoning duties, advertisements for graduate classes, phone numbers for potential babysitters. Black-and-white photographs of famous teachers—Maya Angelou, Ben Franklin, even Sting—covered a corkboard on the left wall. One of the couches was backed up against a huge window overlooking the courtyard. *Not the lobby of the Ritz, but a pretty decent setup.*

A few teachers were sitting at the tables, and loud, boisterous men surrounded the one in back. Leslie immediately steered Emma in an almost complete circle so they faced the wall to the right of the door—it was covered by a large wooden structure filled with square holes. They now had their backs to the tables.

"Shhh... just ignore them," she stage-whispered. "They're the Lounge Lizards."

Emma replied softly, "Lounge Lizards! They sound a little obnoxious, but isn't it mean to name 'em after scaly, cold-blooded creatures?"

"No, they call *themselves* that. It's like a little club—coaches only. The rule is that they can only talk about sports and sex. Be careful of the idiot in blue shorts—he's the superintendent's son."

Emma glanced surreptitiously at the group before returning her attention to the mailbox wall. Each hollow had a name pasted above it, and Emma was thrilled to find "Lovett" above a box in the middle. *Empty, but still a mailbox all my own.* Leslie went down two rows and pulled mail from her box.

A voice called from the other end of the room, "Hey, Parker!"

Leslie and Emma turned toward the voice, a deep growl that emanated from the burly, semibald giant who stood at the full table in the back. He wore long blue shorts that swished when he walked and a

Thomas Jefferson T-shirt that strained over his gut, but at least it was tucked in.

He slammed a pair of meaty palms on the table. "Who's the new chick? Why'ntcha *park-er* over here in my lap?"

The Lounge Lizards erupted into laughter, with the exception of one youngish-looking man who squirmed and looked uncomfortable. Emma had actually taken note of that man when she glanced at the table earlier. Not exactly Sting, but pretty cute.

Leslie lifted one corner of her lip. "Damn! An accident! I must not have hit that sign hard enough." She pasted on a wide smile that looked more like a sneer and retorted, "That's interesting, Charlie. You made a play on words, otherwise known as a pun, and actually seemed to understand it."

The large man leered at her. "I understand *you,* Parker."

He high-fived the men on either side of him, all of whom wore some version of the basketball shorts/T-shirt/tennis shoes uniform. Emma looked at her skirt and blouse, which she liked very much, but... no fair! *How come these guys get to dress like Saturday morning?*

Leslie pulled Emma across the room to the Lounge Lizard table and stood with her fists digging into her sides, arms making triangles on either side of her body. She flung her head to the side, nose skyward, striking a pose like Joan of Arc.

"Really?" Leslie scoffed. "You understand me, do you? Do you understand me here with 'a gallant curtle-axe upon my thigh, a boar spear in my hand,' planning that 'thou shalt be whipped with wire and stewed in brine, smarting in lingering pickle'?" She turned her face to Emma, whispered "Double whammy—*As You Like It* plus *Antony and Cleopatra,*" and winked.

Charlie looked at her blankly. "Huh?"

The younger man snickered. "I think that means she's planning to kick your ass."

The other coaches laughed at that until silenced by a black look from Charlie.

He got up and pulled Emma into the seat next to him. He had a brown fuzz of hair on his ears, close-set dark eyes with a unibrow that traveled from one corner of his face to the other, a large hooked nose, and thin lips. He pursed them, and his eyebrows made a V as he pulled out a look one assumed was created to show interest and concern. "No, really. Tell us about yourself."

Emma shot a look toward Leslie, who shrugged in an "It's too late; you're on your own" gesture. "Well, Ah don't know anything about sports. And what Ah know about sex, Ah'm not tellin'."

Only the guy at the end of the table smiled, the rest cowed by Charlie. Or maybe she wasn't that funny.

"Ain't that a bitchin' accent!" exclaimed the Lizard. "Are you Southern?"

"What a good guess. What class did you say you teach?"

"Well," Charlie tried a humble face and failed, "I have basic PE classes most of the day, but this semester I also have Advanced Strategies of Golf. That one's a killer!"

Emma's eyebrows went up. "I can imagine."

Charlie's ham-handed attempt at seduction was interrupted when a woman entered the lounge and stopped at the first row of mailboxes. Her lips were pursed, and she walked with purpose. Emma didn't get a chance to see her face. The new woman was somewhat tall but looked taller due to her beehive hairdo dyed an unnaturally vivid shade of red. Her glasses were on a chain, and she wore a brown pencil skirt and a white oxford blouse with a Peter-Pan collar. Emma couldn't resist looking down—sure enough, serviceable brown oxfords. *Now this is a real teacher. Just like I remember! I wonder if she sleeps under her desk like we always figured.*

Someone from the Lizard table coughed into his fist, a mangled choking that sounded an awful lot like "electrolysis." Charlie jumped up off his chair and walked a complete circle around the woman, his nose almost touching the sides of her face as he searched her cheeks and chin. The woman raised her hand, flicked him on the forehead, and stalked out of the room.

Emma thought her eyes would bug out of her head as she turned to Leslie for explanation. Leslie picked Emma up off the chair and motioned her toward the door.

Leslie leaned in, murmuring, "It's probably best you know now. That's Martha Bonaventure, a social studies teacher. Rumor has it that

Martha was once a bearded lady at the circus." She glared at the back table on their way out. "The Lounge Lizards are shameful about it. They search her for facial hair, and sometimes Charlie stands on the table and acts like a ringmaster when she comes in."

"That's awful!" cried Emma.

"I know. Like I said—superintendent's son. Gets away with murder. Sometimes she gets back at him though," Leslie said. "Besides social studies, she's also the newspaper editor. Once she had his head Photoshopped onto a tightrope walker's body and printed the picture in the school paper."

"Wait, wait, let me guess the headline—'He's Wound Too Tight for the Tightrope'?"

"Actually, it was 'Charlie Cherishes His Sequined Tights.'" Leslie grinned. "I think next issue, Martha's going to Photoshop his head onto a clown's body. You know, 'Clown Charlie Disproves Myth About Big Feet.'" At that, she threw her head back in glee, clapping, and the two women made their way through the main office.

As they walked back through the commons, which was filling with students, Emma was treated to another odd sight. Well, not odd for this place, she decided. A tall man with wavy blond hair and a handlebar mustache was coming their way. On a skateboard. His long-sleeved blue shirt was rolled up to the elbows, tie flung around his neck and fluttering a little as he rode by. He passed them with a cheery smile and a "Hi, ladies!"

Leslie waved and continued on as though they hadn't just passed a grown man in dress clothes on a skateboard. Emma clutched her arm, mouth open, shaking her head.

"That's the principal," was Leslie's nonchalant remark. "Haven't you met him?"

Emma shook her head.

"Oh, that's right. You interviewed with the vice principal." Leslie shrugged. "You'll meet him later. His name is Nathan Farrar."

Emma waved as he wheeled past. "Hmm. Well, Ah think *Ah'm* the one who's going to get the education here. That's all right though. You know, Ah haven't even taught a class yet!"

"Yes, that's right. New girl, emergency credentials, no real classroom experience." Leslie's eyebrows rose to meet her hairline. "Can't wait to hear how *that* turns out. You go, girl. What's your first hour, American Lit?"

Emma nodded. "Then Sophomore Lit and more Sophomore Lit, followed by all students' favorite subject—lunch. Guess Ah'll see you then?"

"Until then..." Leslie intoned sonorously. "May the Force be with you."

They parted ways, and Emma proceeded toward her first totally-in-charge, no-help-from-education-books, do-or-die class ever.

CHAPTER 3

THE HALLWAY ON THE TOP-RIGHT corner of the "H" held English classrooms and ended at the library. At the back of the library was a mini-teachers' lounge, and Emma took her brown-bag lunch there to join Leslie, who was already seated and chomping voraciously—yet delicately—at an unidentified school lunch. The food sat in the square and circular compartments of a yellow plastic tray. More nostalgia. Emma remembered many days of eating mystery meat. She and Hannah had made a game of trying to identify foods that came in unnatural colors, which was much more fun than actually *eating* said rainbow food. Seeing Leslie so obviously enjoying herself made Emma smile.

"So what's the special today? Macaroni and something masquerading as cheese?" Emma asked.

Leslie said nothing, just pushed her tray and her fork over for Emma to taste.

Emma tasted. "Oh my! That's fabulous. What is it?"

"Fettuccine carbonara." Leslie leaned back and patted her stomach with satisfaction.

"Fettuccine carbonara? Have I died and gone to a country club? Ah think the most sophisticated food they had at my high school cafeteria was pigs in a blanket!"

"Oh, they have that here. For the *students*. Matter of fact, I'm pretty sure there are subliminal control messages in the 'pigs'—students are always way more mellow on pigs-in-a-blanket days." She shook her head, took another forkful, and spoke around a mushy mouthful. "No, I have an 'in' in the kitchen—Mrs. Albert, head cook. Looks sort of like a pit bull. Mr. Albert looks a little like a St. Bernard, but some miracle of genetic mingling created their daughter, Sara Albert, one of the great beauties of our school." Leslie took a gigantic forkful and somehow kept it all off of her clothes. Emma wondered how she did that.

Emma sneaked another bite. "So what, did you give Sara an A in Mythology? Or wait, let me guess. Does this have something to do with your crusade?"

"Yup." Leslie swallowed. "Thanks to me, the captains of the football team, the basketball team, and the tennis team are now missing sections of their tongues—and Sara Albert isn't approached by oversexed men anymore."

"My, my, my. I bet Sara loves you for that."

Leslie twisted noodles on her fork, leaned back, and sucked them down. "Yeah, well... Sara doesn't know how to make fettuccine carbonara."

The two women were interrupted by a PA announcement that was so loud and obnoxious, it about scared Emma off her chair.

"Attention, students! Mr. Dixon is running a special in the library. Check out a literary classic today, and it's not due back for four weeks instead of two. Avoid late fees and sharpen your brain at the same time. Repeat: Bluelight Special in the library."

"Who was *that*?" asked Emma, shaking herself.

Leslie continued forking down lunch as if she hadn't heard anything. "That's one of the secretaries. So, Emma, from where do you hail?"

"From where do I hail?" Emma's head tilted in puzzlement as she opened her boring brown lunch—a ham sandwich. "Is that the Colorado way of asking me where I'm from?"

Leslie flicked a manicured hand in the air. "Oh, you know, it's the 'no ending your sentences in prepositions' thing. I know it's not an *actual* grammar rule, but there are some things I just cannot abide. I mostly just hate the 'at' thing. 'Where's she AT?' 'Where's it AT?' Drives me crazy. I know starting a sentence with 'from' sounds lame, but it's a funny example I use to teach my students the concept of prepositions and their functions."

A teaching example? "Oh, great... a lesson plan!" Emma felt excitement shine from her face. She needed some of those, as was obvious after her first class, when she'd been told by a thick-necked male student that she "didn't really need to teach anything as long as she kept on a'lookin' so *fine*." She smiled at Leslie. "I know, I always hated those stranded prepositions. There's a song, you know, to memorize them, but I always liked the idea of 'anything a plane can do to a cloud.'"

"Oh, yes, Grasshoppah. Or anything a cat can do to a couch. I know, I know, there are times when you have to strand your prepositions, otherwise you sound like Yoda, but many more times when you should not leave them out there like a deserted-island survivor," Leslie said. "So I tell them this cool story. My brother met this girl once and asked her where she was from. She replied—a total snoot, this one—'I'm from someplace where we don't end our sentences in prepositions.' My brother paused for a minute then said, 'Oh. I'm sorry. Excuse me. Where are you from, *you snooty bitch?*'"

Emma gasped. "You say that in your *classroom?*"

"Oh, yeah. Total teachable moment." Leslie nodded, amused. "Ask any one of my students—they'll tell you the rule about not ending your sentences in prepositions. They may not remember any literary storylines or the definition of a gerund after they graduate, but they'll never ask where that Shakespeare guy was born *at*."

The two women beamed at each other. Leslie took half of the boring ham sandwich and shared more of her pasta. They shoveled in the rest of their lunch. Well, Emma shoveled. Leslie looked more like she was having lunch with the Queen Mother, only faster.

"So I have to ask," Emma said slyly, "are you going to show me where all the important stuff in this school is at?"

Leslie slapped Emma's hand. "Only if you'll tell me where you're from."

They got up to take Leslie's tray back to the lunchroom and headed through the library to the cafeteria. It was an interesting layout, because the small lounge in the back led straight into the stacks, and the edges of the shelves were peppered with "No Food! No Drink!" signs. How the heck did one get from the library entrance to the lounge without having food and drink? Emma looked into the bottom of her lunch bag, saw the Oreos calling her name, and decided she didn't really care about the signs.

"Sure. I hail from Holly Hills, South Carolina. Remember how I told you 'bout Hannah and me?" Emma munched on cookies as she spoke. "But I just finished school in Mississippi. I must say I'm very excited to be in a place where my hair doesn't fuzz up as soon as I leave my house. It's taken me a little while to get used to the altitude though. I have to admit something. This is a little frightening. High schoolers. I mean... some of 'em are so *big*! What if I can't get them to behave?"

Leslie looked at her sympathetically. "Don't worry. You'll be fine. Some of them will be so busy looking at you they won't have time to misbehave. Others will be good if you expect them to be good. Others you might have to kick out. You'll get to meet a lot of parents tomorrow for Back-to-School Night, and that's always good leverage. It works like this: 'No, no, don't give me detention. Mom will take away my Xbox!' And if that doesn't work, you can always threaten to take away their school Internet accounts."

Leslie stopped. She turned and stood right in front of Emma, taking the Oreos from Emma's hand and shoving one into each of their mouths. Her eyes were so alarmed that Emma almost swallowed her cookie whole. Leslie gulped hers while blocking both women's faces from an approaching figure. Then, after a quick scan for chocolate crumbs, they turned to face the man now practically upon them. *God, what now? Hall monitor?*

The guy certainly looked geeky enough to be the hall monitor. He was tall and thin, with mincing steps, a tan suit—high-water pants, no less—and a checkered bowtie. Emma could hardly restrain herself from shouting, "It's Alfalfa!" Her father had kept VHS sets of old television shows in the back of his bookstore, so Emma'd grown up with all those Li'l Rascals. Thankfully, this man had a simple short brown haircut. If he'd had even a single protruding hair spike, she was sure she'd have laughed out loud. Leslie saw the look and elbowed Emma hard enough to wipe away the oncoming grin.

"Good afternoon, ladies!" His face was jovial and earnest, with fluffy eyebrows, and his eyelids, despite his happy expression, drooped over round eyes. His wide nose was also in direct conflict with his thin face and pointy chin. He looked like those pictures where body parts from different people were morphed together. "And how has your day proceeded thus far?"

Leslie answered cautiously, although Emma couldn't figure out what possible harm could come from this dorky guy. "Just fine, Edward... uh... and yours?"

"Oh fine, fine!" The man was nodding. "Got two new novels donated by the public library—a Coben and a Carr. Very fine, very fine. Of course, there was the incident with that Toby monster..." He scanned the stacks, eyelids drooping further.

Emma whispered out of the corner of her mouth, "We have a kid named Toby Monster?"

"Shhhhh!" The elbow again. "It's Toby McDonald. Don't antagonize the situation. There's still hope we may get out." She spoke in a kindergarten-teacher voice to Edward. "I'm very sorry about that, Edward. I wanted you to meet—"

Edward's head lolled back toward the women, but his frog-like eyes went right over them. "No respect for the sanctity of fine writing. Why, do you know what he did?"

Leslie sighed. "No, Edward. What did he do?" She was gripping the underside of Emma's elbow and digging in.

"He *graffitied* on a Herman Melville book! *Moby Dick*, no less!" Edward rolled back and forth on his brown saddle shoes. Heel to toe, heel to toe.

Leslie moved all her weight behind Emma and shoved her forward. "That's awful, Edward. Now, this is—"

Edward interrupted, getting more agitated by the second. "Do you *know* what his crass writings said?"

Leslie, apparently resigned to their fate, sighed. "I couldn't possibly guess."

"He wrote, '*Moby Dick* is a great big—'"

Leslie covered his lips with two fingers. "Edward Dixon, have you met Emma Lovett? She's from the South. Delicate ears, all that."

Emma was getting the message. "Hey there, Mr. Dixon. Well, it looks like we're disturbing you here, so—"

Edward interrupted, roaring, "Herman Melville is an icon of our time! Toby the monster will never comprehend that! He'll probably instigate book burnings soon, very soon!"

He paced like a caged lion, pushing chairs out of his way as he walked. His thin frame obviously wasn't as frail as it looked. Students who had come in to study were heading back out.

"He probably thinks Jane Austen is some Betty in his history class!" Emma ducked a flying pocket protector.

"Well, I say down with Toby the monster!" he shouted. "Down with all his hoodlum friends! That's it! I'm banning him from the library for life!"

Leslie remained calm. "Would you like me to take care of that for you, Edward?"

"Already done." He breathed heavily. "I can't take this job anymore! I'm going to work for the post office! Argh!"

Leslie patted Emma on the back, and they walked up to a bulletin board near the rounded checkout desk. Leslie showed her a sheet of paper labeled Banned. Leslie removed the tack from the top of the sheet and unfolded it, accordion-like, until the bottom touched the floor. It looked like a bizarre wish list for Santa. She ran her hand up and down the list to show Emma, like one of the girls on *The Price is Right*, replaced the tack, then stretched to the top of the corkboard and unstapled a paper bag also attached by a tack. She took the bag over to Edward, and he sat and breathed into the bag. Leslie patted his back until he was calmer, while a stricken Emma stood back, horrified.

Leslie sympathetically motioned Emma toward the exit. "Well, I'm so glad you're feeling better, Edward. Have a great day."

Edward pulled the bag away and responded with a cheery, "You too, Leslie! And it was wonderful to meet you, Emma! I'm sure we'll have loads to talk about, you being an English teacher and all. Flannery O'Conner, who is, of course, Southern, is one of my favorite authors. Did I mention that?" He smiled and took a deep drag from the paper bag, waggling his eyebrows at Emma.

"Aaaahh... no," Emma said as she was dragged through the beeper gates. "You never mentioned it. Bye!" She almost tripped as she was yanked through the doors and into the hallway. "Holy smokes! What was that all about?"

Leslie took in a deep breath, apparently inhaling freedom. "Severe schizophrenic psycho-affective personality disorder? I'm not sure. I, personally, think he just needs to get laid."

Emma chuckled as they passed a few other English classrooms on the way to theirs. "Ah may be new, but Ah'm already starting to figure out that's one problem with the school system. Not enough teachers having sex, and too many kids having it."

"Amen, sista."

"So it's planning hour now, then only one more class. Ah think my name games have gone well, and Ah'm already getting to know their names! Plus they have to do an introductory essay to be turned in tomorrow. Don't think first-day homework is makin' me popular right off the bat. But Back-to-School Day is tomorrow? Introductory parent–teacher conferences? Should Ah be worried about that?" Emma tried to run her hands through her hair, which was very mussed by what she would remember as the "Oreo/Toby Monster incident."

Leslie smoothed her still-perfect blond hair. "Oh, my advice is to not think too much about it. Go home, get some sleep. But since you know now about Martha, Charlie, the banned list, and the paper bag, I think I can pronounce you 'prepared for life at Thomas Jefferson High School.' Feel secure in the knowledge that it could only get weirder." Leslie winked and wiggled her long red nails good-bye.

Emma shook her head. "Well, practically prepared anyway."

Leslie turned and walked backward. "Sure. Perpetually prepared!"

Emma countered, "Painstakingly, perfectly prepared!"

Leslie tried once more as she backed toward her room, "Particularly, passionately pre—" but her heel hit a stack of students' books someone'd left by her door. She didn't fall though, even in the stilettos. Emma would have been laid out, flowered skirt overhead.

"Thanks. I take great comfort in your wise, albeit clumsy, reassurance, Indoctriness. Is that a word? Well, I say it is now! Bye!" Emma flung her now-somewhat-tamed hair and unlocked her room to start planning for fifth period.

The eye wink at the hand yet let that be
Which the eye fears, when it is done, to see.

—Macbeth I.4.53–4

CHAPTER 4

Tuesday, August 25

TUESDAY MORNING DAWNED, WELL... EARLY. Emma rolled over after the radio blared in her ear for the third time, and she forced herself not to pound the snooze button again, or possibly throw the thing across the room. She'd bolted up in the middle of the night, awakened by a horrifying dream in which all the parents turned into zombies in the middle of her speech about the importance of them giving a good breakfast to their children before they came to school. They wanted her brains for breakfast.

She sat up and tried to clear her head. Brain-eating zombie parents? Good grief, Charlie Brown! She tried some deep, cleansing breaths. All Emma wanted was to help kids learn to love learning. Sure, it might be hard, but no one was going to eat her brains. She was being silly. Breathe, one, two, in through the nose, out through the mouth. Or was it in through the mouth, out through the nose? *In and out, in and out, there, there. Hoo-ee.*

She got out of bed and went to the closet to find the perfect parent–teacher conference outfit. Why did they do this so early in the year? She couldn't handle brain-eating parents so soon. It seemed to her that the conclusion of the second day of school should be reserved for something more mellow—maybe some get-acquainted games with her new students. Maybe a review of nouns, verbs... conflict management. Something basic.

She left her house at six forty-five, allowing enough time to double-check her already impeccable classroom and make sure her rosters were complete. Walking through the courtyard eased her tension and retrieved her smile. It was that tree. Magnificent, ancient, and possibly an excuse for undone homework—she still wasn't sure if it grew acorns—Emma felt the tree was symbolic of her job as a teacher.

Oh sure, many kids wouldn't remember the first thing about dangling modifiers—most of the time she wasn't sure she knew what they were either—but her influence would live on long after the students left the building. She would wrap a few more rings around the core of their trees until they became glorious redwoods or sequoias or... or... aspens. Let's face it, some of them would just be aspens. She sighed, giggled at her goofy metaphor, and stopped at Leslie's room to say hello.

Leslie's room looked much the same way Leslie did—sleek and stylish. The student desks were the only part that resembled Emma's room. Leslie's walls were covered in black-and-white prints, Ansel Adams and Scott Mutter together in a strange combination of nature and industrialization. There were splashes of red and purple in the forms of Albert Einstein and Ralph Waldo Emerson sayings, and all of the prints were tilted, with black, purple, and red paper setting off the angles.

Emma had a hard time getting her posters to hang straight, much less slanting them on purpose and making it look artistic. *Oh well, variety is the spice and all that.*

The janitor she'd met yesterday, Melvin, was at the bookshelf just to the left of the door. He was dusting it with one of those fluffy feather dusters, and he smiled and waved it as she entered Leslie's classroom.

"Hi, Melvin!" Emma said. "So nice to see you again. The room is lookin' excellent."

He nodded bashfully and continued his work. She wandered toward the desk, also black and lacquered to a shine, which Leslie sat atop, flipping through a gradebook. She was wearing a red suit, which was the exact shade of her fingernails, that fit like a glove.

She smiled at Emma. "How was last night? Did you sleep?"

Emma smiled wanly. "Sort of. This whole parent thing has me crazy nervous. Last night in my dream, they all turned into brain-eating zombies. They didn't want me to teach their kids—they wanted me to *feed* their kids. Literally. What if they ask questions I can't answer?"

"Are you kidding?" Leslie snorted and set the gradebook next to

33

her hip. "What are you going to do when *kids* ask questions you can't answer? Because they will, you know. Your master teacher must have sheltered you in a big way. Oh, right—you didn't even *have* a master teacher. Tell me, what are you going to do when kids ask questions to which you don't know the answer?"

She glanced at Melvin, and Emma turned to look. The feather duster sat on the shelf, and he had something in his hand that he was stroking.

Leslie walked over to him. "Can I help you with something, Melvin?"

Melvin jumped as if struck by lightning, and he thrust the thing at her. It was a bookmark covered in brightly colored sequins. "Oh, no, Ms. Parker. I'm sorry, it's just—I just…them sequins flashed at me, and I just picked it up. It…it reminded me of somethin'." He flushed.

Emma noticed Melvin had big eyes and a gentle, embarrassed smile. He looked as if he might have been handsome once, but his nose had expanded and had lots of those tiny veins people acquire with hard living. *It looks like my dad's nose!* She had to blink back tears for the second time in as many days.

Leslie gently pushed his hand back. "Reminds you of something or some*one*? I think someone…" When he nodded, she said crisply, "Well, of course you should take it with you. Pop it into your favorite book and be reminded whenever you want."

"But it's a very nice bookmark," he protested. "It's yours. You've got it displayed as part of the… the decoration on this shelf. I couldn't take it from you."

She patted his hand again. "Oh, posh. Don't be crazy. I've got scads of bookmarks from every Scholastic book fair for the past fifteen years. I'm sure I can find another to match my décor. Ration. To match my deco*ration*." She winked at Melvin. "Please, take it."

A smile lit Melvin's face as he closed his fingers gently over the bookmark. "Thank you, Ms. Parker. It means a lot. To you it's just a bookmark, but ya know, sometimes it ain't what ya look at, but what's really there." He picked up his feather duster and backed out of the room, waving it at the two women.

The women waved back.

"That was a nice thing you did," Emma remarked. She gestured to the display on the bookcase, which included several items with the same multi-colors, including a small, delicate theater mask and a little dragon that looked as if it had come from a Chinese New Year celebration, and then she gestured more expansively to encompass the whole room and Leslie herself. "Especially since it seems you're real particular with your—shall we say with the things with which you surround yourself?"

Leslie shook her head. "That's just for show. Besides, you don't know Melvin. He and Abigail—you'll meet her later—are what keep this place afloat. 'His life was gentle, and all the elements so mixed in him, that Nature might stand up and say to all the world, "This was a man!"' Or in this case, a man and a woman. *Julius Caesar.*" She took a bow. "Anyway, he's great. I'd give him my car or all my Jimmy Choos if he asked for them." She touched the ceramic mask and walked back to her desk, where she propped up her feet, presumably so Emma could see her Jimmy Choos. "C'mon, let's get down to the nitty gritty, Miz Scarlett. What're you gonna do when kids ask you questions to which you don't know the answer?"

"Ummmm..." Emma's forehead crinkled. "Pretend?"

"I *wish* that would work!" Leslie pounded her palm into the lacquer. "I am a *great* BSer! But no, no, kids always know. So I say *extra credit.*" She breathed those two words with reverence. "Whenever you don't know the answer, offer extra credit to the kid who can find it. That usually excites them to the point that they forget all about the fact that you have no clue." She leaned back in her chair again, satisfied with the day's lesson.

But Emma was still stuck. "Surely you can't be serious about doing somethin' like that *tonight*? You don't want me to offer the parents extra credit?"

"Oh, that. I have a phrase—'Let me speak to my administrator and get back to you on that.' Works every time, because they don't want their name taken up to the principal's office *now* any more than they did when they were fifteen." She sighed expressively. "Sometimes my sheer genius is overwhelming. I'm serious. And don't call me Shirley."

Emma grabbed a pencil from the desk and threw it at her new friend. "Okay, Miss Brainiac. Ah guess Ah'd better be gettin' to my room to teach something, and to work on my plan to meet the parents who might ask me questions Ah can't answer. Just like the kids." She sighed. "Boy, Ah'm lookin' forward to that part."

She started toward the door but was pushed aside by a couple entering the room. Actually, she was pushed by the woman; the man followed after like a duckling follows its mother.

"Ah, Ms. Parker," the woman oozed. "So glad to find you here and unencumbered."

Emma had to restrain herself from asking, "And what am I, chopped liver?"

The woman was tall, wearing a suit and a long camel-colored coat that must have been worn for the sole purpose of sweeping into rooms, because, after all, it was August. She had brown hair pulled into a bun and a thin fox face with a bump on the end of her nose that looked just like the bun on the back of her head. The first adjective that came to Emma's mind was "imperious." The second was "royal pain in the ass." *Is that really an adjective? Maybe a title.*

Leslie took her feet off the desk—ever the gracious hostess—and crossed her arms. "Mr. and Mrs. Fillmore, how can I help you? I don't remember seeing Camilla's name on my roster this year." Her voice was smooth as cream, but Emma heard the acid around the edge.

The little man who Emma guessed was Mr. Fillmore—although she wasn't quite sure who was the mister in this operation—backed a bit toward the door. Mrs. Fillmore grabbed his shirtfront to retrieve him.

As she held tight to her husband, Mrs. Fillmore spoke with a steely voice that had the deep rasp of a former smoker, although Emma was, for some reason, sure this woman would never smoke. "No, no. I wouldn't allow her to take your class again. I tried to find you at the beginning of the summer, but your number appeared to be unlisted, or nonexistent. I'm here to discuss the B-plus Camilla must have inadvertently received in your Advanced Composition class last year. Would you care to fix that now?"

The woman dropped her husband and charged over to Leslie's desk. She drummed her fingers on the shiny black lacquer. Her energy was daunting—as if she were ready to explode like a pinball and bounce off each desk. She and Leslie engaged in a momentary stare down, with an unclear victor.

Leslie stood to her full height of—well, of taller than Mrs. Fillmore—and responded with her own steel. "Mrs. Fillmore, I'm sorry, but there was nothing 'inadvertent' about Camilla's grade. Camilla didn't turn in a persuasive essay until a week after it was due, and there were one or two homework assignments she missed altogether. She's a good writer, but she could use a little more discipline."

Mrs. Fillmore vibrated; her face turned red, and the long coat swayed. "There must be some mistake! I'm sure you just lost the assignments you say were 'late' or 'missed.' This is ridiculous. Camilla is *very* disciplined! She's destined for wondrous things. Ivy League schools, for a beginning. What must I do to make you understand what a B-plus could do to our plans? I'm sure it's your mistake." The woman was humming like a teakettle.

Emma was tempted to move out of the room, but she was more concerned for the poor tiny husband. About five feet four inches tall, he had dark hair and enormous black eyes, a small cupid's-bow mouth, and an infant-sized nose. Mr. Betty Boop. He was, from a safe distance, alternately wringing his hands and reaching for his angry wife then retreating and wringing his hands again. Sweat beaded on his upper lip. The wife paid him no notice as she seemed to advance on Leslie despite the large black desk in her way.

Leslie stood her ground. "No, I'm sorry. The mistake is hers. Now please remove yourself from my personal bubble, Mrs. Fillmore, and understand this—she earned the B-plus, and the B-plus she gets. Enjoy the rest of your conferences, Mrs. Fillmore, and have a nice day."

Mr. and Mrs. Fillmore stood for another moment, one helplessly, the other furiously. Finally, the woman turned, grabbed her husband, and shepherded him from the room.

Leslie stood her ground a second after they left then collapsed into her chair. "Holy anal-retentive drama queens, Batman! They sure don't pay me enough for this job!"

Emma went to Leslie, incredulous. "Please, please tell me all these parents aren't like that!"

"No, no, those are only a chosen few. Most parents just want what's best for their kids and don't steamroller or put the blame on anyone else when their child doesn't do as well as they'd like. I call *these* few parents the My Child Can Do No Wrong Corps. And I think *she's* the president, grand master, whatever. Anyway, don't worry. You'll be fine. Just remember the mantra."

Leslie and Emma clasped hands and repeated it together, "Let me speak to an administrator and get back to you on that."

Feeling better, Emma left for her room. Once she arrived, she relaxed a bit more because the room was so welcoming. She'd stayed after school on Monday for some decorating, and the results were more than pleasing. Flowering vines wrapped around the white boards, and large fake-but-nice plants sat in each corner. Student desks were placed in a U that faced the front center of the room, giving her space to move when she talked. The empty bookshelves had been filled with some of her favorite classics: *To Kill a Mockingbird, Cat's Cradle, Something Wicked This Way Comes.* The desk had a William Shakespeare bust serving as a paperweight in the corner. Parts of the room were a little girly, but she thought it was a comforting place to work and learn. She sat at her desk and waited for the onslaught.

He reads much,
He is a great observer, and he looks
Quite through the deeds of men.

—Julius Caesar I.2.200–2

CHAPTER 5

Wednesday, August 26

WEDNESDAY MORNING, EMMA LEFT FOR school again at six forty-five. She'd slept soundly, unplagued by nightmares. Back-to-School Night had been a rousing success, or at least no one had converged upon her like what had happened in Leslie's classroom. The parents were curious but gracious. Emma had even met a nice couple named Myra and William Lansing who'd offered to make her the fourth on their bridge team. The fact that she knew nothing about bridge didn't faze them, and before long, she'd agreed to a Friday-night game. What a social life she was developing—bridge on a Friday night at twenty-six years old!

Leslie would probably choke, and Hannah would have staged a revolt. Emma thought she'd be ready for the brown dress and oxfords before long. She twirled her hair into a bun and laughed. Oh well, this sure was fun so far!

She walked through the courtyard, smelling the flowers, then through the commons, smelling the students. She was amazed that school had only been in session for two days and there was already—well, not a smell exactly. But a sense. Teenagerness filled the air. When she unlocked the door to 104, her room smelled a little less like hormone stew and a little more like the orchid Air Wick she'd plugged in, so she breathed that in with satisfaction.

After she turned on her laptop and checked her plan book, it was still only 6:50. Emma decided to take a walk and check out the back of the school, since the adventures of the first two days had prevented that. The first six classrooms in the English hallway had doors on two sides, one opening into the hallway off of the commons and the other opening out the back side. Each room had one frosted window along the back, but it didn't open. It was just a big rectangle of glass giving Emma impressions of kids passing and activity happening. Time to check out the source.

She flung open the outside door. Two tennis courts were right in front of her, fenced to keep errant balls in. As she walked alongside the fence, she saw two outdoor basketball courts by the exit to the gym. Beyond that, Emma saw a running track enveloping the football field, goalposts gleaming in the sun. The other side of the courts and the field were covered with asphalt—*student parking, I'm sure.*

Emma walked between the basketball and tennis courts to see what lay beyond that. On the north fence of the tennis courts, she saw what looked like another small building. *I bet that's sports equipment. Maybe a weight room.* As she started toward the building, eager to see if she was right, she heard angry voices on the other side of the unidentified building. She hesitated.

"You have to do it!" someone growled. "I know you're doing it for others, so now you must do it for her."

Emma couldn't hear the response. She thought it was a woman's voice answering, but all she could make out sounded like the "wah wah woh wah" of the parents in *Charlie Brown* comics. She edged closer to the wall of the unidentified building, knowing it was impolite to eavesdrop but unable to stop herself.

The gravelly voice said, "You've been doing it for others for the past two years—football players, soccer players. They're not nearly as important as my star!"

The other voice said something, and Emma got even closer, accidentally hitting a rock with the toe of her shoe. She sucked in an anxious breath, but the demanding voice just kept on.

"Let me explain using small words so you can understand. You can't stop me. It's going to happen, either with you and a job you can keep, or without you, and then you have no job. Don't you get it? Destiny isn't a matter of chance. It's a matter of choice."

The Charlie-Brown-parent voice whimpered and faded as footsteps trod away from the building. But the footsteps belonging to the other speaker increased in volume, and a panicked Emma scurried back up the walkway between the courts, and she ran full speed back into her room.

Very thankful for her lack of interest in stiletto heels, Emma crossed her room in her flat shoes and sank into her seat. *What on earth could that have been about?* She couldn't tell whether the angry voice had belonged to a man or a woman, but she was pretty sure the one being threatened was a woman. *What was it she had to do that she'd been doing for others for the past two years? The "others" had to do with sports—I think it was football and soccer?* Emma didn't know anything about sports. She'd always been more interested in books.

Emma drummed her fingers on the table and opened her laptop. She was busy researching new ways for her class to rehearse their Shakespeare scenes when her students filtered in for first-hour American Lit.

She closed her laptop as she heard, "Hey, Miz Lovett!" The student greeting her had a bright-orange shirt and a shock of black hair, and his name was...

"Hi, Anthony! Did I get that right? Anthony Trumbull?" She grinned when the student nodded. "Well, Anthony, you can put your introductory essay on the chair in front of the white board. We're going to do some 'getting to know you' activities, then we're goin' ta start the year with a little introduction to our first theme of American Identity. Yay for the American Identity!"

Anthony didn't look as thrilled with that concept as Emma was, but she continued testing herself on names as students entered. She was happy to hear some of their friendly hellos.

"Do you know a lot about sports?" Emma asked as she came into the library teachers' lounge at lunch.

Leslie was already stylishly wolfing down the lunch Mrs. Albert had made for her. *How in the green Sam Hill does she do that?* Today Leslie wore an emerald-green shift with one of those short jackets Emma thought was called a shrug. *If I ate as much and as fast as she did, I swear it'd be all over my lap. Maybe all over the floor and the wall.*

"What's on the gourmet menu for the day?"

Leslie swallowed and passed the tray. "Herb-crusted halibut. One of my favorites. Wanna split?" She cut the piece of fish in half. "I couldn't care less about sports, but I know some things, I suppose. Why, what do you want to know?"

Emma sat and looked around the small room. "Don't any other English teachers come in here? I thought there were four more of us." She gave Leslie half of her sandwich in exchange for the gourmet treat. "Not that I mind—need to talk privately anyway."

"Ooh, private! Awesome!" Leslie took a drink from a can of iced tea and ticked off her fingers. "Mrs. Miller just had a baby, so she goes home at lunch to feed him. Mr. Van Pelt writes in his spare time—meaning before school, after school, at lunch, and at home. Mss. Trudeau and Chandler eat in the big teachers' lounge. So it's just us chickens. Spill!"

Emma told Leslie what she'd heard before school. "Ah don't know if the person making the threats was a man or a woman, but Ah'm pretty sure the one receiving them was female. What is that building behind the tennis courts? Ah was trying to explore but then ran away when I heard that voice comin' my way." She took a bite of the heavenly halibut. "Ah was a scared little chicken. Mm-mmm, good. This is fabulous. Mrs. Albert is a genius."

"Hmmmph. That building is a weight room, and half of it stores sports equipment," Leslie said. "There're a few Dumpsters with a wooden surround protecting them on the other side, and the alley between the two structures is used for 'questionable activities' all the time. Kids are always getting caught smoking back there. And doing other things. I'm glad you didn't stick around. That voice sounded mad, you said?"

Emma nodded. "Super mad. Ultra mad. But my question about sports... the mad voice said somethin' about sports and 'doing it for others.' Somethin' about football, I think. Or baseball? Doing what? For years, the voice said."

Leslie shrugged. She scooped up the last bit of fish with the corner of Emma's shared peanut butter sandwich and popped it in her mouth. She gathered up her tray. "I don't know what that could be about, Em. Sounds illegal or at least immoral. Keep your ears and eyes open, I guess."

Folding her empty brown bag for reuse tomorrow—Emma was nothing if not green minded—she smiled at her new friend, because she already felt as though they were friends. "It was just so strange. I need to go plan for the rest of the week now. I'm starting American Lit with some short stories from different eras for a unit I'm calling 'The American Identity,' and I think I'll start the sophomores with Shakespeare, even though I can see it'll take all my creativity to get 'em excited about it. But if I hear anything else about sports or someone who's uber mad about them, you'll be the first to know."

"Ah, Grasshoppah. 'You would seem to know my stops. You would pluck out the heart of my mystery.'" Leslie's eyes twinkled. "*Hamlet*."

"How do you *do* that?" Emma shook her head. "I've only known you for three days, and you've pulled the choice Shakespeare quote outta your... hat, like, six times over! Ah would really, really like to do that."

Leslie and Emma waved at Edward Dixon on their way out. He was helping a student and seemed very calm, in no danger of needing the paper bag or his banned list.

"I just love the Bard," Leslie explained. "He knows more about people than anyone I know." She leaned in and whispered, "Sometimes my quotes don't really have much to do with the topic at hand. That Hamlet quote has nothing to do with sports or threats or anything like that; I just wanted to talk about a 'mystery.' It's a fun game though. I'll teach you." She winked. "Don't plan too hard!" And she continued down the hall to return her tray to the cafeteria.

Still musing over the mysterious voices she'd heard, Emma sat at her desk and tackled plans, including how to help students give speeches without too much fear—fear of public speaking was the number-one fear, higher on the list than death, even—and how to get those sophomores excited about a four-hundred-fifty-year-old guy who'd never heard of texting. She had her work cut out for her, but she already loved the challenge.

O horror, horror, horror!
Tongue nor heart cannot conceive nor name thee!

—Macbeth II.3.60–1

CHAPTER 6

EMMA WAS DREAMING ABOUT A bird. In the dream, her cat, Trinculo, was scratching at the front door, and when she went to open it, the cat entered with something in her mouth and dropped it at Emma's feet. Emma cried out, dropped to her knees, and picked up the tiny sparrow or starling Trinky had given her. The little bird was quiet and still in Emma's hand, then it turned its shiny eyes her way and chirped, a harsh, piercing noise from something so small. The dream Emma thought she could save it with her healing touch, so she stroked it gently. Its chirps grew more strident, but Emma was sure her ministrations were working when it flew up toward her face and chirped right in her ear. She woke and looked at the clock: four thirty. *Sheesh.*

Then the bird chirped again. It took Emma a second to figure out the sound was coming from the smoke detector, informing her it had low batteries. She closed and opened her eyes for a few minutes, assessed going back to sleep as a (chirp) fruitless venture, and pushed herself out of bed to go to the kitchen.

Stumbling through the still-shadowy living room, she tripped over Sir Toby, her sheltie, and brought a dining room chair out to position in the bedroom doorway. She halfheartedly pounded on the smoke detector casing until it detached, then she stretched her hand up to the rectangular battery and yanked on it. It popped out of the wall, slid down the front of the detector, and hit her in the face. *Ow.*

Groggily holding her cheek, she went to the bathroom, switched on the light, and after her eyes had adjusted, she studied her reflection. The corner of the battery had bonked her on the cheekbone under her right eye, leaving a small red mark. She touched it. *Ow.* Great, two days into school, and she'd have to explain a black eye. *Oh well, "you should see the other guy" will probably work as well as anything.* A shower, a banana, and two Cokes later, it was only 5:20. Emma pondered once again whether the sleep gods would let her return to bed for a few blessed winks. *Nope, not gonna happen.*

As the caffeine coursed through her veins, she figured she might as well go to school, take advantage of her cola jolt, and do something productive and teacher-ish. Actually, the parents of one of her fifth-period Speech kids, Matty Coughran, had insisted on giving her some special activities to use to help Matty with his dyslexia. She'd explained that in a speech class, reading problems really weren't an issue, but the Coughrans smiled and nodded and completely understood her point. So when did she think she'd have those activities ready? Emma smiled— well, she'd get those babies inserted into her plans today, whether little Matty needed them or not.

It was already becoming bright outside when she headed for the driveway. The mountains to the south were dappled with alternating fingers of sunshine and shadow, green pines and red rock. It was beautiful country. The Internet said Pinewood averaged six to ten *feet* of snow per year—Emma hoped she would remember days like this when the first major snowstorm forced her to dig her little Honda out of a drift. Maybe she should take advantage of these long days and sleepless mornings and go running before school. Ha. Maybe when the pope wore Spandex. The idea summarily abandoned, she got into her car and drove toward Thomas Jefferson High.

Five minutes later—*Commute, huh? Traffic, what? This is why I love my small towns*—she looped through the bus lot and continued to the faculty parking lot. Large signs with calligraphic lettering proclaimed it for Faculty Only, although Emma already knew that kids parked there all the time. That rebellious teenage thing could be expressed in the smallest way.

She walked around to the main doors coming from the bus loop, pausing to try to remember what it had been like coming off the school bus every morning. *Nope, no real memories of that. Probably one of those things that got blocked out, like most horrific school memories.* It was funny. She had loved being in school, which was obvious from her chosen profession, but some kids were so mean, then and now, that she wouldn't go back to the nightmarish vision that was puberty for a million dollars. Not for Chris Pine even. Well... no, not even for him. She took out her new ring of keys and looked for the one that unlocked this door, allowing sleepless and anal-retentive, workaholic teachers entry outside school hours.

She unlocked the door and stood in the doorway of the commons, the smell of fresh wax and old lockers drifting her way. *Wow, the whole school to myself.* Emma had an instant urge to remove all the light bulbs from the fluorescent rectangles and place them in the gym, which was a senior prank she'd heard of once that sounded so neat. The senior pranksters had done it and only broken two bulbs, the money for which they'd placed carefully atop the massive pile before they left.

Her own stupid senior class had broken into the school library, pulled all the books off the shelf, and done massive amounts of damage along the way. *No* class, that. She sighed. Apparently, she had to naysay all the prankster stuff now that she was an adult, or at least pretending to be one. Maybe she didn't want to do puberty again because she'd never left it in the first place? Could be.

A glance at her watch revealed it said five forty-five. *Holy smokes!* Well, she guessed the best place to start would be her mailbox. At least this early, it would be unnecessary to smack the sign overhead—no "accidents" lurked at that ridiculous hour. Emma looked up, paused for a fraction of a second under the sign, and smacked it anyway. Slavery to superstition was her knack.

She used the same key to unlock the doors to the main office. Leslie had explained that as a design flaw in a building originally designed in the 1970s. Teachers needed to be able to use the teachers' lounge and their mailboxes, but to do so, they had to go through the main office. *That's probably why these secretary computer towers are all bolted to the floor like a tornado's comin.'*

Emma stopped short as a strong smell assaulted her nostrils. Metallic and warm, like a just-soldered copper pipe, the smell insinuated itself aggressively into the fresh wax smell. Rounding the corner of the counter and heading for the back stairs to the teachers' lounge, she stopped.

From between the two secretaries' desks protruded a single foot, splayed sideways with the toe pointing toward the exit. Emma saw the black rubber waffle tread on the bottom of the shoe and a bit of loose gray pant leg.

She drew in her breath and inched closer, dragging one hand along the front counter and hesitating for a second to search for movement on the floor. The pant leg continued up and connected to a man sprawled between the desks. His other leg was bent under him at the knee, with one arm pressed against his torso and the other flung from his side, palm down. He wasn't moving.

Emma's gaze moved farther up the body until she saw one side of a face, turned sideways with one cheek resting on the floor. Emma couldn't see who it was yet, but the gray jumpsuit caused a swell of panic. *Oh my God. I think it's... can it be... no!*

Emma's breathing accelerated to a rasp and hitch as she slid her feet forward to see who it was. One eyebrow arched in a permanent shaggy half-moon that belied the slackness of the lower half of his face, and the anguished sob she tried to stop with her hands seemed to echo off the wall. *Melvin. It's Melvin McManus, who keeps the school afloat, who has a saying for every occasion and reminds me of my dad. Oh my God, it's Melvin.* He looked both shocked and appalled, as if whatever had happened to him had both surprised and angered him.

A split second later, she saw the blood-filled hole that used to be the top of his head, and that was when she started screaming.

She flailed and backed into the front counter, sliding alongside it and yelling indecipherably. When her throat was scraped raw, reality set in. *I'm screaming to an empty building.* Her screams trailed off into little breathy puffs floating up from her stomach, then they stopped with a whimper. Her hands shook at her sides, the fingertips dropping staccato points along her cotton skirt. Emma closed her eyes and smacked her temple twice, as if that would help make a course of action more apparent.

Her vision cleared, and she looked once more at Melvin. Tufts of gray hair mixed with the blood at the top of his head. She retched, and Coke bubbles parked in the base of her throat, burning. Emma edged around the counter, her vision avoiding the red spatters flung in Rorschach blots across the metal desk behind the body.

Hyperventilation loomed large, and it took conscious thought to suck in a huge breath and hold it for a second. The metallic smell was still there, and another scent was coming through. Fetid and swampy, reminding her of some dark, mucky places she'd been to back home. Blood and… and death. The realization set in—she was smelling blood and death. She felt an involuntary heave that started clear down in the intestine and roiled up. With another conscious effort, she stopped the heave in her chest before it reached her throat. Emma flung herself out of the office before she threw up all over the crime scene.

Leslie rushed up to Emma a second later.

Emma was in the commons area, wearing a furrow through the waxed floor and murmuring, "The swamp. Ah swear it smells just like the swamp. Swampy, like the swamp. Only with copper plants. Freshly soldered copper plants. No alligators though… alligators already been there. Alligators ate a hole in his *head*…" With that she fell, crying, into Leslie's arms. "What are you doing here?"

Leslie pushed Emma's hair back. "I was in my room. I heard a scream."

"I can't believe this. Never saw anythin' like this at home."

"Show me."

Emma led Leslie into the office and stood mute, pointing at Melvin's body. Her breaths were coming slower now, the rhythm thrown off by an occasional hiccup. How could there be a dead person here? She'd never seen a dead person. The only dead thing she'd seen was an alligator that she and her dad had found one time when they were hiking, and that was just a sad, shriveled thing, no blood or wounds. No expression on its face, no shock or fear. Leslie took a quick inventory of the situation. Her expression changed from no-nonsense to sad only once—when she walked far enough to see the top of Melvin's head.

She turned to Emma and said softly, "Maybe we should call the police?"

The question sent Emma into a panic attack, and new tears combined with more frenzied pacing. "Oh God. That's the first thing Ah should have done, isn't it? Oh God, oh God, Ah've ruined everything, haven't

Ah? They're never going to find out who did this awful thing, are they? It's all mah fault, ain't it? Oh God, oh God." Emma kept up this keening plea until Leslie shushed her.

"Shhh. Honey, you haven't done anything wrong. We'll figure out who did this. You didn't touch anything, did you?"

Wordless now, Emma shook her head.

"Well then, let's just touch a phone and get someone over here." Leslie gently took Emma's purse from her shoulder—which Emma didn't even realize she had with her—dug around for a cell phone, and commenced to start the biggest uproar Thomas Jefferson High School had ever seen.

CHAPTER 7

BY THE TIME SCHOOL WAS supposed to start, students and teachers were waiting in the courtyard, straining to see the goings-on inside. Emma knew an email or phone tree had been invoked to cancel school, but that hadn't kept anyone home.

Inside, yellow crime scene tape was strung from the lockers to the opposite wall and stuck to one of the wildcat's fierce-looking teeth. Tape also crossed the front doors to the commons, but it might have been broken were it not for Officer Hulk Hogan, who stood planted in front of it. He had a gigantic head and equally large arms crossed in front of him, the blue seams across his shoulders threatening to rip.

Emma saw the large group through the long rectangular windows in the entrance doors, but they seemed quiet. *Must be the Goliath in blue staring them down.* Inside the commons, where Emma and Leslie waited to give statements, the crime scene was quiet but for the photographer snapping pictures of the body and the detective collecting little invisible things into plastic baggies.

Emma stood with Leslie in the corner of the room. Emma felt the dried tears on her cheeks and saw the fists still crinkling her skirt as if they had a mind of their own, but she was feeling better. She looked at her friend, really seeing her for the first time. Leslie's normally perfect bob was sticking out in several directions, and her face looked, well... different.

Emma couldn't figure it out at first, then she got it—Leslie was missing the top half of her face! Her early-morning blond eyebrows and transparent eyelashes made her upper face a smooth pink eraser with startling blue dots in the middle. Leslie also wore a faded AC/DC T-shirt and bright-purple sweats with holes in the knees. Emma looked at Leslie's feet, and despite the trauma of the current situation, she smiled. Leslie was wearing running shoes with Tweety Bird embroidered on the sides.

"Why are you here so early? Why are you in your sweats?" whispered Emma.

The detective and photographer shot dirty looks at Emma, and she tried to stifle her whispers.

"Forgot my purse last night, and couldn't find another mascara. Obviously I need the mascara bad." Leslie gestured to her naked face. "I only live two minutes from here, and I was up, and…" She looked down at her feet and her tattered clothes. She whispered to Emma, "I tawt I taw a teachew in hew *sweats*!"

Emma would have smiled at her friend and her naked face, but then she looked toward the open office doors.

Leslie looked at Emma's eye. "What happened to your face?"

Emma ran her fingers over the orbital bone; it was a little sore. "Flying nine-volt."

Leslie nodded as though she understood perfectly.

The detective's evil looks weren't stopping them, so he finally approached. "Ahem. Ahh… Carl Niome here, ladies. Detective in charge. Which one of you ladies found the body?"

He was short and had thinning dark hair, with a florid complexion and flattened gin-blossom nose probably created by years of drinking. He held a large pewter wildcat paperweight, maybe eight inches tall and almost as wide. One of the sharp feline ears was covered in blood.

The detective's hands were enclosed in latex gloves, and he balanced the paperweight on his palm rather than gripping its neck or head. *He's doing that so he won't smudge any fingerprints.* It was a large paperweight, and Emma wondered why she hadn't noticed it before. *Some detective I'd make!* Guess reading lots of trashy mystery novels late at night had done nothing for her observational skills.

"I, ahhh… Ah found the body, um, him, um, Melvin, early this morning," Emma said.

"How early?"

"Um, about five forty-five."

The detective tilted his head and regarded Emma, adjusting his brown slacks from slightly over to a little bit under the paunch of his belly. "Hmmm. And why were you here that early?"

Emma felt like a deer caught in the headlights, though she knew she hadn't done anything wrong. Cops were so *good* at the fear and intimidation thing.

"Oh, I... I couldn't sleep. Thought I'd get some work done." She kind of wished she had followed her original instinct and gone running. Maybe if someone else had discovered the body, they'd at least have had the presence of mind to call the police right away.

His eyes narrowed. "Hm. And did you touch anything? Check for a pulse, maybe? Attempt mouth-to-mouth?"

Emma felt her gorge rising. Had she forgotten something else, something even more critical than timely law-enforcement notification? Oh God, the tears were back, lining her wide green eyes as she tried to blink them away. She stepped back, hands covering her mouth at the same time Leslie stepped forward and got in the detective's face.

"Check for a pulse? Attempt mouth-to-mouth? Are you insane? Look at him. He's got a hole in his head the size of Cleveland, and his—sorry, Melvin's—*wide-open* dead eyes aren't seeing anything but the Great Beyond. Give her a break!"

The two stood eye to eye for another minute, Leslie looking steely despite her spiky hair and nonexistent eyelashes, and the detective was the one who finally looked away.

"Okay. Let's start over. Everything is exactly as you found it, yes? And you didn't touch anything but the office door and the front counter?"

Emma nodded and stood up straighter. Watching Leslie so obviously win their staring contest made Emma feel empowered. "Yes. I knew him too. I mean, I met him Monday morning. He came to check on my room before school started."

That information sent one of the policeman's eyebrows skyward. "You knew him, eh? Did you two happen to, oh, I dunno... fight over anything? The condition of your room perhaps?"

Leslie started toward him, stink-eye in full effect, but Emma stopped her with a hand on her shoulder. "No! No fight! He was real nice, checking to see if Ah was okay for the conference. He was very sweet, and Ah wish Ah could have helped him, but Ah couldn't! Ah came early to school because good teachers have to put in extra hours to get the job done." Tears sprang to her eyes for the fourth time in as many days. "He was nice. Reminded me a little of my daddy."

"Well," said Detective Niome, "it's—it's okay. I'm sure this is upsetting." His hand passed over his thinning hair, and he glanced at Leslie.

She stared back, and he looked down. He took down both ladies' names and addresses, told them sternly "not to go anywhere anytime soon," and went back to the office to speak to his photographer.

Emma watched him go, then she collapsed against the wall of lockers, hands crossed over her heart. "Hoo-ee, he's grouchy! But do you think he's any good? I mean, poor Melvin..." She tipped her head toward the bloody office. "You were so mean to him. Can't you get into trouble for being mean to a police officer?" Emma had been, of course, taught to respect anyone in a position of authority, and she wondered how her new friend could be so cavalier.

Leslie's naked face was hard to read. "He's...he's not smart. I'm sorry I was mean to him, but you were so upset."

How would Leslie know he's not smart? Has she met him before? Maybe she's been in trouble with the law, and she thinks he's not smart because he couldn't find evidence against her. Emma shook her head, dismissing the thought. *You've been reading too many detective novels, silly.*

Leslie was silent as she watched law-enforcement types come and go from the office. She began to speak to Emma but was interrupted when two women approached them. The tall woman was younger, with a frizzy pouf of hair and a brown suit. She looked stressed out by the police activity. The little rotund woman wrung her hands as if she were trying to squeeze liquid from them. She looked to be in her mid-sixties, with white curly hair and a blue polka-dotted dress. Her eyes were red rimmed beneath 1950s spectacles. *It's Aunt Bee, right here in Mayberry, Colorado, where you drive five minutes to work and find dead guys when you arrive.*

"Oh goodness! Is it true? Is somebody dead? Somebody's been killed here at school." The older woman's voice was so quiet that Emma had to move closer to hear her. "Oh my, my, my, nothing like this has ever happened here. I mean, we had the police out last month when someone was stealing underwear from the girls' gym lockers, but this…"

The taller woman was easy to hear. Her brash voice matched the wild hair. "I always knew this place hid a darker side. This many trees in one place is like *Friday the 13th.* I knew it."

The younger woman considered Emma. They both figured out at the same time that they had never met and looked accusingly at Leslie, who was still staring at the death room with a curious expression. Finally Emma gave Leslie's shoulder a little smack.

Leslie roused herself from her trance. "Oh, hi, Abigail. Hi, Janice. Abigail Patterson and Janice Tichner, school secretaries, meet Emma Lovett, new English teacher. Emma found the body."

Emma shook hands with Abigail and Janice.

"I'm so sorry, dear," Abigail said, and again Emma moved closer so she could hear the birdlike voice. "It must have been horrible for you. Who was it?"

"One of the custodians. Melvin McManus?"

Both women stiffened.

"Oh, he's so nice! Was nice. Is nice. Oh, Janice, you knew Melvin, didn't you?"

Janice quietly said, "Yes, I knew him." Her frizzy hair seemed to droop. She stared sideways at the main entrance, and her fists opened and closed, opened and closed.

"Poor, poor Melvin," mourned the older woman. "Was he shot?"

"No," Emma replied. "It looked like he was hit over the head."

Ms. Patterson pondered that for a moment and waddled off, clucking and shaking her head. Janice followed, but they were turned away from the office by one of the attending officers, so they went back out the way they had come in, Abigail wringing and clucking, Janice's stressed face looking… stretched. Leslie's attention had again gone elsewhere.

"What on earth are you thinking about?" asked Emma. "You're on another planet right now, and I'm not only referring to your outfit."

Leslie looked at her sweats and picked absently at a hole by the waist, pulling out threads and making overexposure a dangerous possibility. "Never mind. You've been through a lot this morning. Let's go for some coffee and bagels." She called over to Detective Niome, "We're going to get some breakfast. I think we'll try Durango Bagels, which is about a mile from here. I take it when you said not to go anywhere soon, you meant like Barbados, *n'est ce pas?*"

He stared at the women like they were fungus.

They walked the two minutes to Leslie's house and jumped into her red convertible.

"I feel so bad," said Emma. "Melvin is dead, and we're going for bagels. Seems cold, somehow."

"I know, you're right. But we're not dead, and if I didn't get away from that place, I thought I might collapse from the oppressive atmosphere. Besides, we have limited time before I have to go home and get ready."

"Ready for what? No school today."

Leslie smacked the steering wheel with her palm. "Duh. Of course you're right. So it's a leisurely breakfast, yes? You're not embarrassed to be seen with me, are you?" She wiggled her wild hair and pulled out the T-shirt. "Sometimes I'm not in the mood for the whole circus that is my morning regimen."

Emma laughed. "Of course not. Hannah and I used to go out on weekend mornings for breakfast, usually still in our pajamas. Did you get your mascara?"

She smacked the wheel again. "Oh, damn. I forgot."

So why was she really there? "So you missed the main purpose of your early-morning trip?"

"I guess I did. What were *you* doing there so early in the morning?"

"I was planning on preparing some activities for Matty Coughran. His parents insisted his dyslexia would cause him some problems in speech class." *I know makeup is important to her; she's so stylish. Doesn't make sense...*

"Yeah, I think the Coughrans are part of the My Child Can Do No Wrong Corps." Leslie turned left into a little strip mall and pulled into a space in front of the bagel shop in the corner.

Emma could smell the fresh-baked bagels before they even parked, but she didn't want to leave the subject alone. "I just think it's a little... strange. I mean, wouldn't you pick up the mascara right when you walked into your room? I guess you could have dropped it on your way out, but..."

Leslie turned off the car then turned to Emma. "Okay, okay, I wasn't really there for the mascara. I was doing a little strange, un-grownup-type thing this morning, I'll admit. But if I tell you, you are *sworn* to secrecy, *capisce*? Cross your heart, hope to die, pinkie-swearing, blood-oath secrecy."

Emma shrugged. "Sure."

"I have a key that works in most of the classrooms. That's the first secret—our keys are only supposed to work in the main office and the department where we teach."

"And...?"

"And sometimes, usually about once a month, I go to school early and play a prank on Charlie Foreman. Before summer break, I put itching powder in his sports jacket. The month before that, it was a bucket of water that dumped over his head when he walked in the door. Juvenile, I know, but *so* much fun! He thinks it's one of his football players, and he doesn't want to get his precious jock athletes in trouble, so he never tells anyone. Anyway, this morning I was rigging a stereo boom box to blast AC/DC at top levels as soon as he opened the door. Then I heard you scream."

Emma stared at Leslie. Leslie's grin was a sneaky little-kid grin, but it wasn't the furtive look of a liar. "Whew. I thought maybe you were..."

"You thought I killed Melvin? Of course you did. I thought maybe *you* killed Melvin."

"You thought?" Emma said indignantly. "Well, I guess you would."

"So I guess we're pretty much thinking the same thing. Carl Niome is no good. And that nose. That nose looks like he takes more shots of tequila than shots at the firing range." Leslie turned her whole body to the side and looked intently at Emma.

"Well, I suppose so," replied Emma. "He might not be very good. What's your point?"

Leslie pulled at threads in her sweats. "I was just thinking... poor Melvin, you know? I mean, he deserves more than Detective Abbott and his very buff sidekick Costello." Her eyes grew steadily brighter.

"What, you mean we should hire someone? I don't know about your paycheck, but mine is woefully inadequate for hiring a guy to mow my lawn, much less—"

"No, I don't think we should hire someone. Let me ask you this—what were your favorite books when you were young?"

Emma thought for a minute with a nostalgic smile. "Nancy Drew. Trixie Belden. Encyclopedia Brown… sometimes the Hardy Boys."

"And now?"

The smile grew. "Oh, I vacillate between Myron Bolitar and Stephanie Plum mysteries."

Leslie held out her closed fist. "Let's do it. Let's solve it ourselves."

Emma felt her face go through a range of expressions: surprise, doubt, then fear. *That's the craziest thing I've ever heard.* "Ah don't know, Leslie. Ah've never even seen a dead body before, much less tried to find his killer. It sounds dangerous. Or maybe stupid. Probably both."

"Possibly. But don't you feel a sense of responsibility to Melvin? I bet he would have a saying to fit this situation. 'If you can save the world, you oughta,' or something cute like that. 'Upon such sacrifices, my Cordelia, the Gods themselves throw incense.' Although that's King Lear thinking they are the sacrifices, so it doesn't really fit."

"I don't know. It seems like that could be the perfect fit. I want to know who killed Melvin, but I don't want to sacrifice my really great career. Or myself. Ah sure don't want to sacrifice my life." Emma pushed down on her cuticles, a nervous habit that never seemed to make her nails look any better. *I know the reason I went into teaching was to help people, but can I help like this?*

"We can be very, very careful," Leslie said. "'To be thus is nothing but to be *safely* thus.' *Macbeth.*"

Emma snorted. "Come on, I may not be able to quote the man at will, but even I know *Macbeth* is one of Shakespeare's greatest tragedies. Using that for a quote about our safety ain't helpful." She shook her head. "Is not helpful."

She got out of the car, walked toward the door of the bagel shop, and peered in, happy to note an empty corner table. Private. She went back to Leslie and stood next to her at the open window.

Leslie's face grew more excited by the minute. "Come on, don't you remember how much you wanted to be Nancy Drew? How cool was she? The coolest, that's how. Maybe the police will solve it—who knows?

But a little insider investigation couldn't hurt." Her eyes grew big and pleading. "Whaddya think?"

Emma closed her eyes. The picture of Melvin surrounded by blood wouldn't go away. For some reason, her focus narrowed to the palm resting away from Melvin's torso. He'd been holding the sequined bookmark in that hand the last time she'd seen him alive, and her heart had gone out to him. She should help if she could. She took a deep breath and nodded. She closed her fist and smacked Leslie's, first on top then knuckle to knuckle.

"Yay!" Leslie cheered. "Let's go then. Let's do it!"

They walked from the car into the bagel shop for a quick breakfast. It had become obvious that, besides Leslie putting on some adult-type clothes, they had a lot to do.

CHAPTER 8

Later that day, Emma and Leslie walked to a park just a few blocks from Emma's house. They sat on low playground swings, eating burritos and looking at a Harlan Coben and a James Lee Burke mystery novel, respectively.

"I'm not sure this is how we should go about this," Emma said around a mouthful of beans. "I've read all of these books, and they didn't help me this morning—I acted like a spaced-out space cadet." Her face burned at the recollection. *How could I not have called the police?* That detective's suspicion shouldn't have surprised her. If she were in charge, she would suspect herself. Some days, mature, responsible adulthood seemed a universe away.

They'd picked up some supplies at the hardware store earlier: screwdrivers in multiple sizes, a corkscrew, a blender, and a crowbar.

"Crowbar?" Emma had said. "Are we going to hit the murderer over the head? I thought we were just going to find him and, you know, point him out to someone, ahh, *bigger*. And a blender?"

Leslie had shushed her and said, "You never know what your situation may require." She'd also bought two Swiss army knives—one for each of them.

"Did you really think I could have killed that poor man?" asked Emma.

"I think that's redundant, spaced-out space cadet. I don't really think you're the killer, just based on your swooning, delicate-lily reaction when you found him and *especially* when you realized you'd forgotten to call the cops. Call me crazy, but I don't think that can be faked." She looked Emma up and down. "I mean, I guess you could be an amazing actress that even I can't read." She grinned. "I doubt that, of course. I'm pretty good, if I do say so myself. But fine, we'll both be suspects, and we saw Carl the Clueless pass us off like so much chicken fluff. And that's what I'm doing to your worries. You were fabulous with that goon of a detective!"

What about that? Why is she so awful to Detective Niome? It was Emma's turn to look closely at her friend, decked out in the black shirt and shorts she'd insisted they wear to get started.

"Ah'm sorry, but if Ah'm going to start this big investigation with you, we have to be totally honest with each other." Emma took a deep breath. "Why would you say that policeman's not smart? Why were you so mean to him? Do you know him?"

Leslie stopped swinging. She dipped her head forward so the bob could cover her cheeks. "I can't. It's too embarrassing."

"Did he arrest you before? You don't need to be embarrassed. Ah'm the one who should be embarrassed about how poorly Ah handled things this morning." She patted Leslie's knee. "It can't be that bad."

"It is that bad. It's humiliating."

"Leslie."

"Oh, all right. All right. But don't say I didn't warn you." She flung her head back, exposing her face again. "When I was a sophomore in high school, I sneaked out of my friend Kendra's house. Or maybe it was Amy's—they both had great houses for sneaking out—and we went skinny-dipping at Arney Lake." She shoved in another big mouthful of burrito and chewed mightily. Then she took another bite.

"Come on, come on. You got arrested for indecent exposure? So what? You were a minor. You're thirty-seven, right? So that was over twenty years ago." Emma counted on her fingers. "Right, twenty-one years."

"Patience. I didn't get arrested. Lemme get this out. So we're naked in the water, and a car pulls up to the beach. And these four senior boys get out. At least, I thought they were all seniors because the two I knew were."

"I sure don't see where you're goin' with this, but continue."

"So they strip to their tighty whities and walk into the water. One of them walks toward me, and only my head is sticking above water, and

I'm *so* glad it's dark. The guy puffs out his chest and says, 'Hey, I'm Carl Niome. Do you know me?'"

Emma's eyes widen. "No! He was one of those senior boys?"

"Yes, but that's not the embarrassing part. He says, 'I play football. If you don't know me now, you will soon.'"

Emma looked at Leslie quizzically. "What an idiot. Maybe that's embarrassing for him, but..." She stopped, and her eyebrows shot up. "You didn't."

Leslie sighed. "I did."

"You *dated* him? You went out with the police lieutenant in charge of Melvin's murder?" Emma was astonished. "Because he played football? He's so short."

"Because he was the football *star*. And because he was a senior, and because, oh, I don't know. That self-confidence, the whole 'if you don't know me now, you will soon' just got me. Sucked me right in."

"Well I have to say, I'm surprised. You seem so much more sophisticated and worldly than that guy. He must've been the quarterback, right? Or some sort of a... runner guy? He's not very big."

Leslie's face was glum. "Yes, quarterback. Star quarterback of our rival high school, Central Mountain High. He was buff then, I swear. It actually gets worse though. He was my first."

Emma gasped. "That man took your virginity? Holy moly macaroni, Leslie."

"I know, I know," she moaned. "And he really isn't smart, Emma. Whatever smarts he may have had got knocked out of his head on the football field." She set her burrito on her lap and grabbed Emma's hand. "Melvin was the greatest, and we love him and should find out who killed him, but Carl Niome will never do it on his own. This morning, maybe you weren't Emma Lovett at her best, but you just took some time to feel comfortable with the Amazonian Emma. Now that we're both hear-us-roar women and all that, we should go for it." She held the James Lee Burke novel aloft. "Forget all this type-A preparation. As Shakespeare says, "You see, my good wenches—how men of merit are sought after; the undeserver may sleep, when the man of action is called on.'" With that, Leslie bustled about, gathering their supplies.

Emma frowned. "So are we good wenches or men of action? Besides, isn't it Falstaff speaking in that quote? He's hardly the heroic man of action who should be our role model! Unless, a'course, you're talking about some action with that cute guy sitting at the end of the coaches' table. Hoo-ee." Emma imagined what she'd like to do to the coach until Leslie thumped her on the back of the head. "Ow! Quit that, you! There were no public displays of affection here!"

"No, not yet, but I can see potential PDA in your eyes. Come on now, focus. Let's go to the school and search for clues." Leslie dropped the last screwdriver into a gigantic backpack, grabbed the crowbar, strapped the pack onto her shoulders, and they headed off to school.

"It's only three," said Emma. "What if they're still there? I mean, doesn't it take a long time to gather evidence—hair samples and all that?"

She stared out the window as Leslie drove them toward school. The idea of amateur detecting was kind of thrilling, but it also made her nervous. The hairs on the backs of her forearms, the ones that had stood up as soon as she smelled the blood that morning, had yet to lie flat. She pondered the wisdom of their plan for a moment longer then came to a decision—screw it. This was her new, be-herself adventurous life, and she was going to make her mark, darn it.

Never mind if that mark involves me getting fired in the first week of my job or maybe even enduring some pain or danger or possibly dying; make a mark I will. As Shakespeare always said... aw, shoot. *How did Leslie do that, always have a pertinent Shakespearean quote at the tip of her tongue?* Emma would probably never wear heels or hairspray with as much grace as Leslie, but she was determined to get the quote thing down at some point.

Leslie replied, breaking Emma's train of thought, "Well, I have to say your heart is in the right place, giving Carl the Clueless the benefit of the doubt. But you're in the wrong town for primo police work. Rumor has it that when a student here allegedly killed his pregnant girlfriend, Carl saw him not long after and told him, 'Git on home and wash those nasty stains outta your clothes, boy.' Somehow I think all his investigating talent could fit on the head of a little-bitty pin. He's a glorified glory-days high school football star, that's all." She grinned.

"But if by some miracle of the criminal-science fairy they are still there, we'll just stay back and do some reconnaissance work."

They pulled into a little apartment building parking lot next to the school.

Leslie reached over Emma's lap, pulled a set of binoculars out of the glove compartment, and handed them to Emma. "Maybe we can learn something important from a distance."

Emma turned the binoculars over. "Where did these come from? We didn't buy them on our supply-gathering run, did we?"

Leslie's face grew mischievous. "No, they were in here already. I told you about Timothy, yes? My ex-bastard?"

Emma gasped. "That's what I call my ex too! Amazin'."

"Anyway, before I sent him packing, he was involved in some extracurricular activities, if you get my drift. This was how I found out. I have a camera too, one with an excellent zoom lens if you're interested... *your* ex? I didn't know there was an ex. What ex? Tell, tell!" Leslie twisted around in her seat and faced Emma.

Emma waved her off. "Later. Right now, I'd like to concentrate on poor Melvin and also on not getting caught. Thinking about Ronald will just make me angry, then I'll lose focus. Come on, it looks pretty quiet over there." She jumped out of the passenger door of Leslie's conspicuous red Audi convertible and headed through the fence toward the entrance to the school.

Leslie followed, muttering, "Ronald? You were married to a guy named Ronald? Did he have red hair and giant french fries as his pals? Didja call him 'Ronnie'? How 'bout 'Reynaldo'?"

Leslie continued gibbering in disbelief until Emma shushed her as they reached the courtyard.

CHAPTER 9

THEY STOOD IN FRONT OF the building, looking at the yellow crime-scene tape that had been placed in five or six uniform strands across the door, starting at the very top and marching on down to the doorstop.

"It's just like on TV!" cried Emma. "Neat!"

Leslie looked the barricade up and down. "The thing that cracks me up is that Andy Taylor here thinks that five pieces of tape will somehow make it more difficult for us to enter than just one." She snorted. "Maybe on TV that's how it works."

They went around to a side door and used Leslie's key to enter the school.

"Gee, do you think we should be wearing gloves?" Emma whispered. "You know, fingerprints and all that."

"Gee, darlin'," Leslie changed her voice to a sugared Southern drawl, "do you suppose the Mayberry RFD squad might have some technology that can tell them *these* fingerprints are different from the ones we put here yesterday? Or the day before that? We've got the gloves to wear in the main office—the crime scene."

"Thank you, smart aleck. All I meant was what if they checked the door for fingerprints earlier, and now we're puttin' new ones on, thus proving our postmortem entry. Well, our post-postmortem entry, I guess. Our earlier one qualifies as that too, since he was dead when we got here." She sighed. "Poor Melvin. He was such a teddy bear kind of guy—I could tell. And such a thankless job—can you imagine?"

But Leslie was already wiping the doors where they had touched them. "Okay, you got me on that one, Agatha Christie. Just be careful."

They sneaked into the commons, gloves on. The coppery stench of blood lingered in the air, making the hairs inside Emma's nose quiver. She remembered smelling pot for the first time at a high school party. It was an unforgettable smell, always flying straight into the memory cells of her brain the moment it hit her nose. This would be one of those smells, she could tell. Only without any good memories attached.

The women went under the wildcat sign into the office—neither jumped to hit the sign. *Too bad. This may be a good time to do everything possible to avoid accidents.*

Leslie ducked under the crime scene tape at the office entrance and paused. Emma followed suit and stood right behind her, staring at the sharp shoulder blades poking out from her black T-shirt with lettering down the back—Bon Jovi *Slippery When Wet* Tour, 1987. Anything to avoid looking at what Leslie was looking at. But, Emma decided finally, if they were to solve this thing, it would probably be important to, you know, study the crime scene a little. For Melvin.

Taking a deep breath, she peeked around Leslie's back. The floor where Melvin had fallen held a taped outline of a body. The silhouette looked smaller than the hulking figure who had entered her room on Monday. Was that only two days ago? A large pool where his head had been was drying to a brownish clot. The spatters on the sides of the desk, the ones she remembered as a vivid red, had turned brown and dull like the inside of an old Band-Aid. Even the air in the office seemed brown, like a haze of pollution had entered the building and settled in the office. The whole scene seemed surreal and sepia toned, an old film noir.

"See anything new?" Leslie's voice sounded as if it was strangling.

Emma noticed her tense posture and clenched fists. No wonder those shoulder blades were poking out of her T-shirt. "No, it seems the same as I remember, only darker. I think the first thing they do is try to determine what happened in what order. Let's just try to figure out a chain of events and then get out of here, okay?"

Leslie walked in a circle around the taped outline. "His head went down here"—she pointed and continued to the other side—"and his feet were facing toward the front counter *here*. So if he walked in the same way we did and went down almost immediately, the killer must have come…" She went to a little cubbyhole with a sink and a coffee machine in the back right corner of the office. "From here. They surprised him from behind—wham!—with the pewter wildcat." She brought her hand around in a circular motion and came down from above on Melvin's imaginary head.

Emma's eyes went bright with unshed tears. But with the unpleasant vision came information. "You knew Melvin; he was a tall enough guy. And even though that wildcat was heavy, Ah'm sure someone would have to come down hard on his head to kill him."

Leslie picked up on this train of thought. "And come down from a pretty decent height. Look, you do it. I'll be Melvin."

Emma positioned herself in the cubby with the imaginary paperweight in hand. Leslie came in and stood where they approximated Melvin to be. Emma swung her arm around and down. The imaginary paperweight struck with mighty force—right between Leslie's shoulder blades.

"Nope, I'm too short. Okay! There's some valuable information. The killer had to be pretty tall, unless he had time to stand on a chair before Melvin entered. Assuming this was a sort of hit-and-run killing, the chair would still be somewhere close, I think."

"The way his body went down looked like he was headed for this desk. Why would he have been going toward the desk? Or been in here at all?"

Emma walked to the other desk. "I don't know. Maybe he saw something at the desk that the killer had left, and he went to look at it, but the killer had gone to the cubby for coffee. He saw Melvin approaching and killed him to prevent him from getting to the desk."

Leslie ran her hands over the desk; it was clean. "Nothing on the desk, but even Carl the Clueless would've probably picked up something that stood out."

"And no chairs close enough for someone to stand on and hit Melvin over the head," Emma noted. "So Ah guess we'll just have to start with the tall theory."

"Well, great. That narrows it down to half of the teaching and student population at this school, me included. Assuming it's even someone *from* here. Maybe he had gambling debts, and the killer was Tall Joe Someonelli coming to extract payments."

They sighed in unison, but Emma felt encouraged. "I think it's a good start. Besides, don't they just break bones on people with gambling debts? He's sure not going to be payin' anyone back now. What should we do next?"

"Let's go upstairs and check his mailbox," replied Leslie.

They headed back across the office for the stairs on the other side, careful not to touch anything as they went.

The teachers' lounge looked the same as it had yesterday, which seemed odd to Emma. Something huge had happened down two short flights of stairs, and this room didn't even know it. Leslie walked to the far end of the boxes and peeked into one labeled simply Custodians.

"Why don't they each get their own?" asked Emma. "That seems unfair."

"I think there must not be as much spam sent out to janitors. You know, we get the professional journals plus surveys, catalogues, all that. It takes up more room." Leslie pulled a couple of papers out of the box and studied them. "Okay, what we have here are two work schedules for September. One's addressed to Melvin, and the other is Debbie's. She's the blonde who cleans over in the 400s. We know why Melvin didn't pick his up. I wonder why Debbie hasn't picked hers up? Hmm."

Emma looked thoughtful. "That's strange. Maybe Debbie killed him and she's now on the run."

Leslie looked about to reply when they heard noises in the office. She grabbed Emma's elbow and drew her behind the door of the lounge. They listened to Detective Niome and another voice Emma didn't recognize.

"Are you sure you've got enough here, Detective?" said the voice.

"Yup," Niome's flat-lipped twang floated up the stairs. "My men spent the whole morning gathering evidence from this sidea the building. No fingerprints out of the ordinary—our technician said only the secretaries and you had fingerprints on the computers and the coffee machine. Nothing out of the ordinary. The murder weapon—yer pewter paperweight—was wiped clean, so that's a dead end. As long as you know we might be comin' back and forth, I don't see why you can't open school tomorrow. I know those kids would love the time off, but..."

"But they'll hate it when they have to make up the lost time come June. I'll call in a cleanup crew for the office. Thanks, Detective."

"No problem, Nate. Say, how do you think it's gonna be for them Broncos this year?"

The voices faded as the men walked out of the front office. Leslie let go of Emma's elbow, which Emma realized hurt like the dickens where it'd been clutched. They breathed a collective sigh of relief.

"Who was the other guy?" asked Emma, rubbing her funny bone.

"You met him—the principal, Nathan Farrar. Or you saw him zip by on his skateboard, at least. I'll introduce you when this all calms down. Hopefully I can introduce you as my partner on this case we've solved singlehandedly!" She winked at Emma.

"Wouldn't that be doublehandedly? And what do you want to do now, Mademoiselle Poirot, since others are prowling the school and makin' our lives more difficult? We can check out the janitor Debbie thing tomorrow, but..."

"Nah, let's go. We'll have an easier time of it tomorrow when we're actually supposed to be here. Right now I need a drink!" Leslie went around to Emma's other side, and they walked—quietly, cautiously, not touching anything—down the stairs to take a small hiatus from a hard afternoon of detecting.

Conceal me what I am, and be my aid
For such disguise as haply shall become
The form of my intent.

—*Twelfth Night I.2.54–6*

CHAPTER 10

Friday, August 28

Thomas Jefferson High School started at the usual time on Friday morning, with the usual bell and the kids bemoaning the fact that summer was officially over. It was *very* officially over, since their parents had now been to the school and met their teachers—that made it more real somehow. But the ambience was ever so unusual, with kids whispering to kids and teachers whispering to teachers and janitors sneaking around on tippy-toe, watching over their shoulders for what Emma had overheard some students calling the "Custodian Canceller."

Emma felt sorry for the janitors, although she couldn't imagine Melvin had been killed by some demented serial killer who had it in for the hired help. *What, the killer's father was a janitor and he was ashamed of his blue-collar background? Somehow, the killer's whacked-out brain thought crushing all the custodians made it okay that he couldn't afford a letter jacket in high school?* That was just too ridiculous for Emma to stomach.

No, his murder probably had something to do with Melvin's background. Or maybe he'd just stumbled onto something he shouldn't have. Janitors were in the building late; it could have been a wrong-place-wrong-time thing. How sad.

She got through her first three classes without noticing what she said—which was okay, because the kids weren't really listening anyway. She overheard some boys in her American Lit class betting each other on who would sneak into the office after hours and try to find some overlooked crusted brain matter. That gave Emma the big-time heebie jeebies, but she maintained enough composure to remind the boys that Melvin had been killed in that office after hours, and shouldn't they be more careful? However, that didn't have the effect Emma desired. They just looked, wide-eyed, at each other—they hadn't considered that. They high-fived and upped the bet from ten bucks to twenty. *Oh well.*

Following the blur of morning classes, she went to meet Leslie for lunch. After an amazing lobster bisque, courtesy of Mrs. Albert, they popped over to the left side of the library to strategize. Emma stopped short of their customary discussion table to take note of the man in the sports section—it was that cute Lounge Lizard reading a book about Peyton Manning. Leslie took note of Emma's googly eyes, sighed, and steered her toward him.

"Hunter Wells! This is Emma Lovett. She's brand new—even newer than you."

He looked up, startled, and dropped his book. Well, his *books*, as it turned out. The sports bio was a cover for another book. Emma knelt and helped him pick it up—Kierkegaard! He jumped up a notch in her estimation, from pretty cute coach guy to pretty cute coach-philosopher guy. He blushed, took the book back, and hid it on the shelves.

"Hello, ladies. How was your lunch?"

When he made eye contact with Emma, she about fell over. His soulful blue eyes and shock of black hair were enhanced by those candy-apple cheeks that guys hated but girls loved. He looked about six feet tall, slender but wiry, with a blue polo shirt that made his eyes bluer, and khaki trousers. Definitely someone she'd like to get to know. Definitely.

"Nice to meet you, Hunter," she responded. "Our lunch was wonderful. And how was yours?"

"Well, our discussion today was about reasons for becoming a free agent. So I guess it was *somewhat* philosophical." He grinned.

Oh, gorgeous grin too. With a dimple, for Pete's sake. *They sure do make 'em nice in Colorado.*

Emma was bursting to ask, especially now that she'd seen his choice in literature, "Don't you get tired of talking only about sports and sex?"

The three of them walked to the back table.

"Well, sports really is a multifaceted, complex issue," he said.

Leslie snorted.

"And sex—let's just say I'm already tired of discussing it with sweaty guys all the time," he said.

"I imagine it does get tiring," replied Leslie as they sat, "especially when mixed with sports. I thought the whole 'scoring' idea went out with junior high locker rooms—yet I've heard Charlie talk about *touchdowns*, and not the kind you make on the football field."

Hunter snickered. "Charlie is maybe a taco or two short of a combination plate. But he's been here a long time, and I'm learning fast that seniority definitely 'scores' with the Lizards."

"Not to mention his superintendent parentage," offered Leslie.

"Yeah, well, I won't mention it if you don't." He smiled again. "And ya know, the only other people I can really talk to at lunch are in the social studies department—that's where I teach—and they all have little kids and talk about bottles and breastfeeding all day. Except for Martha Bonaventure, who doesn't talk much at all. To tell the truth, I'm slightly more adept at sports and sex—discussing them anyway."

Leslie elbowed Emma. "So, are you a free agent these days, Hunter?"

The color came back to Hunter's cheeks, matched by a blushing Emma, but his response was cut short when he saw Charlie and another coach walking by the library window. Leslie shoved Hunter under the table.

Emma eyed Leslie in astonishment. She craned her neck to look at Hunter now crouched below them. "My, my. I daresay I don't know you well enough for you to be under there, Mr. Wells."

"Please"—his voice was muffled—"call me Hunter."

Emma giggled. "Hunter. What are you doin'?"

Leslie stage-whispered, "Lounge Lizards can't be seen with English teachers. In the *library*, no less. My God, the ceiling might fall in."

Emma's head was still bent down. "Hunter, maybe you should tell the Lounge Lizards that English teachers know lots of nifty words for sex."

Leslie knocked on the tabletop. "Okay, they're gone. You can come up now. Unless... you've decided you like it better down there."

Hunter came up, his hair disheveled and one side of his shirt collar standing up, looking completely embarrassed. "I'm sorry. I shouldn't even be worried about stuff like that—I should have come right back up and called them over. It's just that I'm still pretty new here. Emma, you must think I'm a total putz."

Emma placed a thoughtful finger to her lips. "No, just a partial putz. But it's nothing that can't be fixed. Quick! Give me five multisyllabic words that mean 'putz.'"

"Nincompoop," he quipped. "Revolter. Supercilious featherhead. Impudent saucy-boy. Ahhh..." He screwed up his face, thinking hard.

"Come on!" Emma said. "You can do it!"

"Um. Butthead?" He collapsed on the chair as the women applauded, at least until they were eyeballed by Edward Dixon.

The three chatted for another minute until Leslie started rambling about open and closed nouns—which, to be frank, Emma had never even heard of—and which was a clear ploy to get rid of Hunter. It worked.

He made his excuses and headed through those electronic gates at the front of the library. Emma watched him go, salivating ever so slightly, until the gates bleated. Edward must have had them turned up to the highest possible volume setting, because they trumpeted through the whole south wing of the school. Hunter stopped short, face red and grin sheepish, while Edward minced over to the gates. Hunter pulled a book from the back of his pants, where it was hidden under his shirt, and handed it to the librarian.

Emma strained to see the title. *Walden*! He was stealing *Walden* from the library, probably so no coach would see him check it out. She couldn't decide whether to be impressed once again by his choice of reading or endeared that he felt he had to sneak it out of the building. She chose both.

Emma was drawn from her reverie by Leslie, who grabbed hold of Emma's earlobe and pulled her focus back to the table. "Concentrate! He's a suspect. I don't care how gorgeous or well read he is. We must focus."

Emma watched him checking out the book. "Awww, come on, we're suspects already. Does he have to be a suspect too?" All of a sudden, she turned businesslike. "No, Ah'm only joking. Of course he has to be a suspect. But does he *have* to be a suspect?"

"Of course he does, dummy. Did we not deduce that anyone over five-nine or so had to be a suspect? Melvin had to have been killed by someone tall, and your Lothario over there is at least six feet. It's the only clue we got, baby. Let's not toss it, 'kay?"

Emma sighed and put her hand over her forehead, Scarlett O'Hara-ish. "All right. But let's get to work so we can eliminate him from the list. So I can date him. Hey, that kinda rhymes. The Nancy Drew rap!"

They got up and left so they could talk privately, Emma chanting "elim*inate* him so I can *date* him" the whole way. After stopping at the office to ask about Debbie—the janitor who hadn't picked up her schedule—and finding out she was on vacation in Las Vegas until Monday, they went to sit in Leslie's room.

"Well…" Emma sighed. "At least we've eliminated one suspect. Unless that Las Vegas story is just an alibi and she sneaked back to murder Melvin, her deceiving lover."

"Nah, she's pretty short, now that I think about it."

"Then what do we do now?"

Leslie sat at her desk, one long arm ending in a fist under her chin as she pondered. But she couldn't really make a fist since her fingernails were too long, so she rested her chin on some knuckles, with the red talons splayed out underneath. She was wearing a long sleeveless tank dress with sandals, which would be pretty summery if it weren't all black. For Melvin, she'd said, but Emma suspected black was a primary color in Leslie's wardrobe—seasons and mourning notwithstanding.

"I guess we should have eliminated her immediately. My bad," Leslie said. "I think we need to find out more about Melvin—his associations, how he spent his days, what kind of guy he was. That way it'll be easier to figure out if someone killed him for personal reasons, or if he was just in the wrong place at the wrong time." She flipped up the top of the laptop on her desk, turned it on, and her fingers clicked across the keys.

"What are you doing?" asked Emma.

"I just googled Melvin's name. Hey, it says 'Find two listings for Melvin McManus in the North Carolina white pages'! Is that anywhere near Holly Hills? No"—she scrolled—"nope, nope. Here's a George Melvin McManus who died in 1958."

"No, silly, you're in a completely different state." Emma looked over Leslie's shoulder. "Hey, what are you doin' now?"

"Checking the database for Melvin's address. We have a planning hour right now—I think we should plan to pay Melvin's house a visit." The clicking stopped, and a printer in the corner hummed.

Emma crossed the room and pulled out the paper. "He lived at 1129 Washington. Is that far from here?"

"No, actually, it's the street on the other side of those apartment buildings we parked at yesterday. Whaddya say? Shall we play hooky? Do a little B&E?" Leslie pushed away from the desk and twirled in her chair.

Emma knit her brows together. "B&E? Blowing off school and embarking upon a life of crime?"

"Breaking and entering, goofball. Common crimespeak for all your typical murder mysteries, which you know. But I like yours better."

"Oh, hell—excuse me!" Emma's hand covered her mouth. "I know what breaking and entering is—I just missed the acronym. That's pretty serious, isn't it? Ah mean, seriously illegal. Like, losing our jobs, being in the police blotter that they publish in the newspaper illegal." She paced in front of the student desks, her flowered skirt rippling as if she were giving an intense lecture.

For all her twang and inexperience, she did feel intense when she lectured—especially when it was about how important English was to your overall education. She felt lecture-type energy now as she worried aloud about losing her job during the first week of school.

But Leslie quelled her fears. "No, I promise we won't break anything—just enter. And if we get caught, we'll do a dumb-girl routine. 'Oh, Mister Ossifer, we just wanted to put some flowers on Melvin's mantel in remembrance.' Smile, smile, bat, bat of eyelashes. You can do that in your sleep, Miss Consummate Southern Charm. I just think it's the best place to go from here."

Emma smiled. "Okay. But let's not forget to bring some actual flowers with us, because otherwise..."

"Yeah, yeah, flowers." Leslie grabbed her purse, and Emma grabbed the address.

They got as far as out into the commons, where the principal rolled up to them. He was wearing a short-sleeved green oxford with khakis and a tie with geometric blue and darker green shapes. His skateboard had multicolored geometric shapes on it too—Emma wondered if he did that on purpose. His blond hair was longer in back, and it curled around his ears and over the nape of his neck. A darker-blond handlebar mustache lifted as he smiled at the pair.

"Hi, ladies! Are you doing okay today?" His brown eyes were a little sad, like a beagle begging for a bone. "I wanted to talk to you, make sure you're okay."

Leslie said, "Nathan, this is Emma Lovett, our new English teacher."

"Lovett." He chuckled. "I love it! Heh heh heh." His face suddenly grew serious. "I'm sorry I missed your interview. I was out of town, and I knew the vice principal would make a great choice."

Emma looked at Leslie, who shrugged in an I-told-you-who-was-really-in-charge way.

He continued. "Are you doing okay after you... after... yesterday? I'm sorry I didn't call you at home, but I was involved in the police investigation."

Leslie widened her eyes at Emma. *What investigation?* But she said nothing.

"Ah'm fine," Emma replied. "It was a little disconcerting, to say the least."

Nathan nodded, his mustache wiggling.

"Leslie and I will do anything we can to help Melvin and his family," Emma added.

Nathan shook his head. "I don't think he had a family, at least not anyone close."

Leslie squeezed Emma's hand—no one would be at Melvin's house.

"Well," said Emma, "anything we can do to get school back to normal. Y'all just let us know! Nice to meet you, Nathan."

He waved good-bye and skated away.

Leslie gazed at Emma in wonderment. "Did you just say, 'Y'all just let us know?' Holy cow, woman, you turn that Southern stuff on and off like a faucet, don't you? I mean, the accent is always there, but that drippy debutante stuff comes and goes."

Emma twirled her hands. "Some people think it makes me sound stupid; other people hear it and want to go to bed with me. Others just think it's sweet. I choose the impression I want to make and go from there." Her green eyes sparkled. "Whatever works."

Leslie shook her head as they walked to the parking lot. "All I have to say is this: there's more to you than meets the eye, Emma Lovett."

The August heat shimmered off the parking lot as they got into Emma's green slower-than-molasses Honda—they had determined that her car was definitely less conspicuous than Leslie's red bomber. After a quick run to the market for flowers, they headed to the street just west of the school.

CHAPTER 11

THE RESIDENCE AT 1129 WASHINGTON Street was a tiny house that stood amid a row of almost identical box-like houses. They were all set back from the road with rectangular strips of neatly tended grass and mailboxes shaped like ducks or pine trees. The houses were white or cream colored with shutters of varied shades and brightly colored flowerboxes in the windows. Melvin's house was one of the white ones, and it had blue shutters and no flowerboxes. *That's because there's no female living there.* Emma felt sad again, remembering the sequined bookmark.

His mailbox was shaped like an old-fashioned schoolhouse though, which was too precious for words. Emma touched it lovingly as she walked by, then she slapped her own hands. *Fingerprints, dummy!*

As they approached, they noted the front door was free of crime-scene tape.

Leslie snorted. "Figures."

She strutted up to the door like the Avon lady coming to call, then right before she reached it, she feinted left and sneaked toward the back. Emma followed suit, even though she thought Leslie looked pretty funny feinting and sneaking in her long black sundress. A little gate led to the backyard, and Leslie was about to enter when Emma put a hand on her shoulder to stop her.

"Hellooo. A gated backyard. What could *that* signify?"

If Leslie was embarrassed at possibly forgetting something significant, she didn't show it. "Well, of course it could mean a dog." She whistled. "Here, Rover. Rover, Rover, come on over!"

Nothing. *Oh, the poor man. Not even a puppy to keep him company.*

It took them a minute to squeak the gate open; obviously no one had come or gone that way in quite a while. The backyard was as well tended as the front though, with a sidewalk going all the way to the back fence and a little picnic table in the far corner, shaded by a large tree. Maybe oak, Emma thought. Maybe... maybe this wasn't a good time to get started on her name-that-tree game. She sighed and, pulling out her Swiss Army knife in preparation for the B part of their B&E, followed Leslie to the back door. But Leslie took out a handkerchief, wrapped it around the doorknob, and walked on in.

Emma was astonished. "How did you do that? Do you think someone was here before? Maybe it's the killer!" She whirled around as if she'd been tapped on the shoulder by an invisible stalking hand.

Leslie shook her head. "Come on, ninny. You're a small-town girl. How many people in *your* small town lock their back doors during the day?" She rolled her eyes. "I told you we wouldn't be breaking, just entering." She went in, threw the flowers on the kitchen table, and faced Emma. "I think we should split up and search for clues."

Emma nodded. "Sounds good. Are we looking for something in particular or just clues? Specificity might be helpful here."

"Hmmm." Leslie cocked her hip, musing. "I think any papers that might have information—mail, pictures, scrapbooks, et cetera. You start in his bedroom, and I'll start in the living room."

They stood at the edge of the dollhouse-sized kitchen. Emma went right, and Leslie turned left.

Melvin's bedroom wasn't nearly as well kept as the yard. A blue comforter was scrunched up on the floor at the base of a queen-sized bed. The bed had no headboard, and aside from a bookshelf to its left, which held a few hardback books, a reading lamp, and an alarm clock, the room was devoid of decoration and color. Even the window treatments were simple white blinds. Emma sat on the corner of Melvin's bed and sniffled. *What a lonely life this man must have led.* Although Emma's interactions with him had been brief, she'd sensed the good heart beating in his bulky chest. This detecting stuff was depressing.

"Emma?" called Leslie. "Are you searching?"

Emma sniffed. "Yes, searching. I'm searching, Leslie." *Searching for meaning in a sad ol' guy's life.*

She scooched over on the bed and riffled through the library books in Melvin's bookcase. *Of Mice and Men, A Wrinkle in Time, Island of the Blue Dolphins*—some of her childhood favorites. Odd choices for a grown man's room but nothing she would consider a clue. A Bartlett's Book of Quotations sat next to the bed, and Emma smiled, remembering Melvin's quote from Monday—something like "it ain't worth doin' if you don't do it right." That was a version of something her father had always said—anything worth doing was worth doing well.

She sighed. *Lordy, do I miss my daddy.* She checked under the bed and found only dust. His small closet held a few T-shirts, some jeans, two gray jumpsuits, and three pairs of shoes. She even checked in the toes of the shoes and in the shoe boxes for hidden papers. Nothing.

She headed back to the living room. "Ah'm finding zilch. A book of quotations, which we already knew he liked. Some young adult books, which is interestin', Ah guess, but Ah know a lot of adults who are into YA. You?"

Leslie shook her head. "I got jack squat as well. Nothing interesting in his phone bill, which, aside from some coupon flyers, was his only mail. I found four quarters in the couch cushions though. I'll spring for a soda on the way back to school, eh?" Leslie took a long-suffering breath.

Emma shrugged. "What about that angry voice I heard earlier in the week? Could that have something to do with Melvin's death?"

"Well," Leslie replied, "you said the voice talked about sports. There's not so much as a *Sports Illustrated* here. Just the books you found in the bedroom." She picked up a TV remote from an end table and flipped on Melvin's old set. "ABC." She flipped through the channels. "He doesn't even have ESPN, only your basic networks."

"Oh well," Emma said, "this detecting stuff can't be easy or everyone would do it. Where do we go from here?"

"I think we should go back to school for fifth hour. Someone might get suspicious if all sixty of our students are wandering about 'cause their teachers didn't show." She headed into the kitchen. "The soda idea sounds great though, if I do say so myself. Let's see if he has anything to drink."

She opened the refrigerator, which held a chunk of moldy cheese and a bottle of salsa. Emma opened cabinets—a few plates here, some crackers in this one, and—her eyes widened. "Whoa. Looky here, Leslie."

The cabinet farthest from the refrigerator held something to drink, all right. Lots of somethings. Bottles and bottles of whiskey lined the shelves—big bottles of Jim Beam and Jack Daniels. Only a couple of the JD—Emma knew they were more expensive—but all in all, it was a staggering array. Leslie walked over and goggled at the stash.

"Wow" was all she said.

"Do you think this is a clue?" asked Emma. "And if so, what does it tell us? Just because he drinks doesn't necessarily mean anything. He has enough money to keep a house, anyway."

Leslie scowled. "You're right. It doesn't tell us much of anything except that he was an alcoholic. Which makes his whole life even sadder, in my opinion." She seemed to consider something. "But wait. Maybe it does tell us something." She pulled out the bottles and looked behind them, then she checked all the other cabinets and drawers.

"Nope, these are the only containers in the house," she said. "You didn't find any flasks or fifths or anything in his bedroom, did you?"

"Nothing like that." Emma felt her eyes light up. "And there was nothing around his body or in his jumpsuit either; I think I'd have seen it. I hope I'd have seen it… I mean, it's not like I was being ultra-observant when I came upon his body, but… I think I'd have seen it."

"And that means…"

"That means he'd have to keep a stash somewhere around school!" crowed Emma.

"Exactly. Someone with this big of a habit could never have gone through an eight-hour shift all alone in that school without taking a nip at the bottle every now and then." Leslie had a handkerchief and was wiping off the surfaces they had touched as she talked. "So now we know where to go from here—back to the school tonight to search out Melvin's little hidey-hole. Well, first back to school for fifth hour. Say, do you know what you're going to teach during fifth hour? I don't have a clue. Ah, well—when all else fails, punt." She scrubbed the refrigerator handle, and they headed on out the back door.

Emma laughed. "Well, actually, Ah have my classes planned through next month. Ah know, Ah know. A little anal retentive, maybe? Got some great ideas though. Ah'm not comfortable punting just yet, and this leaves me more Nancy Drew time."

Leslie lifted her eyebrows. "Plus maybe a little time to make time with one Mr. Hunter Wells?" She bonked her hip against Emma's as they walked through the gate.

Emma gave her friend a wicked "who knows?" grin as they climbed into the car to return to Thomas Jefferson.

CHAPTER 12

EMMA WAS HEADED HOME AFTER finishing her fifth-hour class and holding a brief huddle with Leslie concerning their plans for murder solving later that evening, which were to eat a pizza as big as a Chevy and have some beer from a local microbrewery. Emma had discovered that Coloradans only drank beers with names like Fat Tire or Tommyknocker or Tin Whistle, or that at least had a fruit flavor of some sort and cost seven or eight dollars a six-pack. Words like Michelob and Miller Lite were apparently sacrilegious. After eating and completing their plans, they'd go back to the school to find Melvin's secret hideout—if such a thing existed.

She pulled into the driveway of her dollhouse, as she liked to call it, and sat momentarily to gaze at it. Her house! She could hardly breathe the words aloud, even though she had closed escrow in July. Always before it had been "her mother's house," then "Ronald's house," then again "her mother's house."

The phrase "Emma's house" almost made her tongue ache as the words passed through her lips. Never in her whole twenty-six years had anything made her feel more satisfied than buying that house—it was an absolute I-am-Emma-hear-me-roar moment. She got out of the car and twirled a couple of times going up the walk. She stopped to kiss the gladiolus that lined the front porch, not really caring who saw her perform that daily ritual.

One person who saw her was Emma's neighbor Delilah Thornberry, an aging hippie who had come out once before to kiss the flowers with her. Today Delilah just waved through the front window as Emma straightened the welcome mat on the front porch and adjusted the welcome plaque next to the door.

Her first image upon entering was a forty-gallon fish tank filled with angelfish, sitting on an oak stand at the edge of the living room. It was a small room with only a tiny forest-green couch, a fat striped loveseat, and a television, but it had two huge picture windows and enough plant life to qualify as a rainforest. Emma was so glad it was hers.

"Trinculo! Sir Toby! Ah'm here, darlings!"

A fat calico cat made figure eights around her legs almost immediately, internal motor churning as Emma bent to pick her up.

She swayed under the weight of the cat and stumbled over to plop onto the green couch. "Oof, Trinky, I guess that diet will have to become a reality since right now you weigh more than a typical six-year-old."

"Mrreow," replied Trinculo, and she licked Emma's face with her sandpaper tongue.

About that time, the plastic dog door flapped and a Sheltie bounded in from the back.

"Toby! How's my good little girl?"

Toby jumped onto the arm of the couch then into Emma's arms as she struggled to hold one pet on each shoulder. Their similar black, white, and brown markings made Emma look as if she were wearing an exotic—or maybe tacky—fur stole. She petted and loved them for another few minutes then rolled them off of her to land in a heap on the couch. They pretended to squabble, then Trinculo settled down to grooming Sir Toby. Emma poked them both fondly and stood to prepare her home for guests. Well, to prepare it for Leslie.

She picked a couple of hairs from the recliner and pondered the futility of making the place acceptable for her new friend, the socialite. Then she remembered the hard-rock T-shirt and Tweety Bird sneakers and thought everything would be fine. She went to change into the black shirt and shorts Leslie saw as their sleuthing uniform.

Leslie knocked on the door just as Emma was heating up her pre-World War II oven to keep the pizza warm. The house was more than eighty years old, and the oven acted like it was, but it could probably keep dinner warm. She hoped. She opened the door.

"Hi!" said Leslie. "I come bearing gifts."

She was holding an enormous square box on the flat of her palm like a waiter and a six-pack of what Emma assumed was elite microbrew.

Emma took the beer and led Leslie into the kitchen to deposit the pizza in the oven.

"So do you want the fifty-cent tour?" asked Emma. "It's pretty small, so I probably should call it the nickel tour. Want the nickel tour?" She led Leslie around, droning like a tour guide, "And now you see the kitchen, only five by ten feet, but with original hardwood flooring."

Leslie stopped in the bedroom. "I love this—especially the Battenberg lace coverlet and flowered valances, dahling. It's a little pure though. Hunter's going to think you're a virgin if you bring him in here."

"Oh, but once I break out the massage oils and the toys I have hiding in my little bitty bathroom, he'll forget all about the lace and flowers."

Leslie started for the bathroom. "Flying nine-volt?"

Emma stopped her. "Oh, honey, that's for me to know and... well, for me to know." Emma yawned and stretched, heading back into the kitchen to retrieve the pie. "Come on, let's eat. I need some protein and carbs and good ol' *fat* if we're going to work tonight."

"Yup, pizza—the ultimate energy food. I can't tell you how many college study sessions it got me through. Or how many inches it added to my thighs freshman year."

Emma looked at Leslie's thighs and curled her mouth in a moue of disgust. "Invisible inches, stick woman."

Leslie let out a bark of laughter. "No, really. I almost had to develop an eating disorder my sophomore year just to get rid of it. Now I thank God for treadmills."

She punctuated her statement by shoving almost a whole piece of cheesy pie into her mouth, rolling her eyes in ecstasy. Emma followed suit, and they sat at a small table in a breakfast nook off the kitchen. Each cracked open a bottle of snooty raspberry-tinged beer—Emma would have only one since she was driving. The dog and cat circled in for the dinner kill, but Emma shooed them away.

"How come you call them Trinculo and Sir Toby if they're girls?" asked Leslie, pulling strings of cheese off her chin.

Emma pulled a long draught off her bottle. "Because have you noticed that most of Shakespeare's women are either deranged, overly haughty, or just plain tragic? I mean, I thought of Viola, but I'm never sure which way to pronounce it. Besides"—she scratched Toby under her chin—"these two are pretty comical, so I wanted jesters and fools, or something equally apt."

Leslie twirled her fingers around Toby's tail, which the dog commenced chasing in circles. She laughed. "'Ah, this fellow is wise enough to play the fool; and to do that well craves a kind of wit.'" She nodded. "So we're just going to find the place where Melvin hid his alcohol? Any other ideas about clue gathering?"

"His house was so empty." Emma sighed. "I swear, every book I read or TV show I watch has clues, letters, or out-of-place objects, something. What if he was just in the wrong place at the wrong time? How will finding his alcohol stash lead us to his killer if it was a totally random event?"

Leslie finished her third piece of pizza. "Well, if it was a random event, it's still one that happened at the school. We'll look for his liquor, and we'll pay attention to the school—see if we can find any clues as to what Melvin found that got him killed."

Emma finished her second piece of pizza. "Guess so. Tell you one thing though—unless we find something to solve this tonight, Ah'm gonna have to take a break from detecting and spend the weekend reading introductory essays. Ah really want to do well and give my students a reason to be there beyond betting on who killed Melvin."

"You're right, of course," Leslie said. "I remember how much work it took during my first year—or five—to start feeling like the instructional dynamo you see before you now." She closed the pizza box. "Come, come, ya wench. Let us solve this murder most foul, strange, and unnatural."

Emma put the leftover pizza in the fridge. "Plus it's just plain horrible, don't you agree? Let's get ta doin' this—for Melvin!"

"For Melvin!" They clinked their beer bottles and left Sir Toby and Trinky to inhale pizza crumbs.

As Leslie was moving her car so they could go to the school in Emma's, Delilah came out of the house next door. She wore a tie-dye T-shirt with a long multicolored skirt and sandals. Her brown hair was peppered with gray, braided down her back, and secured with a leather knot. Next to her was a dog—large, shaggy, and with bangs that fell forward over his eyes and ears.

"Yoo-hoo!" She waved. "Emma, come 'ere, you sweetheart, you!" A smile split the sun-kissed wrinkles of her face. She wore no makeup—surprise!—but it seemed her eyes sparkled in the many colors of her clothing.

Emma dutifully padded over to her neighbor. Leslie exited her car and followed.

"Delilah, I'd like you to meet my friend, Leslie Parker. Leslie, this is Delilah Thornberry, my neighbor."

They shook hands.

"Oh, I'm so glad Emma's making some new friends!" exclaimed Delilah. "This girl was here alone almost the whole summer, and she's so cool!" She beamed at Emma then grew serious. "I heard about the murder and how you found the body. Man, that must have been such a bummer! Are you okay? I could, like, make you a cobbler."

Emma laughed. "Yes, Delilah, it was pretty much a bummer. But Ah'm all right, and Ah'm sure *someone*"—she winked at Leslie—"will figure out who did this terrible thing to poor Melvin."

Leslie pulled on Emma's sleeve. "It was so, so nice to meet you, Delilah, but Emma and I are late for a movie. Ta-ta!"

Delilah gave them a merry wave as they drove away.

"Delilah Thornberry?" asked Leslie. "That sounds like something out of a bad romance novel. Is she for real?"

"Of course she's for real. I thought you saw these types of aging hippies all the time; we are in the mountains of Colorado, after all."

"Yes, but usually at this point, they've become what we call 'granolas,' and they aren't so big on the tie-dye and the word 'bummer.' Still no makeup or fancy hair, more into flax milk and recycling."

"She's really nice. She has two grown children named Moon Lily and Rainshadow; I've seen pictures. She does cook cobbler for me; it's terrific. Plus her dog is, of course, named Dylan."

Leslie almost choked with laughter. "After Bob, I presume?" She sobered with obvious effort. "No, she seemed nice. Just be careful if she bakes you brownies!"

CHAPTER 13

THEY GOT TO THE SCHOOL right after dark. The crime scene tape was gone, but Emma still found the night-shrouded building a little creepy. She shivered as Leslie unlocked and pushed open the side door, and its shadow swam across the floor as it opened. The lockers stood sentinel, dark and quiet as the women passed. They crept toward the main office to begin their search.

Emma saw Leslie hesitate underneath the Wildcats welcome sign then sigh, stretch, and pat it lightly with her fingertips. Emma wasn't tall enough to reach it without leaping and making noise, so she mouthed a silent wish that Leslie had done enough for both of them.

Leslie headed straight for the desk farthest from the entrance—the one Melvin had been facing when he was hit.

"This is Abigail's," she whispered. "I'm pretty sure she hides spare keys around here, and I know she has a master that will go in every room. My key is special, but not that special." She rummaged through the desk, under the computer keyboard, and under the pads of the chair. She finally found the keys on the file cabinet, inside a small philodendron plant.

Emma watched Leslie wipe soil off the keys. "Are we just going to start unlocking everything? What's the plan?"

"I know there's a janitors' closet and office around here. I think maybe it's by the gym. That's our starting place to look for Melvin's stash." When the keys were clean enough for Leslie to drop them in her pocket, they were off. "Watch for the other custodians—we don't want to scare someone, and we certainly don't want to have to explain ourselves right now."

Emma nodded. She wasn't sure what she'd say to someone if they were caught sneaking around. She thought about it as they proceeded. *Hi, Mr. Janitor! We're lesbian lovers and needed a place to meet!* She shook that one off—no need to start those kinds of rumors. Plus, if the janitor really was a mister, he'd probably want to join in or watch or... eeewww.

She tried again. *Hey, Mr. Janitor, she's training to be the first female boxing champion of Pinewood, and we needed the gym to work out.* She watched Leslie, tall and lean, walk ahead of her. That one might work.

Emma whispered, "Yo, Adrian," a few times until Leslie gave her a strange look and shushed her. Finally she settled on one. *Oh, my deah Mr. Janitor—we knew your job was so hard since Melvin was gone, we thought we'd come help you clean.* She batted her eyelashes, stuck out her chest, and knew she'd found a winner.

Leslie stopped in front of the large gym doors to unlock one. The duo walked around the basketball court, looking for something that could be the janitors' office, and found a nondescript blue door in the far left corner.

The room was as plain as the door marking its entrance. It had a low-slung Naugahyde couch in a vomity squash-yellow color and a square card table along the back wall. One corner was populated with every type of mop, broom, and cleaning device one could imagine, except for the big metal machine that buffs the floors after they've been waxed—that one squatted in the opposite corner. A vending machine filled with various and sundry junk food reigned over everything else like an ugly seventies housewife.

Leslie planted her hands on her hips and surveyed her surroundings. "What a depressing lounge. Man, I thought teachers had it bad. But look! The vending machine has actual junk food—Twinkies and Doritos and stuff... no twenty-first-century pseudo-vending machine food like the Kashi lean cardboard bars the schools have for the kids these days."

"Well, the Waldorf -Astoria it certainly isn't. And no making fun of the cardboard food—kids are seriously obese! So where do we look?" Emma went over to the broom corner and rummaged through them as if maybe Melvin would hide his booze in the mop bucket.

Leslie just shook her head and went into the little closet that stood catty-corner to the vending machine. She searched through the few extra gray jumpsuits that hung there. She reached effortlessly high to sweep the top shelf with her hands then showed Emma the dust on her fingers. She shook her head, mouth set in a grim line. "We got bupkus."

Emma shrugged. "I still think this is a good plan. There was entirely too much alcohol at his house for there to be none here."

"Are you sure he wasn't carrying any?"

Emma thought. "Pretty sure."

"I suppose the killer could have swiped it. Maybe it was a sterling silver flask."

"I don't know." Emma was resolute. "Ah still think it makes sense he would have hidden some at school. Isn't this a lounge for all of the custodians? Surely it would be a secret place only he knew of."

"Of which only he knew," lectured Leslie. "And don't call me Shirley."

Emma made a choking noise. "Second time you've made that joke. You might want to take it out of your repertoire—it was a favorite of my bastard ex. My ex-bastard. Whatever. I know that *Airplane* movie is a cult classic, but... come on, let's just make a tour of the school and see what strikes us."

Leslie moved out of the lounge, a stricken look crossing her features. "Oh God, I guess Tim used to say that too—must be where I got it. I must not be as rid of him as I like to think." She crossed her eyes. "Quick, smack it out of me."

Emma tapped her on the temple; Leslie acted as if something distasteful was flying out of her ear, uncrossed her eyes, and continued out of the gym.

The commons was even darker now; the sun had made its entire ambit for the day. Emma was more relaxed than before though, possibly from smacking ex-husband cooties out of Leslie's head. They stopped to unlock a few more unmarked doors and found nothing but a box of yearbooks from last year—Emma took one as good for research—and a closetful of boxes of computer paper.

Leslie was indignant, muttering, "What paper shortage?"

They returned the master key to Abigail's plant and were approaching Leslie's room to retrieve a pile of essays—might as well get something productive done tonight—when Emma grabbed her arm and halted the two in their tracks.

"Look," Emma whispered. "Do you ever leave the lights on in your room?"

Leslie shrugged her off and spoke in a normal tone, "Paranoid much? I'm sure it's just a custodian cleaning my room, and I need to get this stack of—"

She stopped when the light blinked out, momentarily blinding the two women, and a simultaneous movement from the door shocked them into paralysis. A shadowed figure burst into the hallway and steamrollered them both. Leslie smacked onto her tailbone, and Emma crashed to the floor and slid a couple of feet until a locker made her head cease its backward movement. She struck it hard, and on some subconscious level, she took note of the noise her head made as it hit—sort of like the sound her dad's mallet made when he smashed tin cans to sell. The shadow took off across the commons to burst through the exit.

The stream of curse words that flew from Leslie's mouth would've made a sailor's ears bleed.

"Leslie? Are you okay?"

Leslie turned onto her stomach and rubbed her rear. "Peter, Paul, and my aunt Fanny, this hurts!"

Emma straightened her head from its unnatural angle and cupped her hand around the sensitive bump blooming on her skull. She thought about trying to get up and run after the intruder, but the stars that sparked through her vision as she sat up convinced her otherwise.

The bump was directly on the top of her head, an agonized throbbing radiating down both sides of her skull until tears came. She closed her eyes. *Could that have been Melvin's killer?* "Holy smokes. Who on earth would go breakin' into your room?"

Leslie stood and swore some more, still rubbing her butt. "Probably not someone who was worried I'd critique their cleaning. Dammit, this hurts. If I have to sit on one of those blow-up donuts, I'm going to be pissed."

"Just curious," said Emma, squinting to get rid of the flashes, "but do you know how much you're cussing? Ah swear, you just opened your mouth and gangster rappers fell out."

Leslie laughed, only it quickly turned into a bark of pain. "Guess what, sweetheart. The honeymoon's over—I could give a lumberjack or a truck driver a run for his money any day. I was on my best behavior before. Well, screw that. We've had microbrew and been in danger together now. I think you can hear me sans filter."

"You're right, of course. I'm no effing prude."

Leslie howled. "You sound like a six-year-old trying the word out for the first time. I'm not trying to corrupt you, promise. 'More than it is ere foul sin, gathering head, Shall break into corruption.' *Richard the Second.* C'mon, let's see if anything happened to my room."

Emma looked around with a hand on top of her head, trying to protect the injury. "What if he comes back?"

"He's not coming back. He's been caught. Just quickly, let's look."

Emma followed her into the classroom, which, aside from the fact that the door was open, looked pristine and untouched.

"Can we go, please?" Emma begged. "We'll come back tomorrow morning if you want to search some more. In the daylight." She pulled Leslie's arm to move her toward the exit.

They ran across the commons and through the courtyard, grateful when they made it to the relative safety of the parking lot lights. Emma kept turning in circles, checking all angles and shadows for movement. They got in the car.

"Did you see him at all?" asked Leslie.

Emma clicked on her seat belt and pulled out of the lot. "Not really. The lights on then off really threw me for a loop, and he knocked us over right after. Do you think this had something to do with Melvin?"

"I don't know how it could. I mean, for all anyone knows, you found the body and that's the extent of your involvement. No one would have reason to think *I'm* included, and it was my classroom. Plus, well, I did notice something about our shadow man."

"What?"

"He was pretty damn... excuse me, Pollyanna... darned short. I mean, maybe even as short as you. He shoved right into my chest when he knocked me over, and I'm pretty sure he used his head, like a tackle."

Emma had to agree. "He must have pushed me with his hand as he barreled toward us, and with you being the bigger target—no offense—used his head."

"None taken. So it was probably just a kid trying to hack into my computer or something. We have grade burglars every so often."

Emma was surprised. "Really? And have you ever had your grades stolen or deleted? Shouldn't we call the police?"

"I have a hard copy anyway, but I think security as far as grades goes gets more and more sophisticated, and it's really hard to hack in. But I know they've been infiltrated and altered once, at least." She continued as Emma pulled into her driveway. "There's some sort of CIA–level firewall to prevent hackers from gaining access from outside the school, but one baby genius did it from *inside* the school once, so several of the teachers keep a hard copy now. I'll show you all of that so you can learn how to transfer into the computer gradebook. It's pretty slick—click, click, and the program figures percentages and everything."

"That is slick." *Interesting conversation. We maybe just about got killed, and we're talking about gradebooks.*

"Yuh-huh. So I think this break-in was an isolated incident, no connection to Melvin. Anyway, if the kids were smarter, they'd find a more hidden computer and hack into that one. We're all connected by a LAN—local-area network—and I can get to my gradebook anywhere in the school. I wish there were a way to get into it from home. I've heard some schools give you a program for that, but like I said—CIA–level firewall. This may look like Backwater to you, but the Powers That Be are very serious about grades and records."

She headed toward her convertible then turned back. "And no, I don't think we should call the police. I'd rather not have to explain our late-night excursion to Carl the Clueless, who already suspects us both. Grade burglars can't figure out my password these days anyway."

"What, it's not a PDA?"

"No, it changes all the time. This week it's 'Timsnivelingbastard.' Next week it might be 'Timhomewrecker,' or 'Timnoballs.' Technology is fun!"

Emma shook her head. "Geez, Leslie, bitter?"

Leslie smirked and gave Emma a good-bye wave. Her perky look faded a bit when she tried to sit in her deep bucket seat, but Emma was pretty sure she'd avoid those donut thingies at all costs.

Emma walked into the dollhouse and looked around, still shaken by the confrontation, although she'd never admit that to Leslie. She had promised to try to help Melvin. Maybe they could do that in the daylight. Maybe they could enlist some bigger help. She sighed. *Maybe I need to grow some nerve.*

She double-checked the deadbolts on the front and back doors, took the ten-second walk-through of her house with a butcher knife in hand, and thought about checking the basement. *No, too scary.* She simply threw the lock on the door at the top of the stairs and trapped the boogeyman down there.

Then she took a deep breath and collapsed on the couch with Trinky and Toby, stroking them absently with one hand and rubbing her aching head with the other.

"Oh, girls. What have Ah gotten myself into?"

I have a faint cold fear thrills through my veins
That almost freezes up the heat of life.

—*Romeo and Juliet IV.3.14–16*

CHAPTER 14

Monday, August 31

THOMAS JEFFERSON HIGH STARTED MONDAY morning with a way-too-mellow atmosphere, considering the circumstances. At least, that's the way it appeared at first glance—people were spilling out of the double doors that marked the entrance to the commons, chattering and milling about. The sun was bright and shiny on the old tree in the courtyard, and it looked as though all was right with the world. Only Emma knew it wasn't. Melvin was dead, and they had yet to figure out why or how. The serene aura seemed out of place in light of that.

Emma saw a large group of students gathered outside the commons, talking over pamphlets, though she couldn't see what the papers said. She shook her head, perplexed, and plowed through the crowd to see what the fuss was about.

Two of the long rectangular cafeteria tables had been end-to-ended in the middle of the commons and covered with pamphlets and papers. A large white sign hung across the edge: PERSONAL SAFETY TIPS! STOP THE FEAR! A familiar woman and much shorter man were smiling and handing out whatever paraphernalia was intended to stop whatever fear the sign referred to. *Fear of commercializing the death of this sweet man?* Emma was unsure.

She was going to go to the table rather than suffer death by curiosity when she saw Leslie glowering in the far corner, long arms crossed, fingers tapping on her elbows, one hip thrust to the side. She looked dangerous, which made Emma pretty sure she knew what was happening.

Emma walked over to Leslie. "What's going on? Stop the fear? Why are there parents here? This is very strange."

"It's Ophelia and Lewis Fillmore," seethed Leslie. "Remember last week when Mrs. Fillmore about blew up all over my classroom?" She looked both angry and in pain—Emma was pretty sure she was trying to massage her sore behind when no one was looking.

Emma nodded. "Oh, yes—she was the woman who wore a long coat in the middle of August so she could sweep into rooms. Her name's Ophelia?"

"Like she deserves a name originally penned by the Bard. As if. And she's way too snotty to drown herself. We'll have to do it! This, this fear-inducing propaganda is only going to make the kids scared."

Just then, they were approached by William and Myra Lansing, the couple who wanted to play bridge with Emma. Myra had a halo of flaming-red hair and freckles everywhere you looked. William looked a lot like that basketball player from the eighties, Larry Byrd, but slightly shorter, paler, and lankier, if that was possible. They both looked harried.

"Oh, hello, Emma!" said Myra. "We're so glad you're here. We missed you on Friday! We organized this safety seminar with the Fillmores so we could give the kids some good information. We just want to help—"

William picked up her sentence. "But it seems as if Ophelia and Lewis might be going a little overboard." His hands flew through the air like lost doves. "I don't think we need to have a petition for a campus police officer; I'm sure we could just bring it up at the next PTA meeting. Plus, we don't want this to distract students and run into class time."

"Hmm," said Emma, thinking. "Where is the principal? Is he all right with this? Never mind. Where is that secretary who does the announcements? Ah bet she could do some crowd control."

"This morning, they all have a big crisis committee meeting, ironically," replied Leslie. "Only one vice principal is on duty." She uncrossed her arms and crossed them the other way. "I'm sure I can't do much to Ophelia but set her hackles up, but let's go talk to her anyway."

She marched over to the table, cleaving her way through a crowd of kids. "Hi, Mrs. Fillmore. What are you doing? Can't you see this is only—ow!"

Her voice was already on the rise and she hadn't even completed two sentences, so Emma delicately dug into Leslie's lower back with one fist and smiled at the couple on the other side of the table. "Hello, Mr. and Mrs. Fillmore. Ah'm Emma Lovett—we met at parent–teacher conferences on Tuesday?"

Mrs. Fillmore extended three fingertips for Emma to grasp. Mr. Fillmore nodded toward the two women and retreated to the end of the table to solicit signatures for the petition.

Emma continued, "Um, we're very sure you have the best interests of the kids at heart, but this seems a bit militant. Have you spoken to Principal Farrar?"

Mrs. Fillmore nodded. "Mr. Farrar wants to assist his students in any way he can. When Myra and William called to suggest some safety literature and self-defense information, Lewis and I knew this would be a memorable way to help the students and staff during this stressful time." She arched an eyebrow. "I don't see what could possibly be inappropriate about that? You think this looks militant? I think it's exactly what we need. 'The question, after all, is not what you look at, but what you see!' Thoreau." She nodded in satisfaction.

Lewis Fillmore nodded from his corner of the table. His dark hair looked curly this morning, emphasizing his Betty Boop-ness even more.

Emma was at a loss. "No, no, of course, Mrs. Fillmore. We welcome your good intentions. Class is about to start though, so if the Stop the Fear table could please wait until, say, lunchtime?"

Ophelia looked down her nose at Emma. "Hmph. 'It is not a thing to be waited for, it is a thing to be achieved.'"

Who is this woman? And why does she talk like she's reading from cue cards? "Ummm, yes. Of course. Can we continue achieving it at lunchtime?"

After a stiff bob of Ophelia's head, Mr. Fillmore gathered up papers. The Lansings shot Emma a grateful look and fell in to help. Janice Tichner, the other school secretary, materialized out of nowhere and stacked flyers like an assembly-line robot. The Lansings greeted her; the Fillmores ignored her.

Already I can see what is typical behavior for this pair. Afraid Leslie might still do her attack-dog impersonation on the Fillmores, Emma grabbed her arm and hauled her over to the office, where they went up the stairs to the teachers' lounge.

"That woman annoys me," remarked Leslie.

"Gee, really, darlin'? I would never have known. They *are* just trying to help, it seems."

Leslie replied with something that sounded suspiciously like a growl. When they got to the lounge, they ignored a catcall from Charlie Foreman, acknowledged a smile from Hunter Wells, and huddled up around the mailboxes.

"Are we going to be able to look around more today?" whispered Emma.

"I guess during lunch and planning again. I'll give my first and second hour a pop quiz so I can figure out where we go from here. Do you have pop quizzes in your arsenal of anal-retentive future plans?"

Emma popped Leslie on the shoulder with September's *English Journal*. "I can probably find one or two, O Queen of Sarcasm. I can even find a lesson plan that will allow me to think and might allow *them* to think as well. That's what we do here, right?"

Leslie grabbed the magazine and popped her back. "Okay, O Princess of Perfection. I—"

She was cut off by the PA, the force of the voice and the decibel level reflexively making her shut her eyes and ears and tensing Emma's shoulders clear up to her chin. Both of them winced as the secretary completed the morning announcements.

As the teachers in the lounge shook their heads to clear the blast from their ears, Martha Bonaventure marched in. Her beehive seemed skyscraper high today, and she was wearing a taupe skirt instead of a brown one, but otherwise she looked the same as when she and Emma had first met.

Emma smiled. "Good morning, Ms. Bonaventure. I hope you could make your way through all the nonsense downstairs."

Martha sniffed. "I'm completely certain that all those people are doing is stirring up the hornet's nest. Monkeying in the wrench. I have a hard enough time getting the attention of my students when it's ninety degrees outside without filling their heads with fancies and making them more fearful." She grabbed her mail, turned on her heel, and marched back out.

A couple of coaches snickered as she left.

"Bye, Martha," called Leslie. "I can't wait to see your next edition." She glared at the back table. "I hear she's doing an ex-po-zay on the staggering incidence of homosexuality amongst high school coaches."

One of them, an older balding man with pop eyes, choked on his coffee. The rest were silent.

Emma shook her head as they went back downstairs to their first class. "I hope she gets revenge some day for that bearded-lady rumor." She cocked her head and looked at Leslie. "Do you think it could really be true? I mean, they had that kind of carny in South Carolina all the time. I've seen headless chickens, three-tailed snakes, men with two noses, and more bearded ladies than I can shake a stick at. At which I can shake a stick? Whatever. My point is: do you think Martha has a past?"

"Knowing the way rumors start and fly around here, I would guess someone caught her plucking a stray facial hair in the girls' gym locker room about fifteen years ago and she became a circus freak fifteen minutes later. I doubt it has any roots in truth."

Emma sighed. "Poor Ms. Bonaventure. No wonder she's grouchy— hair that must weigh ten pounds and false rumors to boot. Plus, have you really ever looked at those oxford shoes? I know they're supposed to be comfortable, but I bet they pinch."

"Oh yeah, baby," Leslie agreed. "Give me some good Ferragamos any day. Anyhoo, I guess I'll see you at lunch. Put on your thinking *chapeau*. 'Piece out our imperfections with your thoughts!'"

Emma blew out a breath. "Ooh, Ah know that's from one of the Henrys, but Ah'm too tired to figure out which. Hey, Ah'll see you later!"

After a successful American Lit class and two semisuccessful Sophomore Lit classes—her Shakespeare introduction hadn't gotten them as excited as she'd hoped—Emma and Leslie wolfed down their lunches and spent the remainder of the lunch hour trying to find a place Melvin could have adopted as his own.

They got a school map from counseling and marked off areas with closets or small rooms that looked unoccupied. They found that the costume room behind the stage was a meeting place for young lovers. A blushing Emma and angry Leslie sent them packing with the requisite smacks upside the head. The couple was in such an inappropriate state of undress that Leslie included threats of expulsion.

There were several small closets that held textbooks for every subject, some dating back to the 1950s. One dusty little room was located in the far south corner of the school, between the library and freshman hall. Emma opened the door, sneezed, and went through some of the boxes. Leslie pulled out a home economics book from 1953, glanced through it, then practically tore it apart.

"Look at this! 'The Good Wife's Guide: *Listen to him. Remember, his topics of conversation are* more important *than yours.*' Holy shit." Her voice strangled with increasing fury as she continued reading. "'*Be a little gay and interesting for him. His boring day may need a lift, and one of your* duties *is to proVIDE IT FOR HIM?*'"

"Relax!" commanded Emma. "Look at the date—1953. Pre-bra-burning days. We've come a long way, baby."

Leslie was pacing maniacally.

"Stop, really. You're going to give yourself an aneurysm, for Pete's sake."

Leslie's face was indeed turning purple as she read down the list. The last item was apparently the clincher. "Jesus H. criminetly on a crutch!"

She threw the book across the room, oblivious to the startled gazes of student passersby. Emma retrieved it and shuffled through the pages before depositing it back in the closet.

"I almost fear to ask. What ended the list?"

"It said…" Leslie took a deep breath. "It said, '*A Good Wife Always Knows Her Place.*' In capital letters, like one of the lesson plans would be to needlepoint it onto a pillow." She sighed. "I know I freaked out a little, but I just can't believe they taught that stuff in the schools! Girls have enough trouble standing up for themselves without being taught Subservience 101." Her eyes got misty. "I should know. I'm not sure why I've made such bad decisions as far as men go, but I sure didn't learn it in *school*. Can you imagine?"

Emma patted her back as they left the room. "I know, I know. Ah can't imagine. But that's not us now. We're Amazonian women, remember—stamping out PDA, solving murders, all that. Come on, Miss Feminist Fury. Let's find us a hidey-hole."

CHAPTER 15

THEY HEADED OUT INTO THE courtyard, Leslie breathing deep, calming breaths. The afternoon sun glanced off of the concrete benches, making Emma blink. Her vision adjusted as the principal skated toward them. He made an impressive jump over one of the benches, blond hair haloed by the sun, tie fluttering behind him.

Emma was fairly awed. "Hello there, sir. Very nice trick!"

"Hi, ladies!" Nathan grinned. "So do we feel safer today after visiting our parent safety table this morning?"

Leslie growled. Emma just smiled and nodded, elbowing Leslie in the ribs until a grimace appeared that would maybe pass as a smile.

The principal seemed satisfied. His blue eyes twinkled. "So tell me what you think about fakies."

Leslie looked as startled as Emma felt. "Um..." Leslie said. "I guess a lot of girls do it. We don't usually talk to guys about it though."

Nathan's surfer curls jiggled with his confusion. "Huh?" Then understanding broke over his face. "Oh! I get it. Heh heh heh. No, I mean *fakies*. See?" He did a twisty-jumpy sort of trick off of one of the benches.

The women breathed a simultaneous sigh of relief—not ready to have *that* discussion with the principal.

"Very nice, sir," said Emma.

"Impressive," said Leslie.

He beamed. "I'm practicing that one for the Halloween BBQ. Dads love me!"

"And moms?" asked Emma.

"Do not." He picked up his skateboard. "Well, I'm off to practice skating down stairs." He started to open the doors to the commons when Emma stopped him.

"Stairs, sir? Where do you find those?" She and Leslie exchanged significant glances. "We, uh, know the building pretty well and were under the impression the only stairs were the two short ones to the teachers' lounge. You're not going to skate from the teachers' lounge into the main office?"

"No, of course not! Abigail would freak. No, I mean the concrete stairs down to the old basement under the gym." He received only blank looks. "The gym was the original one-room schoolhouse for this place, so of course it has a basement. The door's in the corner of the boys' locker room? There's nothing in it except for pipes and stuff, but the concrete stairs are great for practice." He opened the door into the commons, dropped his board, and skated away.

Emma and Leslie stood stock still for an instant, then they broke into motion, circling and hopping, chanting, "The basement! The basement! Yay for the basement! That's it, the basement! Woo-hoo, we love us some basement!"

A few students gathered to watch, some with cell phone cameras aloft, and when the ladies' impromptu dance had them so wound up they had to stop to breathe, everyone applauded. The two bowed their way into the building and ran for Leslie's classroom.

Leslie shut the door and flopped against it. "I can't believe I've been here fifteen years and didn't know there was a basement. And I call Carl clueless."

"So I guess we don't want to try to sneak into the boys' locker room during school?" asked Emma.

"No, let's wait and come back tonight."

Emma shook her head. "That doesn't sound like a good idea. My head still hurts from the last time we were here at night and got bowled over." She rubbed her head.

"I got a stun gun this weekend while you were busy with lesson planning," Leslie said. "We'll be so, so careful! Please, please, Emma! I just know the basement has some answers!"

I don't know. I don't know. "Just thinking about that angry voice I heard at the beginning of the week, then finding Melvin's body, then running into that guy coming out of your room and getting pushed down and…" Emma stopped. "I think we could really be in danger."

Leslie took Emma's hand. "I'll show you how to use the stun gun. I'll get you your own stun gun. Melvin got surprised and hit over the head. We're paying attention, looking around. With stun guns." She squeezed Emma's hand. "We're Amazons, right? Don't you really, really want to know?" She swung Emma's hand to and fro. "For Melvin."

I do really, really want to know. For Melvin. "All right." She sighed. "So, so careful. Stun gun ready. In and out."

Leslie nodded. "In and out. Like wind. Magic."

Emma had to smile. Her worldly friend was practically bouncing out of her high heels. "So we have some planning time left. Do you think we should, I don't know, actually plan something school related?"

"Fabulous idea." Leslie went to her desk and reached underneath. Emma heard a click, watched Leslie feel around, and when Leslie straightened up, she had a gradebook in her hands. Like magic. "Here's the handwritten version of my gradebook. Let's get on the computer, and I'll show you what the gradebook software is like and how it's transferred."

"What's that?" Emma asked. "Secret door?"

Leslie nodded. "Looks like the underside of a desk, but… not!"

"Neat!" Emma went to the desk to check it out.

Sure enough, it looked just like an ordinary desk, but Leslie showed her how two drawers on one side were slightly smaller, making room for a space between the drawers and the desk's underside. When Leslie clicked a button hiding under the lip of the lacquer, the wood slid down, exposing an encyclopedia-sized pocket.

Marveling at that trick gave Emma a chance to calm down. Her anxiousness was changing from pure nerves to a nervous excitement. The thought of being able to figure out who had killed Melvin was at the forefront, sure, but… then she thought again of Melvin.

"Did I tell you my dad owned a bookstore?" Emma asked.

"No, how cool! Is that why you became an English teacher? What made you think of that?"

"Ah was thinkin' about Melvin and how he had quotes for everything, then Ah thought about your cool desk and what Melvin said about that bookmark you gave him. 'It ain't what you're lookin' at, but what's really there.'"

"Oh, and that's true for this desk. I get it."

"My dad had quotes for everything too, and he had that drinker's nose Melvin had, and I just..." She rubbed her nose. "I just wondered if you knew he had a bookstore."

Leslie took Emma's hand and squeezed it. "When did you lose your dad?"

"He died in 2010. Congenital heart failure caused by emphysema. Oh, and that drinker's nose? I'm sure that didn't help." Emma sniffed. "It was a used bookstore, you know? The kind where you can trade your already-read books in for not-yet-read books."

"And he brought books home for you," Leslie said.

Emma wiped under one eye, catching a tear before it spilled. "Hundreds of books. Thousands. Every week he brought more, and every week I devoured them. But I was just thinking of the books he read."

"Let me guess," Leslie said, "murder mysteries?"

"Oh, by the millions. Elmore Leonard, John D. McDonald, Dashiell Hammett, all the classics... those guys took risks to help others. I guess I can too. Carefully. With stun guns. For Melvin."

They were sitting at her desk, mastering gradebook technology, when someone knocked on the door. Hunter Wells poked his head in, looking precious in a plaid shirt and blue pants. *Would guys hate being referred to as "precious"?* Emma was pretty sure they would.

"Hello, lovely ladies! What's the haps?" The question was addressed to both, but the smile was all for Emma.

She felt the corners of her mouth turn up. "Not much here, kind sir. And for you?"

He came into the room. "I'm very satisfied that a Monday work day is winding down." His eyes gazed into Emma's. "Miss Emma, I'd be even more satisfied if you'd consent to having dinner with me tonight."

Emma smiled. "Why, Hunter, thank you! I'd like that very much"—

she had to struggle to keep her smile when she felt a stiletto heel digging into her foot—"but can we make it early?"

The heel dug more gently.

"I have a, um, a book club meeting later in the evening."

The heel retreated.

"Sure, that'd be fine. Can I pick you up?" he asked.

The heel returned, threatening.

"Um, how about I meet you? Then I can just go on to the meeting."

The heel retreated.

"How about Rephele's? Five thirty or so? I'll make reservations."

"Sounds great. See you then, Hunter."

He tipped an imaginary hat. "Until then, ladies, have a terrific Monday." He ambled out of the room.

Oh, how Emma loved to watch him go. She was thoroughly prepared this time though, and she deflected the hand coming upside her head to smack it.

"PDA be darned," she begged. "He reads Thoreau!"

CHAPTER 16

R EPHELE'S WAS A LOCAL FAVORITE, with knotty pine furniture and skinny fir trees in the corners. Each booth had forest-green tablecloths and old black-and-white photos on the wall, set off by candlelight burning from round, triple-wicked cinnamon candles. The fare was eclectic, from seafood cheesecake appetizers—scooped and spread on homemade French bread—to classic beef or fish dishes. Emma and Hunter had delved into the seafood cheesecake and had already destroyed almost a whole loaf of bread in the process, partially because it tasted amazing and partially because they were overcoming their first-date awkwardness with food and inane conversation.

"So..." Emma said, "where are you from—I mean, originally?"

Hunter swallowed a mouthful of seafood. "I grew up in Stockton, California. Otherwise known as the armpit of the world."

"Wow." She giggled. "The whole world, huh? That's pretty serious."

"Well, I guess it wasn't that bad. It does have the highest murder rate in the whole state though. Higher than LA, even, I mean, per capita. Colorado is much nicer. Here people actually cruise the main drag in search of chicks and parties instead of targets for drive-by shootings." He sighed. "I have terrific parents though. They're still there, still married, still in the house where I grew up. Nice people."

"Do you have any brothers and sisters?"

"Yeah, one of each. My sister's older. She taught me a lot about women. At least, I think she taught me some valuable stuff." He grinned. "You'll have to let me know. Anyway, she's still in Stockton, teaching at this inner-city–type school, doing the *Dangerous Minds* tour of duty."

Emma pointed her fork his way. "And the brother? Have you passed the woman lessons on to him?"

"He's younger—still in high school, still in Stockton. He was one of those 'accidental' later-in-life babies. My parents love him of course, but boy, was he unexpected."

"We used to call those 'whoops babies.'" She smiled. "Mah parents wished for some of those after I was born, but no luck."

"What about you? What's your family like? From where do you hail?"

Emma almost choked on her bread. "Obviously you don't hail from anywhere that ends sentences in prepositions." She barreled right over his puzzled look. "I'm from Holly Hills, South Carolina. My mama moved to Mississippi after my dad died, and... after my divorce, I moved there to get my degree." She thought that statement lacked in first-date decorum, but she felt she should bring it up early.

He didn't seem upset by the "D" word. "Oh, you were married? What happened?"

"It's more like what didn't happen." She sighed. "I don't know. I was young, stupid; there was that Talicky hickey thing—"

This time he almost choked. "Whoa, back up. Talicky hickey thing?"

"His name is Ronald Talicky. He was famous for the Talicky hickey— it sucked the common sense right out of your head. But it turned out to be all he really had to offer. Plus..."

"Plus?"

"Oh, we got married at Christmastime. Then summer rolled around; girls started wearing tank tops, and the famous Talicky hickey was poppin' up on shoulders and necks all *over* the place. So I left."

Hunter looked concerned. "I'm sorry. Why did you go so far away? Is he dangerous?"

She smiled. "Well, he never hit me or anything, but he didn't take rejection well, and he's a taxidermist. After I left him, I kept waking to visions of myself stuffed and perched on his mantel. Plus I wanted to start over—new town, new career, new attitude. I'm goin' to get all Southern and twangy now—Ah suppose if I'm really honest, Ah needed to find somethin' to crush the can of whoopass Ronald leveled on my self-esteem. So far it's all been terrific here." She watched Hunter's face. His concern and compassion squeezed her heart. *This date was a really good idea.*

Hunter took her hands. "Here's me being Southern and twangy.

Ah do declare, Miss Emma Lovett, Ah think you're pretty gosh dang terrific."

They exchanged smiles until Emma could shake herself free of his gaze.

"What about you?" she asked. "How did you get into teaching?"

A flash of something she couldn't read skimmed his face. "Well, um... you know, same old save-the-world story. Plus I've always been good at history."

He stopped abruptly, and she sensed not to press him further. *Another mystery to solve some day?* She hoped anyway.

They ordered pasta and talked about Thoreau and Emerson and transcendentalism, although it turned out Hunter was much more practical and Emma more spiritual and willing to believe in strange abstractions. They were headed into a heated discussion when Emma spilled sauce on her shirt, and instead of laughing at her clumsiness, he soaked his napkin in soda water and gave it to her to blot at the stain. *Practical but sensitive. And well mannered. Smart. Oh, and did I mention gorgeous?*

The rest of their dinner was punctuated by inconsequential chatter and goofy looks across the table. The time for her to go to her "book club" came entirely too soon.

They walked together to her car.

"Well, Miss Emma," he said, "I enjoyed our dinner very much. I hope we can do it again."

"Me too," she breathed.

He leaned forward and kissed her softly. "I'm not inclined toward giving hickeys on the first date. Well, toward ever giving hickeys actually. But there're other things I can do pretty well."

Her eyes sparkled. "Ah look forward to findin' out what they are."

He squeezed her hands again and walked away. She, of course, watched him go.

Leslie's house was every bit as stylish as the woman herself. Done in a Mediterranean style with bilevel flat roofs, rounded stucco edges, and olive-cloth awnings, it sat proudly on the corner like a green-eyed Siamese cat. *How on earth can she afford this place on a teacher's salary?*

Trellises ran down its sides with ivy leaves so shiny they looked plastic, but Emma felt she knew Leslie well enough to know she would *never* have plastic plants. Her thoughts ran to her classroom's fake trees, but real ones couldn't get sun in there! Those thoughts stayed briefly before Hunter was reinstated to the forefront of her mind. *Ah do declare, Miss Emma,* said her internal Southern belle, *what a doll he is.*

She got out of the car before she could allow herself to project her thoughts to the Lovett/Wells nuptials and the adorable boy and girl—boy first, because she'd always wanted a big brother—they'd have. The tendency to do that every time she met someone charming sort of blunted the real time frame of any relationship. *Plus men seem to sense it, you know? They can smell the eventual wish for marriage and babies on you like popcorn at the movies and run screaming for the hills before that little hot dog starts dancing across the screen.* She sighed. No marriage and babies right now anyway; she was too busy being Pinewood's answer to Miss Marple.

Leslie came to the door in shorts, a T-shirt, and running shoes, twisting around in a rendition of their "yay basement" dance. "Hey, you! Are ya still hungry? Didja eat only salad, like a demure little debutante? I have sustenance, then we can go solve this crime, by God!" She eyed Emma's skirt and sandals. "I will, of course, clothe you properly before we go. How was your date, Slick?"

Emma swooned against the doorframe. "Oh, I've already started picking colors for the bridesmaids' dresses, if that tells you anything. And I ate plenty. It was marvelous."

She followed Leslie across a hardwood floor into a wide-open, high-ceilinged living room. A semicircular couch that looked like cream-colored clouds curled around an absolutely humongous television set. *I'd probably turn on a movie channel and never get up.* And that couch would never survive Trinculo and Sir Toby, not for one minute.

A couple of palm trees—*Real palm trees? In Colorado?*—sat in concrete planters at the edges of a picture window that looked out over a pine-forest backyard. *Now* that *looks like Colorado!*

She turned toward the kitchen, which was part of the open-floor concept of the house, where Leslie waited with their food. She had one of those kitchen islands that Emma had always wanted, and it was covered with hors d'oeuvre-type food: quesadillas, fruits and veggies, even Lit'l Smokies!

"Lovely. Are you having a party I didn't know about?"

Leslie shoved a cheesy cracker into her mouth. "No, it's just that I don't cook, so I overcompensate by making pounds and pounds of appetizers. Enjoy! We need energy for basement busting."

A session of content munching commenced, most of the munching done by Leslie, as Emma had just eaten, followed by a trip to Leslie's bedroom to clothe Emma and show her how to use her new stun gun, which was called a Terminator. It had a flashlight attached and was pink!

"My neighbor, Ike, volunteered for the test tase." Leslie laughed. "He fell right down and shrieked like a banshee. Plus it makes this really loud noise when you press the button."

"I love that it's pink," Emma said and looked around.

She had been expecting a bedroom *quelle chic*, maybe with Japanese lacquer and black silk sheets, but instead—in line with the cartoon sneakers motif, she guessed—it was more like a college dorm room. But much bigger, of course, and with a fireplace.

A life-sized poster of Johnny Depp was tacked to the ceiling above a king-sized bed covered with a patchwork quilt and, unbelievably, stuffed animals! The Pink Panther, a ratty brown teddy bear, and Tweety Bird gazed up from the pillows. There was even a guitar leaning against one corner of the room. Emma fully expected to see a hot plate and an empty pizza box peeking out from under the bed. Leslie's Cheshire Cat grin had returned as she watched Emma inspect the room.

"Cool, isn't it? Of course, when I have male visitors, I take the poster down and shove the animals under the bed."

"I just have one question."

"Shoot."

Emma waved her arms. "Where did you get the money for this place? It's pretty amazing—Johnny Depp notwithstanding."

Leslie's face bloomed like a flower. "Where do you think, honey? Tim the bastard paid dearly for his indiscretions."

She gave Emma a T-shirt that went down to her knees and a pair of shorts that went longer, but after some judicious folding and tucking, Emma was ready to go.

As they walked to the car, Emma had to ask, "What were his indiscretions exactly?"

"The most significant one was a personal trainer named Anthony. The rest I chose not to know." Her tone was flippant, but Emma couldn't see her face as she walked ahead.

For a moment, Emma didn't know what to say. Then she caught up to Leslie and tucked an arm in hers. "That's all right, darlin'. Wait 'til I tell you about the Talicky hickey."

CHAPTER 17

"I THINK THIS PLACE GETS LESS spooky every time we sneak in," Emma remarked.

After stopping in the office to remove the key from Abigail's philodendron, they walked through the hallway that led to the old gym, sneakers squeaking softly.

Her shorts threatened to fall to her ankles about every three seconds, and she found it annoying that the clothes were so big but the tennis shoes fit like a glove. Either Leslie had very petite feet for her size, or Emma was hauling around gunboats. She chose to believe the former.

"Yeah, let's hear you say that if the troll-like intruder comes back and starts shoving your head into lockers."

"Oh, he won't—no grades to steal in the basement. Although I suppose we could catch the principal doing some weird midnight stair-boarding." Emma had to laugh—quietly—at the vision of Nathan Farrar bumping down concrete stairs, hair and mustache jiggling in the dark.

They slunk through the boys' locker room, Emma averting her eyes—it was the boys' room, after all—but Leslie checked out everything. The place smelled gross, like mildew and dirty socks, but was pretty spartan—two stands of small lockers and two big rooms of showers. The back right corner had a protruding concrete wall, and sure enough, the wall hid a set of stairs. Emma shared the stair-skating image as they descended.

"Shh! Here we are. Now pray that Abigail's master key works." Leslie had to force the key into the tarnished brass knob of the splintery wooden door at the bottom of the stairs, but it turned.

The ceiling was low. Leslie had to crouch as they walked in. "Boy, Nathan was right about pipes," she said.

Pipes of many sizes snaked throughout the room, curving and cornering like a demented highway system.

"What do you suppose they're all for?" Emma asked. "There are only two locker rooms."

"Yes, but remember the swimming pool. I'm sure the cafeteria is plumbed through here. If it saved money, they would plumb the whole school from here."

Emma gazed through the network of pipes. "How do we get through it? It's such a maze. I feel like we should be dropping bread crumbs."

Leslie moved toward the wall. "Nonsense. We can follow the wall here and watch for a hole, then always go back to the wall."

With her back to the concrete, she inched along, avoiding the metal maze. Emma followed suit. They were about fifty feet in when the wall suddenly ended. Leslie turned her flashlight toward the break.

"Jackpot!" she breathed.

Amidst all the plumbing, away from anything anyone could see from the main entrance, was another door. It was Alice-in-Wonderland small—Emma was sure Melvin had had to squash himself to enter—but a door nonetheless.

The door had an old-fashioned keyhole. The two women looked at Abigail's keychain and almost cried—no skeleton key.

Emma shook her head grimly, knowing they couldn't be stopped here, so she reached out and... "Whoopee!" she whispered as the doorknob turned under her fingers.

A wash of stale air blew through their noses as the entrance creaked open.

Leslie gagged. "Wow, dust, mold, and booze. How pleasant. At least we know we've found the right place."

The room was windowless and dark, no light bulbs or switches anywhere. Emma's flashlight fell on a kerosene lamp, so she went over and turned the knob. The flickering light danced in and out of the corners but still allowed them to get a sense of Melvin's hiding place. The room was small, about as big as a jail cell. Or at least that's how big Emma thought a jail cell would be. *Or maybe I'm hearkening back to the movies again.*

No furniture. A sleeping bag was folded on top of a large square pillow, probably from some couch that was now half naked. Next to the couch cushion was a cardboard box and an unstoppered silver flask. The kerosene lamp completed the bleak picture.

"I'd say it definitely needs a woman's touch, wouldn't you?" said Leslie.

Emma headed for the pillow/chair to look through the box. "At least he didn't live here." She sat on the floor and pulled the box into her lap.

"Why aren't you sitting on the pillow?"

Emma gestured in that direction. "Look, it still has an indentation. I'd feel like I was sitting on top of Melvin."

Leslie shook her head. "You're one weird chickadee." She sat on the makeshift chair. "I'm quite sure he won't mind."

Emma put the box between them. "Well, we knew we'd find this." A large bottle of Jack Daniels hid in the corner of the box, an empty space the size of a flask right next to it. "This job must've been really hard if he had to drink the good stuff here." She sighed. "Do you think he cleaned gum out from under desks or just let it pile up? I think I'd let it pile up. Poor Melvin."

Next to the Jack Daniels were several books and an old wooden cigar box. Emma took out the books and perused them. "Look, this is the same kind of thing he had in his bedroom at home—kids' books." A couple were part of the Great Brain series, and she found another of her personal favorites, *The Phantom Tollbooth*. "This is a fantastic one; it's about this guy named Milo—"

Leslie snatched the books from her hand. She glanced at the spines. "These are all library books!"

Emma shrugged. "So?"

Leslie's eyes goggled as she opened the front covers. "From the library *here*!"

"I know. He had some in his bedroom, remember?"

"The school library!"

Emma lifted her hands. "At the risk of repeating myself—so?"

"So," Leslie hissed, "they're all monumentally overdue!" She flipped through the books and listed the due dates, which ranged from October of 2000 all the way back to January of 1992.

Emma's forehead wrinkled. "So he died with a heck of a library fine. Are you okay? Is this like your PDA crusade? Overdue library books?"

Leslie took a deep breath then spoke in that kindergarten teacher's voice. "Remember Edward Dixon, our schizophrenic librarian? He almost popped an artery over a little graffiti on a Herman Melville book?"

"Oh, for Pete's sake. You can't think he'd kill Melvin over some books?"

Leslie jumped to her feet and almost hit her head. "Oh, what you saw the other day was just the tip of the iceberg. He's truly bonkers. One day we found him, shirtless, in the conference room, playing the guitar as he stared off into space. He was singing 'Short People.' You know, the song about them having no reason to live. That was after he'd gotten into a huge row with Stan Carruthers, one of our former vice principals, about the way he organized his books. Stan said it was too hard to find things, but Edward maintained that the Dixon Decimal System was better than the Dewey kind any day. Stan was about five-two, by the way. He's dead too."

Emma gasped. "Edward killed him?"

"No, he had a heart attack. But I'm sure Edward contributed to it. He's a loose cannon," she said grimly. "No one knows what he's going to do. I, personally, keep on his good side for that time when he goes postal on the whole staff."

"Maybe he's just a lonely soul," Emma mourned. "I have a hard time seeing him actually hurting anybody."

"Aarrgh," groused Leslie. "*Someone* killed Melvin. So far we have no one with a motive except Edward. Maybe Melvin wouldn't pay the overdue fine, and Edward couldn't find the books since they were hidden here, and he went crazy. I think we should follow it up."

Emma stopped flipping through the books. "Okay, I guess. What's in the cigar box?"

Leslie looked at the box. It was one of those fancy wooden kinds with old-fashioned pictures on the lid. She opened it and shuffled through the contents. "Looks like papers. Let's take it, and the books, to my house, where we can go through it properly. Maybe there're better clues in this box." Her eyes opened wide. "Maybe hate mail from Edward."

Emma thumped Leslie on the temple. "Now, remember—innocent until proven guilty. Being odd is not a factor in guilt."

"Odd? Odd? If he's just odd, I'm Dumbo the flying elephant. Edward is demented. Unhinged. Crackers." They left Melvin's room and backed out of the basement, hugging the walls. "Loopy. Daft. Dotty."

Despite wanting to defend Edward, Emma couldn't help but join in the game. "Balmy. Buggy. Loco. Touched."

They were hooting now—whispers forgotten—partly from their goofy word game and partly in excitement from having some real clues.

"Run amok," Leslie said. "Certifiable. Deranged."

They closed the basement door with a simultaneous yelp of "*Non compos mentis!*" and collapsed on the bottom stair in a heap of giggles.

CHAPTER 18

WITH THE CONTENTS OF MELVIN'S cache spread from one end to the other, Leslie's kitchen island looked similar to the Stop the Fear table at school. Emma had organized Melvin's belongings in piles of "what seems to relate." His bottle was on one corner and the books on another.

In the middle was the stuff from the cigar box: a couple of letters, a mini notepad, and a small key, all of which Emma was ecstatic about. *Love letters! How romantic.* Never mind that they hadn't actually read them yet; she just *knew* they were love letters. Maybe that notepad was Melvin's little diary, plus a key with no lock in sight! They had an honest-to-goodness Nancy-Drew-would-be-proud mystery on their hands if there ever was one, *and* they knew if they had this information, then Carl Niome, kindergarten cop, did not.

At that thought, Emma stopped organizing. "Do y'all think we should give this to that police investigator? I mean, they might be able to make better use of it."

"*Y'all* would think so, wouldn't you? But I keep going back to the 'alleged' murderer kid with blood on his shirt, the one Niome sent home, then I feel confident it should remain right here on my kitchen island." Leslie waved at the piles. "Besides, do we not have the inside track with all the people at school? I'm sure we can finagle information out of Edward with much more finesse than the police could if they barged into his territory."

"Yes, if he doesn't kill us in the process!" Emma said indignantly. "Don't forget, you think Edward could be a murderer. Mur. Der. Er. If he can bonk someone as big as Melvin over the head and kill him, he could probably hack us into teeny pieces without even mussing his Alfalfa hair."

"Shhhh," Leslie soothed. "We know how to deal with Edward. We won't piss him off, that's all. We won't do anything to make him go over to the dark side."

"Oh, yes, of course." Emma threw her hands in the air. "I can see your point. Asking him if he killed someone won't set him off whatsoever. Forget Shakespeare, Les. As Charlie Brown would say—good grief!"

Leslie walked over to Emma and patted her back just like a darn kindergarten teacher would. Don't worry. *Pat, pat.* I know what I'm doing. *Pat, pat.* Smile and nod. *Pat, pat.*

It was completely infuriating, but she had to admit Leslie had been able to control the situation so far, and Emma really didn't know Edward that well. The patting calmed her, annoying and condescending as it was, so she went to the stack of letters. The envelopes had a slight patina of age and were addressed in flowing calligraphic letters "To Mickey," with a Pennsylvania address. They had all been stamped "forward" many times, looking like much-traveled passports. The flaps were soft and worn, as if they had been opened and reopened.

Emma was gentle as she pulled out the letter inside, feeling as if something historical was unfolding.

Dear Mickey,

I think of you often. Every time I'm someplace where the lights whirl or the music twirls me like a little child, I think of you. Sometimes all it takes is a kaleidoscope of the noises around me, and if there are many and they are varied, I feel like I am back with you. I hope work isn't the same when I'm absent, yet you are still happy with it. Please write. Your Flying Raquel Welch is thinking of you.

I love you,
Marlena

"Marlena," Emma whispered. "What a beautiful name. Do you think Mickey is Melvin?"

"I don't know. Mickey/Melvin. They're close." Leslie touched the note gently. "It's almost worn transparent. I don't know if he's Mickey, but he's read these a thousand times."

"Maybe it's like John and Jack. You know, someone has the given name John, but everyone calls him Jack. His real name's Melvin, but Mickey sounds more, I don't know"—Emma shrugged—"tough? More in charge?"

"Yeah, more in charge like your bookie is in charge of your money." She snorted. "What kind of job do you think he could have had? Wall Street?" Leslie ran her hand over the letter. "All the noises together?" She peered at the postmarks. "Can't read any dates."

"Yes, but what about the music? I think theater. Marlena sounds like the star of a musical, don't you think? And Mickey was a stage name?"

"Hmm," mused Leslie. "I don't know. I mean, how did he get from Fred Astaire to school custodian?"

"Ah don't know, Miss Leslie," said Emma. "How did he get from Wall Street to school custodian? Oh, wait, I guess the alcohol could do that. But you're right. Maybe he was a technician of some sort, not really an actor. Maybe she was a film star, not a stage one, and he was, oh I don't know, a key grip or something, whatever that is. Or a gaffer. What exactly is a gaffer? I've always wondered." Her eyes got big, and she smacked Leslie's arm.

"Ow! Whaddja do that for?"

"Raquel Welch was a film star, right?"

"Yes, but it's not signed 'Raquel,' it's signed 'Marlena.' I know there was a classic film star named Marlena Dietrich, but I'm pretty sure she's dead. Hang on, I'll check the computer in my bedroom."

She bopped over to her college dorm bedroom, and Emma stayed to bask in the romance of the custodian's letters. There were four altogether, each one more plaintive as it became obvious Melvin wasn't writing her back. *Why was he keeping them in such a sacred place then? And reading them over and over?* Emma could feel Marlena's frustration as she read the letters. Her heart ached for this seemingly unrequited love. She wondered what had happened to Marlena—she couldn't imagine Melvin ignoring her doleful declarations of love then keeping them so close to his heart all these years.

Leslie came back. "Yep, she died in 1992. And her name was spelled with an 'e'—Marlene—although I've always heard it pronounced Mar-lay-na. What about the 'flying' part? Maybe she was a flight attendant?"

Emma thought. "Maybe. And Melvin was a pilot, until the alcoholism grounded him for good. Can I ask why you had to go to your room to look this up? Don't you have a smart phone? That seems right up your sophisticated alley."

Leslie shook her head. "Don't believe in all the technology. I don't like being available to other people twenty-four, seven and knowing everything there is to know at the same time. Plus it's all destroyed too easily—some hacker here, some terrorist there, and pretty soon we're back to candles and boiling our water. That's why I keep my hard-copy gradebook. When Kevin Madison gets a C, I write a C, and it stays a C."

Emma sighed and shook her head. "You do have your platforms, don't you? Well, Ah admire that you have passionate beliefs."

"Yeah, well, my beliefs didn't stop me from bopping on over to the Army Surplus store for a couple of stun guns, baby."

Emma laughed. "Well, we want to be around for people to be able to get ahold of sometime, right? Me for Hunter, you for... whoever." Emma sniffed. "Listen, this looks like the last letter she sent:

My sweetest Mickey—

I have so longed to hear from you over the past few years, but my heart has come to accept your denial. I will try my best to move on without you. Please know you are, and always will be, a part of my heart.

With love,
Marlena

Emma blew out a breath in a whoosh.

"Wow," said Leslie. "How sad. 'Oh hateful hands, to tear such loving words. Injurious wasps, to feed on such sweet honey, and kill the bees that yield it with your stings.'"

Emma stamped her foot. "How do you *do* that? Just pull something Shakespearean out of the air like that? Jiminy Christmas."

"Goodness, such frustration in one so young." Leslie arched her eyebrows and pursed her lips. "You do know what it's from, don't you?"

"Y-yes. *Two Gentlemen of Verona*, right?"

"Right! See, you're on your way already. Just teach for, oh, ten or twelve more years, and you'll be pulling those babies right out your butt."

"Oh. I don't want to do *that*, Leslie. I just want to be able to quote the Bard at my behest."

Leslie shook her head, looking amused. "It will all come in time, Luke. Rely on the Force." She went back to the island. "Now, we've dealt with the letters, but what about this notebook? And for sure, what about this key?" She handed it to Emma, who held up the small piece of silver and twirled it above the kitchen island. Light bounced off the metal every time it went around.

"It says Master and it's pretty little, so it must go to a padlock. Did you see a shed behind Melvin's house?"

"No," said Leslie. "I didn't see anything but some grass in need of serious watering. Did you look under his bed for a lock box or something similar?"

"I didn't see anything but some dust in need of serious vacuuming."

"Oh hell." Leslie plopped down on a barstool, shoulders slumping. "How do we find out what it opens?"

"My, my, I do declare." Emma's eyes sparkled. "It sounds like you're getting a little twitterpated finally, Miss Perfect."

"Twitterpated? Jesus, that sounds like something a lovestruck ferret would do. Whatever, I personally would not twitterpate under any circumstance, Miss Jewel of the South. Jesus." She shoved three Lit'l Smokies in her mouth for an effect that was something like a blond chipmunk. "Anyway, I think this key could be important, and much as I hate to admit it, I'm at a loss." She picked up the small wire-bound notebook and flipped through the pages. "Look at this. It's like a kindergartner's homework." She handed it to Emma.

"Do you think this is his writing? It would have to be." The first few pages had lists of words. Many of the letters stuttered and shook, like a small child's. *I wonder if that's the alcohol?*

Leslie took the book back. "They're very curvy. Wonder if it's the alcohol." She continued flipping through. "These three pages have quotes—remember how Melvin always had quotes? Look at this one. 'Sooner or later, everyone sits down to a banquet of consequences.' Robert Louis Stevenson. Page 426."

"I remember that book from his room—Bartlett's Book of Quotations. How sad that he paid the ultimate consequence, maybe just for doing his job. What else is in there?"

Leslie flipped through. "Sentences. 'The quick brown fox jumped over,' and the like. Nothing but lists, it looks like." She went through each page. "Thomas Jefferson Wildcats. New York Yankees. *Law and Order.* Edward Dixon Library. America the... wait! *Edward Dixon Library?* What the hell? See, I told you, Emma, I told you! Edward had a relationship with Melvin, then he killed him! That guy's an uber whack job. I can't believe it. Let's go get 'im. Let's go—"

Emma put a finger over Leslie's mouth. "Wait. Just wait one stinkin' minute. So Melvin knew Edward. That doesn't mean Edward killed him. It doesn't mean anything, really... they both worked at the school. Plus, if Melvin hated him, why would he write 'Edward Dixon Library'? Wouldn't it be more like 'I hate Edward'?"

Leslie drew in a breath. "Maybe Melvin was projecting what the school would do to memorialize Edward." Her perfectly made-up eyes were slightly smeared and imperfect, her expression bright and a little wild. "After Melvin killed him to avoid those monstrous late fees!"

Emma laughed. "Come on, you. You're being ridiculous."

"I know. I'm just jonesing for a killer. I wanna find us a killer!"

"Patience, Master Obi-Wan." Emma raised an eyebrow and winked. "Rely on the Force."

"Hey, that's my line! C'mon, let's look through the rest of this notebook."

Emma gestured to some of those little notebook hanging chads. "This one's been ripped out. Wonder what it said."

"Did you see any stray paper in the basement room?"

Emma shook her head and turned another page. "Now what do you make of this?" In messy handwriting was a cryptic note:

CBSSA SAY NO GPA NO PLAY ON PENELTY OF J. LOSS/CRIM. PROS. TALK TO ADAM.

"I have no idea what that says," remarked Leslie. "Of course GPA to us means grade point average, but mixed in with all that other nonsense, it could mean anything. Gay porn addict?" She snorted. "I guess you could have some 'penalties' for that."

"Great poetry anthology?"

Leslie stuck her fork in her mouth and made a choking sound. "I'll give you two words for that: Bor. Ring."

Emma stared at the note. "What about CBSSA? What does that mean?"

Leslie shrugged, so Emma pulled out her smart phone to look up the acronym.

"Comprehensive Basic Science Self-Assessment?" Emma said. "What does a medical test have to do with it? That doesn't make any sense."

"Like I said, those abbreviations could mean anything," Leslie said. "We'll just have to figure out who this Adam is and ask him."

"How are we going to do that, O Wise One?"

"I don't know, O Smart-ass. We have to look in the yearbooks. Maybe we'll get some kids and put them on phone-book research, calling all the Adams. The town's not that big, for God's sake." She sighed and rolled the Lit'l Smokies back and forth across the plate. "I'm wishing the killer would go ahead and be Edward the schizophrenic librarian."

"Well," said Emma, "if I had my druthers, it wouldn't be Edward Dixon. I sensed a good heart under all his pomp and bluster."

Leslie stopped rolling the Smokies. "I've got to ask, what is a druther? It sounds even weirder than twitterpated. Maybe morticians in love, this time." She sucked down the remaining Smokies with one big swallow. "I don't know if it's Edward or not, but we have to go to him and see what he says."

"How are we going to do that exactly? I mean, if he did kill Melvin over books, couldn't he lose his marbles if we even ask about it?" Emma was a bit worried about their plans on this subject.

"He could lose his marbles if his pants are too tight, apparently. Why don't we just call it a night and rest and think about it? We'll start tomorrow with a grand plan to approach Edward with caution." She grinned brightly. "Sound good?"

"Well..."

But Leslie was already cleaning up their appetizers. "Good! Because while we're thinking, I'll just... I don't know, go out on a date or something." She waltzed Emma to the door.

"A date? You have a date? With whom?"

"Aw, shucks. Just a guy I met. Who's much too young for me and cuter than a puppy in a punch bowl." Her white teeth flashed in the sun. "Did that sound sort of Southern? Anyway, dearie, I'll tell you about him if he gets past a third date. That's usually when they get the go-ahead or the no-go. It's a waste of our time talking about him now, because he may be *sayonara* after tonight. He's pretty cute though."

"Oh, tell me!" Emma groveled. She even stamped her foot. "Please!"

Leslie opened Emma's car door for her. "Let's play the Get Over It game, shall we? I'll tell you if he turns out to be interesting. You go home and think hard about how we'll get Edward to confess." She shut the car door, turned, and danced back inside, ignoring Emma's pleas through the open passenger window. After the door shut, Emma shook her head and, smiling, drove home through the August night.

Emma felt vaguely guilty after seeing Leslie's beautiful living room, so she was vacuuming her couch. Trinky and Toby thought the vacuum hose was playing a game with them, so they pranced and pounced and cajoled the attachment as it ran along the arms and back and cushions of her comfy, hairy couch. Guilt momentarily assuaged, she turned on the TV and sat down, a calico furball at either side.

The television flickered and gibbered, but Emma didn't hear it. Trinculo and Sir Toby gazed upward in adoration as she petted and stroked them while her brain roamed. She considered all the items they'd found in Melvin's cigar box. The letters intrigued her the most, all romance and melancholy. Ronald had never written her anything but a grocery list. But Leslie was probably right to put the letters aside as a dead end. Messages from a past life, it seemed.

The mysterious notebook with the unintelligible letters would have to wait until they could find the person who could decrypt the message. The key—now that was a point of interest. Maybe Melvin had money hidden somewhere, which was a huge motive for murder in everything Emma had ever read.

She smiled, recalling the little house in Holly Hills where she had grown up with her parents. It was almost a shack, really, with a shake roof and an old wooden slatted porch. She and her father swung on that porch many a mosquito-ridden summer evening, slapping bugs and sipping lemonade. Money had never been an issue for them, just something her mom counted out of the cookie jar to send her to the corner for candy. How could someone kill for that? Emma watched a small mocha-colored spider crawl across the coffee table, and she got up to get a cup from the kitchen to capture it and take it outside. *I don't understand why people kill anything or anyone at all. That's the* biggest *mystery.*

Spider safely on the lawn, she went back in to further contemplate their plans. How to approach Edward? They couldn't just ask him about the overdue books unless... well, those were some of Emma's childhood favorites. Maybe she could involve him in a dialogue about those titles and see if he reacted. Maybe she could ask to check them out, and if he couldn't find them all... She sniffed and gathered her pets up in her arms. Worth a shot. She would talk to Leslie about it tomorrow morning, then maybe she could get the scoop on the date! Speaking of dates, she allowed a little Hunter-dimple picture show to play in her head. She was eager for some more scooping there too.

In Nature's infinite book of secrecy
A little I can read.

—*Antony and Cleopatra I.2.10–11*

CHAPTER 19

Tuesday, September 1

IN HER BATHROOM ON TUESDAY morning, Emma checked her reflection, brushing powder over the freckles that dusted her nose and applying lipstick to make her lips look fuller. Her small upper lip always depressed her when she looked at the bee-stung mouths of models and actresses, but hey, variety is the spice and all that. She knew you could pick anyone apart feature by feature if you really wanted to. She didn't want to, so she kiss-kissed her reflection and walked back into the bedroom.

She'd put her long brown hair in fat rollers so it fell in curves past her shoulders. Her tank dress covered in flowers was set off by a short-sleeved sage-green cardigan. *How Laura Ashley of me,* she thought as she twirled this way and that. Maybe she should think about wearing some solid colors and fitted skirts, something sophisticated like Leslie. *Nah.*

Floral stuff was great for Emma, not only because it represented what she thought of as her "natural spirit" but because it hid whatever she inevitably dropped in her lap or dripped onto her chest during lunch. Calzone sauce surely wouldn't hide so well on the stark white Prada ensemble Leslie would probably wear today. Of course, Leslie would never drop calzone sauce on her boob anyway.

Although Emma liked to picture herself floating through the halls of the school, perching on her sit bones with ankles crossed in the picture of grace, in reality, she was more like a small flowery cyclone. Maybe because she was a Sagittarius—the klutzy sign. Probably because of her big feet. She preferred to think her mind, so full of information and cleverness, was moving much faster than her feet, so when the two conflicted—*bam!*

She smiled and rubbed gloss over her lipstick, which was all the makeup she'd worn today. Edward, she thought, would prefer women in their natural state, and she wanted to start out right with him. *Was it really possible he had, in a fit of rage over library books, killed Melvin?*

Sir Toby was running back and forth across her toes, and Trinculo had jumped up onto the bathroom sink and sat on her makeup; both actions were demands for breakfast.

As she scooped cups of food from two different bags, she asked, "What do you girls think? Is it possible to kill someone over books?"

The girls huffed and meowed in response.

"I know, I know. Sounds crazy to me too. But I've only talked to him once, and it was a rather awkward situation. I guess all we can do is investigate and hope for the best. Whatever that may be." She left them munching contentedly and headed out into Tuesday-morning adventure.

School looked almost normal today. The parent safety table was gone; evidently the Lewises and Fillmores had decided everyone was safe now. Emma crossed the courtyard to Leslie, who was waiting in the doorway of the commons. Emma had been right on the money as far as the outfit—a white fitted summer suit.

"I knew you were going to wear white today," remarked Emma as she approached.

"You like? It's Calvin Klein." *Close enough.* "How did you guess?"

"Oh, I don't know." Emma shrugged. "I figured either you got lucky with the youngster last night and had to dress pure in penance, or maybe we're going to have calzones for lunch."

"Huh?" Leslie's brows dipped together. "I don't get the calzone thing. And as for my getting lucky..." Her brows moved up and down, Groucho-Marx style. They headed to Emma's room.

"Whatever, Mrs. Robinson." Emma hummed a little Simon and Garfunkel as they entered room 104.

Leslie collapsed into the desk chair. "So have you thought about a game plan for Edward? I tried to think some more last night, but I was so tired." She leered at Emma.

"Yes, you trollop, I did think of something. Notice how *I* was forced to cut my date short for the purpose of investigation, while you and your paramour caroused on through the night."

Leslie's evil grin continued.

Emma sighed and made a tsk-tsk motion with her hands. "Ah don't know how good it is, but it's worth a shot." She told Leslie about the search-for-childhood-favorites plan.

Leslie tilted her head. "Hmm. Sounds like a definite possibility. Certainly better than my idea, which was to throw on trench coats and ski masks, kidnap him, and tickle him 'til he confesses. Or maybe read him articles from *Cosmo*—that would make him squeal. Oh, I can see it now. Five versions of 'How to Please Your Man in Bed' and he'd be pulling a Kurtz. 'Oh, the horror, the horror! I confess, anything to make it stop!'"

"Now, now," said Emma. "Even if he is the killer, I think we should pay attention to the doctrine against cruel and unusual punishment."

Students filtered in, many of them with friendly waves and greetings for one or both teachers. "Hi, Miss Lovett!" "Yo, Ms. Parker, whassup?"

Emma watched them taking their seats, pulling backpacks off their shoulders, and hunkering down for homeroom. Nice kids here. She hadn't had enough time to think about it with all that had happened in the last week, but she was genuinely excited to be in Colorado and at Thomas Jefferson High. She glanced at Leslie, who was high-fiving two boys just entering the room and giving hugs to some girls coming in right after. Leslie was very cool too. Emma was willing to forgive her the perfect clothes and hair and house and all, because Emma had seen the good and loyal heart underneath. A warm glow suffused Emma.

She didn't feel Leslie tapping her shoulder until it became more like a violent poking. "Ow! What?"

"I've gotta go greet my own precious curtain climbers. We'll talk to Edward after lunch, 'kay? Be practicing your Southern charm."

Emma threw her hair over her shoulders. "Nah. Why mess with perfection?"

Leslie gave her one more poke and walked out.

They left campus for lunch so they could discuss strategy for Edward. Their strategy turned out to be scarfing down Subway sandwiches while Emma listed the books she would ask him for.

"*Island of the Blue Dolphins* is the best," she said. "*Gilligan's Island* meets *White Fang* meets feminist survival camp. You'd love it."

Upon their return to the commons, Emma got a couple of strange looks from students.

"What's wrong? Am I trailing toilet paper?" She checked her heels.

Leslie looked her way. "No, dear. Mustard. Right up here where your blush should be." She sat them down on the bench and wiped the mustard off Emma's cheek with a tissue she pulled from then deposited back in the jacket pocket.

Emma gasped. "Calvin Klein! Careful… you're goin' to get mustard on your Calvin Klein!"

"So? No one ever sees inside the pocket anyway. Come on, let's do this."

That one carefree action with the tissue, and the pocket, and the perfect white dress, clinched it—Emma had the highest respect possible for her new friend. Happily, Emma followed Leslie to the library.

Edward Dixon was in one of the back stacks, looking the same as when Emma first met him. She thought maybe his bowtie was a different color. He had a yardstick in his hand and was placing it along the edge of each row of books to line them up perfectly. *Oh my. This man should never work in a high school. This man should never be anywhere with kids, who rend and toss and unleash themselves upon any room they enter. This man should be on the moon. All by himself, categorizing rocks by the Sea of Tranquility.*

She arranged herself into what she hoped was an attractive sort of come-hither stance and plastered on a wide smile. "Hello, Mr. Dixon! We're mighty glad to see you lookin' so chipper on this fine Tuesday afternoon!"

Leslie looked Emma over and followed suit with the stance and the smile.

He looked up and smiled when he saw Emma. "Miss Lovett! Do please call me Edward. To what do I owe this pleasurable visit?" He grasped her hand in both of his and shook until Emma thought her teeth might clink out onto the floor. "Are you looking for some Flannery O'Connor today? I have some collections of her shorter works—"

He stopped shaking and talking when Emma shook her head. "No, sir. Ah've actually..." She thought an eyelash flutter might be good here, so she tried it. "Ah've actually been sort of, well, homesick, to tell you the truth. Ah've been positively over*come* by nostalgia." Flutter, flutter. "Do you get mah meanin'?" One more flutter.

"W-well, of course I know," he stammered. "It can be so difficult to be so far from home. Are you looking for geography books? Recollections of the South—travel books perhaps? I have some Faulkner. You know he was the definitive writer of the Deep South."

She shook her head and placed a hand on his shoulder. "No, thank you, sir. Faulkner is a wonderful writer, Ah agree, but he's often too dark and maudlin for mah... personal tastes. Ah'm afraid his writings might throw me into a depression." She fanned at her face as if she might swoon at any second. *Scarlett O'Hara, eat your heart out.*

Leslie had removed herself from the scene and was leaning on the corner of a bookshelf, watching bemusedly.

Edward was sweating now, and he seemed intensely conscious of the hand resting on his shoulder. "Of course, of course. Modernist writers tend to be intense, at the least. So"—he took a huge breath—"what can I help you find?"

Emma removed the hand. His eyes sadly followed it down to where she demurely clasped it with the other. "I was thinking of books from my childhood, to tell you the truth. You know, old favorites I remember fondly from my elementary school years? Can't you see me, curled up in front of a fire? Oops!" She laughed gaily. "I mean curled up in front of my air-conditioner, enjoying a cup of tea and some classical music, recalling my days of yore?"

She glanced at Leslie, who mouthed, "Days of yore?"

Edward was still looking at her hands. "I'll help you in any way I can, Miss Lovett..."

"Oh, please call me Emma."

He sucked in another breath and blew out his cheeks. "Uh, Emma. Most of our younger reader books are over here. We don't have that many, you know. The high schoolers feel they've outgrown them. Many don't even like to see what they term 'baby books' in here. But I'd be more than happy to show you what's available."

He minced over to a stack in the back corner of the library; Emma could visualize the Alfalfa spike bouncing as he walked. It really would complete the picture. She followed, motioning her head at Leslie to keep close.

"Here you go, my dear." He gestured to a shelf of books considerably skinnier than the rest. "I have the Ramona series over here. Perhaps Judy Blume?" He chuckled, looking uncomfortable. "I know those have helped many young women through their, ah, changes of life."

Emma peered at the row of books. "These all look wonderful, Mr. Edward. But Ah was, believe it or not, kind of a tomboy as a youngster." She positioned herself to gauge his reaction. Peripherally, she saw Leslie doing the same. "Some of my favorites were the adventures of that Great Brain? Oh, those were funny. Do you have those?"

His face dropped as if puppet wires had sprung from the floor and attached themselves to his eyes, lips, and brow. He didn't answer, just shook his head.

She tried again. "Oh, what about *The Phantom Tollbooth*? I loved that ol' Milo. Ah'd simply die to read that one again!"

His lip was almost quivering now, and he had that wide-eyed glassy look of a person on the verge of tears. Again he simply shook his head.

Emma went in for the kill. "You know my favorite? *Island of the Blue Dolphins!* Oh, Ah loved how that Indian girl survived all on her own with only the wild dog to—"

A keening wail erupted from Edward's mouth. He stood there, hands clenched at his sides, and howled as though the moon was full. Students who were studying during their lunch period gaped, and Emma shivered. This was nothing like his past tantrum; this was pain incarnate. She stood in shock for a minute, then Edward ran for his corner office and slammed the door.

CHAPTER 20

EMMA AND LESLIE STARED AT one another, neither sure what to do next. They walked across the library to his office and saw him through the glass that made up the wall on one side. His shoulders shook.

"Well, I think if we want a confession, this is the time to do it," said Leslie. She listened to Edward's muffled lamentations through the door. "Poor Edward. It must have been an accident. That's remorse if ever I've heard it."

Emma sighed. "Let's talk to him." She turned the doorknob and pushed the door open, knocking quietly at the same time. "Edward? Edward, I didn't mean to upset you so. What's the matter?"

He turned toward them, sniffling. His eyes were rimmed in red and threatened to pop from his face. "I-I can't give you those books, Emma. I don't know where they are."

Emma pulled his hand off the desk and patted it. "Oh, that's all right! I'll just go to the bookstore and buy them. We teachers aren't that poor. My, my, no need to get upset about a few lost books!"

But he was jerking his head back and forth before she finished. "No, no. I don't know where they are because Melvin had them!" He threw up his hands and lamented, "And Melvin's dead!" He wailed again.

This time both Leslie and Emma patted his back until he was whimpering.

"Do you know something about Melvin's death?" asked Leslie gently.

"I know he was my friend." Edward hiccupped. "I know we were doing great work, and he never got to show her..."

"Show who, Edward? What work?" Emma asked. She and Leslie shared a look. Delusions?

He sat up straighter. "Melvin was mostly illiterate. He'd run away from home when he was fifteen, and no one there ever cared about his education anyway. So he fell in love, I guess, a long time ago, but he had to leave or she had to leave. I don't remember the whole story. But she was really smart, see, and he wanted to become literate so he could be with her. She wrote him letters for a while, and he couldn't even write her back."

The women looked at each other. *Marlena!*

"So I was teaching him to read and to write. Those books you loved, we were using those books for him to learn from. He's turned into a great reader, and his writing still needs work, but he's taken to typing his thoughts out on the computer. Took. Had taken." Edward hiccupped. "Now he's gone, and he never talked to her or proved himself to her or *anything*. And he was so nice, and it was all so romantic and..."

They patted his back again frantically to ward off another wave of crying.

"Ah'm so sorry, Edward," said Emma. "We didn't mean to upset you. It's only that..." She shot a look at Leslie, who gave her a "go ahead" shrug. "It's only that we found those books in a secret place Melvin had here at school. We're trying to figure out who killed him, and well, those books were so overdue..."

Edward sat up straighter. Tears glistened on his cheeks. "So you thought I killed him?" He sniffed and wiped his nose with a little hankie from his shirt pocket. "Because of overdue library books? My goodness, why would I overreact so over something that trivial?" He blew into the hankie, a loud honking sound like an elephant missing his peanuts.

"Of course it was crazy, crazy talk!" exclaimed Leslie. "It's just that we had so few clues to go on, and the police haven't been around since Melvin was killed. We'd like to, I don't know, avenge his death or something medieval like that."

"Or at the very least, find his killer and send him to jail." Emma wanted to hug Edward; she was so glad he wasn't Melvin's murderer. How sweet and romantic, helping search out a lost love! She resisted smoothing his hair.

Edward honked into his hankie again, a gleam starting in his eyes. "Solving Melvin's death! How Agatha Christie of you, my dears! Oh, of course I must be of some service to my deceased friend. What can I do to help?"

They looked over the top of his head, alarmed.

"Um..." Leslie said.

"Uh..." Emma added.

"Let us talk about it, Edward," said Leslie. "I'm sure you can be helpful in our investigation."

Emma thought. "Maybe research! We've got some papers."

Leslie's eyes blazed. "I know! You can call the dumbass detective in charge and find out what the hell he's doing to solve this crime."

Edward, momentarily flustered by her display of unladylike language, wrung his hankie. "Oh dear, I..." Then the gleam came back, and he sat up straighter. "I would be honored to make that call, for Melvin. I'll get the scoop for you ladies, right this minute." He took one more long-suffering breath, honked his nose again, and shooed them out of the room.

They were standing outside the office—Emma waiting patiently, Leslie's ear plastered to the door—when Hunter walked up.

"Is he okay? Are you okay? Some students told me there was a problem at the library. What's going on?" Hunter wore navy slacks, a crisp white T-shirt that fit in all the right places, and a look of genuine concern. *Wowzers.*

Leslie, who had her back to them—ear to the door—managed without ever really moving to give Emma a subtle jab to the hipbone, which Emma took as a sign she wasn't supposed to tell him.

Oh, that's right. He's still a suspect. "Oh, I asked him for some books. He didn't have them, and he was so upset about it—"

"Upset he didn't have the books you were looking for? That's why the tantrum?"

Emma smiled, still the Southern coquette, and tried that eyelash flutter. "Well, he didn't want me to feel bad. Ah have that effect on men, you know."

"I do know."

They chuckled and shared an intense slobbery gaze until Edward opened the door and Leslie almost fell in. She pulled Emma into the office.

As Emma waved good-bye to Hunter, she noticed a small group of large students come into the library—*football players*. The jerseys gave it away. As soon as they came in, Hunter did one of his duck-and-cover numbers and hid behind the computer desks at the left of Edward's office. As Emma watched through the glass, he sneaked around the entire library—behind the row of computers, around the magazine rack, and from the back of one stack to the other.

What in the heck is he doing? He ended up in a magazine rack about three feet from the circle of mammoth boys, obviously listening to their conversation, and took a little notebook from his pocket to scribble in.

Edward was tapping his toe impatiently as Leslie went to the window and peered through.

"What's going on?" she asked.

"It's Hunter. See him over there? He's spying on that group of athletes, Ah swear he is. He's hiding and writin' in some sort of notebook." She looked at Leslie. "What on earth could he be doing?"

Leslie shrugged. "Looking for some hot tips on steroid use? I don't know; we have to figure it out later. Right now we're here for an update." She and Emma turned toward Edward. "So, our third Musketeer, what's the scoop?"

Edward looked so proud to be a third Musketeer that he was rendered momentarily speechless. Then he folded his hands in his lap and threw his shoulders back. "I spoke to Detective Niome. I introduced myself as a representative of Thomas Jefferson High School and told him we wished to know the status of his investigation. He was very rude and abrupt, by the way—is he always like that?"

They nodded.

"Hmph. Anyway, he said they were following a very promising lead regarding Melvin's gambling habit. Do you think he had a gambling habit?"

They shook their heads.

"I didn't either. I'm pretty sure he tipped the bottle." He made the classic drinking motion with his pinkie and thumb stuck out and his middle three fingers wrapped around an imaginary mug.

Again, the nod. *Go on, Edward.*

"But he was depressed—lots of people do funny things when they're depressed. Why, one time I even..." His mouth opened and shut, making him look like a fish trying to breathe air. "Anyway, he blathered on about mob connections and said they were about to break the case wide open."

Leslie's mouth dropped open. "It sounds like he couldn't break his ass wide open if he had a hand pulling on each cheek."

Edward gasped; Emma covered a loud guffaw with her hand and turned it into a cough.

While they were both recovering, she pulled Emma out of the office. "Thanks, Edward!" Leslie called over her shoulder. "We'll give you an update soon, you little Musketeer you!"

He waved like a beauty pageant winner in a parade.

"Well, so much for police assistance," said Emma. "What are we going to do next?"

"I think we should go over the evidence again. But first I need to check my mail. Maybe Jake Gyllenhaal's sent me a letter since this morning."

They slogged up the stairs to the teachers' lounge.

"Detecting and teaching at the same time makes me tired. I could use some positive male energy. Oh, damn," Leslie said as they entered the lounge to see Charlie Foreman and his crew splayed across the chairs in the back and staring right at them. She looked up at the sky. "I said *positive*, not putrescent. Didn't we hit the sign? I thought we hit the sign."

"Yo, Parker," called Charlie. "C'mere."

Leslie and Emma cautiously approached the coaches' table. Charlie was wearing his PGA outfit today. Brightly colored green-and-yellow plaid pants strained at his hips and belly, and the armpits of his green polo shirt were half-mooned with sweat. Gross. He looked like a giant leprechaun. The table was sans Hunter, because he was at the library, spying on football players. *What is going on with Hunter?*

Charlie's unibrow dipped in a V. "I need to talk to you about George Mandelan."

"What about him?" Leslie asked.

"We really need him to play cornerback this year," whined the head

Lizard. "Don't even think about flunking him in Modern Lit like you did last year. He's kicking some serious ass in practice."

The other coaches were nodding. No interference allowed in football. Big mistake. Grrrr.

"Well, gee!" Leslie said. "We couldn't possibly interfere with the perpetuation of a troglodytic pastime like knocking heads for fun, could we? Tell you what, Charlie." She crossed her arms. "You tell George to work on a *Lord of the Flies* essay a bit more content-rich than '*Lord of the Flies* was a stupid book cuz they stuck them on a island with no chicks,' and I'll think about bringing him in for some tutoring. Otherwise you're out one cornerback."

Charlie's face darkened. The women turned and flounced from the table.

"I'm warning you, Parker," he shouted. "You keep me from a state championship, and I'll shake you up!"

They checked their mail and passed Abigail Patterson as they walked out.

"Oh, Abigail," Leslie cooed. "Big ol' Charlie's threatening me with death by shaking. Go get 'im!"

The tiny woman smiled and whispered, "Of course, dear. I'll take care of it."

"I don't understand how that woman wields so much power," said Emma as they continued down the stairs. "She twitters like a sparrow and is about as big and scary. How about that woman who announces over the PA? That Janice woman? Now *her* I'm a little scared of. Both times I've seen her, she looked like her head was about to explode."

Leslie looked at Emma as if she was daft. "Abigail *is* the woman on the PA. I thought I'd told you that."

Emma was aghast. "That drill-sergeant voice is Abigail? Surely you... I mean, you must be joking! Where does the voice come from?"

"I don't know. I think it's a Wizard of Oz thing. But no one messes with her, for sure. C'mon, let's go back to my room and look through the cigar box again; it's hiding in the secret desk pocket. Maybe something new will come to us."

CHAPTER 21

THE KEY, THE LETTERS, AND the cryptic notebook were spread over Leslie's desk as they pondered them once again.

Emma turned the key around in her hand. "Maybe we should go back to his house and double-check for a padlock."

"Maybe he left money in a locker at the bus station," said Leslie.

"Could be, I guess. Hey! Maybe it's his engagement ring for Marlena, locked away until they're reunited." Emma swooned across the desk and let her cheek rest on the black lacquer.

"You're one romantic fool, honey. Maybe he's a hit man and has all his weapons locked away. Yeah, one for every type of murder: gun, knife, ice pick, rope, syringe filled with an odorless poison." She was getting into it. "Trocar."

"Trocar?" Emma raised her head. "What on earth is a trocar?"

"It's like a sharp tube thingie. They shove it into dead bodies at the mortuary so they can drain the body and embalm it. Wouldn't that be the way to do it? Exsanguination while you watched?" She smiled fiendishly. "That's how I'd do it, if I were a hit man."

Emma made a face, disgusted. "If I'm a romantic fool, you're a gory ghoul. I can't see Melvin as a hit man. We're reaching. Hey, what about Abigail?"

"You think she's a hit man? God, she'd be a great one."

Emma shook her head, impatient. "No, no. What if she killed Melvin? I mean, he did die in her office. Maybe he came upon her doing something illegal, and she whacked him."

"Like what? Pilfering the computer paper? Besides, didn't we say the killer needed to be tall?"

"Maybe her boyfriend, Lurch, was with her." Emma grinned. Oh, spinning those fantastical stories was fun, even if they weren't going anywhere. "I'm still nowhere on this paper and these initials." She turned to it again.

CBSSA SAY NO GPA NO PLAY ON PENALTY OF J.LOSS/CRIM. PROS. TALK TO ADAM.

"I think we should figure out who Adam is," Leslie said. "I don't think we have anyone on staff by that name, but let's look at a yearbook." She went to a bookshelf in the corner and pulled out last year's Wildcats yearbook. "Here's the staff section."

They riffled through it. They found an Alan Ricks—kitchen—and an Alex Hawkins—math—but no Adam.

They spent the remainder of their planning period going through student photos. Believe it or not, in a school of fourteen hundred students, there were only two Adams. Tons of Jasons and Matthews and Nicks, a few Jeremiahs and Zachariahs, but only Adam Butler and Adam Evanovich, both seniors. After creating a plan to find both Adams the next day and let Emma interrogate them—they thought Leslie would just scare them—Emma reminded Leslie to hide the cigar box in the secret desk pocket, and they parted ways for fifth period.

Emma's fifth-period Speech class was finishing up their "What Am I Afraid Of?" speeches. She figured since fear of public speaking was the most common fear, maybe talking about fears in general could help her students come to terms with their own.

One in particular stood out. Kayla Quinlan introduced herself as a champion golfer and said her biggest fear was being unable to keep her grades up during training so she'd be eligible to play. But she said her coach so, so, *soooooo* helped her. She seemed very attached to her coach.

The speech itself wasn't the standout—it was what happened during Anthony Trumbull's speech. The door opened right in the middle of his speech, and Charlie Foreman barged in!

"'Scuse me, Emma, but I need to talk to my star." He nodded at Kayla, and she got up to follow him out, without waiting for Emma's approval.

As Anthony continued his speech, Emma watched through the door's window as Charlie and Kayla talked in the hallway. Just when Emma realized something about what he'd said sounded familiar, Charlie put his hand on Kayla's shoulder and his mouth right up to her ear to say something Emma couldn't hear. Then Kayla hugged him.

His interruption was bad enough, but the way he's touching Kayla... she's a student! He's such a creep. That hug isn't quite over the line, but it's too close for my comfort. Just how helpful is her helpful golf coach? Eeeeww.

After their hug, Kayla smiled at Charlie and came back into the classroom. He watched through the door window as she settled back into her seat.

Emma decided to talk to Leslie and see if anything could be done. Superintendent's son or no, if Charlie Foreman was in an inappropriate relationship with a student, something had to happen.

The final bell came at three fifteen, sending a wave of teens pouring from classrooms into hallways. Emma allowed herself to catch the wave, curious about the feeling of traveling along with the little balls of energy. Okay, not so little—it seemed Emma was one of the shortest in the crowd. *Evolution maybe, or just the fine mountain air?* She caught the eye of some of the boys as they walked along and wondered if any of them were the mysterious Adam.

The wind had picked up when she got to the courtyard—late-summer monsoons. Leslie had mentioned them, and Emma thought the word "monsoon" sounded much wetter than it really was. The sky didn't produce much water, just lots of wind. The leaves on her majestic tree shimmied and danced; her hair caught the breeze and whipped in crazy circles as she ran to her car.

The bushes that lined the patio of her dollhouse were leaning to one side then to the other, bending with the wind like small, fat towers of Pisa. Delilah waved from her front window but didn't come out to greet Emma. Trinculo and Sir Toby were at her own picture window. She skipped up the front steps with arms out to greet them the minute she opened the door. Their joyful barks and meows as they jumped against her were better than any man's greeting. Well, almost as good anyway.

She changed into a T-shirt and shorts and fell onto her hairy couch. The calico crew tumbled onto the cushions surrounding her.

"Hello, my little loveys," she cooed. "Did you miss me today?" She was rewarded with rough licks from Trinky and a zealous yip from Toby. "Ah've been very busy. Along with this wonderful and fulfilling teaching job, Ah'm solving a *murder*. Isn't that great?"

Total agreement from her pets.

She talked to them in baby talk. She could announce her *own* plans of murder and mayhem, and they'd eat up every word. "I think we should have a treat, don't you? Then I have to grade lots of papers. Important work we're doing, don't you think?"

She was pretty sure Trinky nodded, and Toby jumped on her lap. She uprooted her and went to the kitchen for some treats—potato chips for her, dog and cat biscuits for them. Well, they got some chips too.

Diligent grading took place for the next three hours. She turned on piano music and lost herself in the process of correcting essays. Most of the ones from her American Lit class were pretty good, but she had a pile from Sophomore Lit that scared her a little. Sentences that started with "I done" and ended with... well, with nothing at all. No such things as periods here. She feared for the new generation.

Then again, the juniors looked okay. Maybe there was some amazing transformation between tenth and eleventh grade she hadn't heard about yet; she'd have to ask Leslie. She paused in her grading and spent an hour creating a fun grammar game for the sophomores.

Her stomach growled like a mean grizzly after a while, and she stopped for dinner—cat and dog food for them, salad for her to counteract the potato chips. The three planted themselves on the couch after dinner and tried to watch the tube, but nothing suited her fancy on a Tuesday night. She vacillated between wishing Hunter would call and wishing he wouldn't. She was so confused about his evasion and spying. *Could he really be a killer?* She hadn't gotten that vibe from him at all, but maybe that was why people got away with murder.

Hmph. Maybe it was better to be a she-woman man-hater and forget about them all. But his dimples and big blue eyes, along with his reading habits, made him impossible to just forget. *Let's just put him on the shelf for a while then, reserve judgment. Okay, so how does that help with tonight's impending boredom?*

Then it hit her... she could spend more time trying to figure out the little notebook in Melvin's cigar box. But shoot—they were still in Leslie's classroom. She tried to call Leslie and got no answer. *Probably out with her boy toy.* She could run to the school and grab it, especially since her key worked for all of the English classrooms.

It was after eight, and dusk was settling like gauze over the town. It would be dark soon, and Emma wasn't sure how she felt about running back to the school at night by herself. In the movies, it was always the stupid girl who left the safety of her house who got iced. But then again, in *Halloween*, Jamie Lee Curtis had been attacked *right in her own home!* Emma thought about all she'd done since leaving her hometown and leaving Ronald, and she was pretty proud of her bravery.

She was a grown woman, and the school was five minutes away. Melvin had been killed in the wee hours of the morning. And she had her trusty pink Terminator. And she could bring Sir Toby to guard her... and... and... just then, an old episode of *Wonder Woman* started up, its theme song echoing through the living room. That was all Emma needed to leash up the dog. Toby's tail whipped from side to side with the excitement of the adventure.

After throwing a hair tie around her hair, Emma braved the outdoors. The wind had died down and left the air thin and clean smelling. Determined not to lose her nerve, she let the dog jump into the Honda before she hopped in, threw it in reverse, and headed back to school.

CHAPTER 22

THE SCHOOL'S SHADOW AGAINST THE darkening sky was like a miniature cityscape, the mountains behind it slightly darker and much larger. The first stars winked on as Emma drove into the staff parking lot, and she got out and made a little wish on the largest one. Okay, two wishes. One was that coming here alone wasn't the stupidest thing she'd ever done, and two was that Hunter wasn't a secret pervert who preyed on young football players. Or preyed on anyone, for that matter. A leftover monsoonal breeze made her shiver.

The flap-flap of her flip-flops and click-click of dog toes echoed across the empty lot as she and Toby crossed it quickly. Throwing her bag over one shoulder, she fumbled through a mess of keys—hey! She'd only been in Pinewood a few months; how on earth had she accumulated so many keys?—until the school key popped out, and she was in.

It was almost black inside the commons, but for some reason, she felt more sheltered there. She turned on the flashlight attached to her Terminator and wished briefly for the crowbar. Flap-flap, click-click-click they went across the tiles toward Leslie's classroom. She looked and the dog sniffed at all the lockers they passed; she hoped one would have a padlock instead of a combination lock.

No luck, but she'd put herself in a kind of trance by counting locker numbers—228, 229, 230—until flap-flap, flap, click... stop. *Was that a footfall in sync with ours?* She inhaled and walked slowly, flap-click-click... flap-click-click... flap-click... she was too frightened to flash the light behind her, so she exhaled and sped up—flap-click-flap-click-flapclickclick-flapclickclick-flapclickclickclick—and stopped suddenly. A foot behind her fell once all by itself.

Oh god, oh god, what to do now? *Hello, Mr. Janitor, please don't kill me!* She kept walking toward Leslie's room because the follower was between her and the exit. She heard an even step behind her. Her thoughts whirled as she and Sir Toby walked. This was just like the scene between Scout, Jem, and Bob Ewell after the pageant in *To Kill a Mockingbird. At least the bad guy ended up dead in that one.*

Leslie's room was around the corner. She tried to speed up without making it obvious she knew someone was stalking her, because if she broke into a run, he'd be on her right away. Her breath came in ragged gasps, but she tried to quiet them as she stuck the English department key between her fingers. Whether to open Leslie's door or gouge out someone's eyes, she wasn't sure, but the decision would be made soon.

Leslie's room came into view as soon as Emma and Sir Toby rounded the corner. They sprinted across the hallway; she jammed the key in and cranked it around, threw herself and her dog into the room, and twisted the lock on the door.

The light switch didn't respond at all when she flicked it up and down, and she heard the rattling of the doorknob, felt it twitching behind her back. She had to make a barricade. The light from her flashlight illuminated a chair under a student desk, which she grabbed and shoved under the doorknob.

She thought about trying to push Leslie's black-lacquered desk in front of the door when Toby barked at the *back* of the room instead of at the jerking door. She swung her light in the direction of the dog's yelps, where it strobed to the beat of her heart and the shaking of her hands.

The flash landed briefly on something crouched in a ball next to the file cabinet. Toby yipped and yipped, hair and tail standing rigid. Emma tried to find the shape again, but it rose from its recumbent position like the Grim Reaper ascending. The flashlight fell from her hands and clattered to the floor.

Holding her key and the stun gun in both hands, she ran toward the figure. Screaming, she deployed the button on the Terminator. A piercing blare ripped through the classroom as Emma felt hands shoving her backward, then everything descended into darkness.

"Emma? Emma, wake up. Emma, your head is bleeding. Don't move."

The voice came from far away, but she wanted to meet it, wanted to come up from whatever hole she'd fallen into and hear it some more. Someone was licking her ear.

"Emma?"

She felt a pat on her cheek. The light touch brought a million points of pain to the surface of her face. The patting continued. *Ow! Maybe I don't want to come up.*

"Emma, there's blood on the floor behind your head. I'd like to look at your head."

She stuck out her left hand, thankful that the one licking her ear was Sir Toby. Eyes still closed, she reached under her neck with her right hand and felt wetness there. Wetness and pain.

"Hello." Emma opened her eyes then closed them again as she was revisited by the miniature Marquis de Sade who'd taken up residence behind her eyes. "Ow! Quit patting me, will you? I'm awake."

The hand receded. "I'm so sorry, Emma. We need to go to the hospital."

Taking a deep breath, Emma opened her eyes a millimeter at a time. Light came through in chunks, and when her eyes were all the way open, she still didn't see anything she recognized. The fluorescent lights in the ceiling came into focus first, although their symmetry was interrupted by a clump on the right. She clenched her eyes shut again and opened them to see the clump sharpen into Hunter's worried face.

"Hunter! For the love of all that's holy, what are you doing here?" She struggled to sit up, holding her head while pain slammed into her brain with every movement. She tried rubbing her temples, noticing the pain radiate from her forehead *and* the back of her head. *Great, maybe I'm concussed.* She had definitely not signed up for this in the Nancy Drew School of Detecting.

She pulled Sir Toby into her lap. The dog seemed to know not to lick her face, because she settled right down. "Hunter. Where's my stun gun?"

Hunter gave her a strange look, looked around, and found it on the floor over by the file cabinet, then he handed it to her.

From her seated position, and very carefully, she pointed the stun gun at her new love interest. "Hunter, what are you doing here? Were you following me?"

Hunter looked at the shaking hand holding the stun gun toward him. "Of course not! I was in my... I was in the... I was on the other side of the school when I heard you scream and heard that ridiculous noise."

She shook it at him. "Doing what on the other side of the school?"

He ran a hand through his thick dark hair. "Doing... schoolwork. That's all."

Emma had to work really hard not to notice his hair. "I don't believe you."

He squirmed, looking uncomfortable. Beads of sweat popped out on his forehead as he endured her look. "I tried to chase him, Emma, but he was long gone. So I switched the breaker he'd tripped before his little breaking-and-entering excursion, then I came back here to you. I... I just had some work to do. Grading stuff, you know?"

He really was the most terrible liar she'd ever seen. "My good gravy, Hunter. I just do not, in any way shape or form, believe what you're sayin'!" She covered her eyes with her hands, still in so much pain. "Look, you blew me off at dinner when I asked you about your job, then I saw you sneaking around the library and takin' notes while you were watchin' those football players. And now you show up here, with an explanation that wouldn't stick if it were superglued on, and I'm possibly concussed, Hunter! And Melvin's dead!" She shook the stun gun at him again. "And I really liked you."

His face fell. "Okay, Emma. I'll tell you the whole truth. I wasn't following you, and I certainly didn't kill Melvin. But I'm not who I said I was, and you can't tell Leslie who I really am." He gestured around the room. "She's gonna find out about this soon enough though."

Even though it was excruciating, she looked around Leslie's classroom. It was a mess. All the file cabinet doors were open, and files were strewn everywhere. Desk drawers lay in various stages of emptiness on the floor, and bookshelves were empty, the books like fallen birds on the floor.

She gasped. "Leslie's going to hate this. What would someone want with her room? There's nothing here that's really valuable. Well, maybe the desk. Maybe the computer. But there are a lot more computers in the library." Emma knew she was babbling. Her head was trying to wrap itself around something else, but she was too discombobulated to figure out what it was. "Melvin's box! Maybe—"

She stopped herself. She didn't want Hunter to see the secret drawer, not until she knew what was going on with him, so she wiggled the stun gun at him and forced him to take Sir Toby out to pee.

After he was gone, Emma bent under Leslie's desk, hammers tattooing across her head, and extracted the cigar box. It seemed that everything was there—the key, the letters, and the little notebook. The bottom of the box had some doodles across the bottom, which she and Leslie had missed the first time around. *God, we really are the worst detectives. We didn't even turn the box over!* She tried to decipher them, but they swam in front of her eyes like snakes.

Hunter and Sir Toby came back in.

Emma set down the cigar box and picked up the stun gun. "I don't know what's goin' on with you, mister, but until you can start telling me the truth about your comings and goin's around this place, I don't care if you're the hottest and most interesting man west of the Mississippi, there will *not* be a second date!"

He smiled. "You think I'm interesting?" He scooched next to Emma on the desk, and she swung the weapon around. "Don't tase me. I just want to look at the back of your head." He pulled off his T-shirt, balled it up, and held it gently against her wound. "You're gonna need some stitches."

She glanced sideways at a shirtless Hunter. His abdominal muscles flexed as he held the shirt against her skull. *Oh Lord, give me strength.* She took a deep breath, which made her head feel as though it was ready to split. "Come on, Hunter. Spill."

He took away his bloody shirt. "I'm not really a teacher, Emma. I'm a Special Investigator for CHSSA."

CHAPTER 23

"YOU CAN'T TELL LESLIE," HUNTER said. "The only reason I'm telling you is because you're new, and this has been going on for at least two years, maybe three."

"Wait. Wait just a minute," Emma said. "You're not a teacher? What's a chassa? I thought that was a car part."

He smiled. "That's a chassis. No, CHSSA. The Colorado High School Sports Association. I've been investigating reports of fraud, grade changing, you know, people changing grades to improve their sports team by keeping good players on who don't really have the grades to play? I thought it was the football coaches, and it's a very big deal. So I came here as a teacher to, you know, infiltrate."

Emma set down the stun gun and stared at Hunter. "Ah don't know what to say. Nobody else knows you're not a teacher? That's why you were sneaking around the library? That's why you were here tonight?"

Hunter nodded. "I've been going through files in the athletic office, in the PE teachers' rooms, and some other coaches who coach sports but don't teach PE." He put a hand on her knee. "And then I heard you scream. I'm so glad I was here."

"And you think Leslie could be changing grades? Come on, she's the least sports-interested or sports-minded person you will ever meet."

"Nobody else knows, and I mean nobody, except CHSSA and the president of the Colorado Teachers Association. Not the superintendent, not Nathan Farrar. Last year in Aurora, we had a basketball scandal that went all the way to the mayor's office."

Emma shifted her weight on the desk. "Do you think this has something to do with Melvin's murder?"

"I don't know," said Hunter. "I haven't been able to ask the police where they are in the investigation because they don't know who I am either. I'm just a random social studies teacher who—"

"Who could have actually been the one who killed Melvin. You're tall."

"I'm *what*?" Hunter jumped off the desk. "You've lost me."

He picked up Sir Toby and set her on the desk next to Emma, where she sat quietly and didn't jump up to lick Emma's face. *My smart little girl totally gets it.* Emma filled Hunter in on her and Leslie's investigation, including the threatening voice she'd overheard early last week.

"So that's why you were here by yourself tonight?" Hunter picked up the cigar box and shook it at her. "After you've heard someone making threats, and Melvin got killed, and you two have already been assaulted once here after hours? Are you both crazy?"

Emma picked up her stun gun and showed it to him. He shook his head.

"Ah know." She sighed. "Not the best idea Ah ever had. But you don't understand. The policeman in charge of this investigation is goin' down all these wrong alleys. He's so clueless, matter a' fact, Leslie calls him Carl the Clueless. And Melvin was so great. We're learning even more great stuff about him as we go."

All of a sudden, she had an idea. "Hey! We could help you with your investigation, and you could help us! What a fantastic idea!" An excited shiver started up her backbone, which she had to squelch before it could reach her injured head.

"You're babbling. And how can we mount a joint investigation without telling Leslie who I am?"

She turned puppy-dog eyes his way and batted her lashes for emphasis. "You know you don't really think Leslie is involved in a grade-changing scandal, do you?" she purred. "She doesn't coach any sports and doesn't spend time with anyone who does. She can be trusted, I promise."

Hunter huffed. "Well, I've seen her verbally decimate coaches whenever she gets the opportunity. Let me think about it. But you need to make me a promise. You need to never, ever—"

"Ever again come here alone at night. Got it." She gestured to her head. "I've learned my lesson. Twice."

"Are you still mad at me? Will you put that little pink equalizer away and allow me to escort you to the hospital so they can look at your head?" He held the sides of her face and looked into her eyes.

"Ow. No, I'm not still mad, but I'm not feeling well enough to be seduced by a deep, soulful gaze right now, if that's what you're doing." She noted his baby blues anyway.

"Silly. I'm checking you for a concussion. Your pupils look fine, so that's good. Just stitches, then. Come on." He helped her off Leslie's desk. "Let's pay a visit to Pinewood Memorial." He held her hand and led her from Leslie's room.

"When you decide it's okay for Leslie to know about you, can you drop me off at her house after the hospital? I need to fill her in."

Holding hands, they walked slowly through the commons with Sir Toby click-clicking and Emma flap-flapping along.

"Oh, I see," Hunter said. "So it's *when* I decide you can tell her, not if. I see how this is going to go…"

Leslie was still out at eleven forty-five when they got there. Emma was tired, sore, and frustrated, but she wanted to tell Leslie what had happened. Hunter did a complete search of Leslie's yard and two blocks on either side before Emma could convince him she was safe, and he left.

So Emma and Sir Toby sat on Leslie's porch and waited. Emma held a gauze pad against her stitches in case of oozing and turned over events of the previous hours. *Who would break into Leslie's room, and why? Did the break-in have anything to do with Melvin's death? Did Melvin have something to do with the grade-changing scandal Hunter is investigating, and is that why he's dead?*

I keep going back to that voice I overheard last week. Something about soccer and football, but I swear the voice said "her." You've helped soccer and football do it for years; now you have to help "her." Her head still really hurt, but she didn't want to take the pain pills the doctor had given her, because she was afraid she wouldn't be able to think clearly. *Oh, who am I kidding? If I was thinking clearly, I would never have gone back to the school on my own, and I'd be able to make some sense of all this.* She held the cigar box in her lap, fingering the letters from Marlena.

All she could figure was the "clues" they had found had nothing to do with his death. But she couldn't see what Leslie and her classroom had to do with it either. It was all so confusing, and there was still that nagging feeling in the back of her mind, the one she couldn't pinpoint except as residual pain from knocking her head.

The convertible drove up, and Leslie hopped out, hair slightly mussed and lipstick gone. She ran over to Emma. "Oh my god, what are you doing here? What's wrong? Holy crap! You're bleeding. Jesus, what happened to your head?"

Emma raised a hand, not sure where to start. "Hunter's not really a teacher."

"Hunter Wells? Did he do this to you? Why, I'll—"

"No, no, he didn't do this. He took me to the hospital actually. He works as this special investigator, so now we're goin' to all work together, and I still don't know who killed Melvin even though I went to school to look for more clues and your room—oh, Leslie, your perfect room—"

This time it was Leslie who held up her hand. "Whoa, start over. What about Hunter? And what's this about my room? And you went to the school by yourself to find Hunter investigating something? What? I hope you took the Terminator." She helped Emma up and took Sir Toby's leash. "Look, hon, let's go inside, and you can start from the beginning."

They walked inside the house, Emma explaining her Wonder Woman mission and the ensuing results. Leslie gaped and gasped when Emma got to the part about the attack, and she squalled a little when she heard about her classroom.

Leslie sighed. "Well, it's just a room. And I don't know why it's been messed with twice this year, but that's something we should figure out, along with all the other mysteries in our lives right now." She looked at Emma's stitches.

"Do you think we should call Detective Niome about the break-in?" Emma asked. "I mean, last time nothing was missing or damaged, but you sure can't be sayin' that now."

"I don't think Carl Niome gives a rat's ass about my precious classroom, but yeah, I guess we should." She took a cordless phone from a charger on the kitchen wall and used it to dial the police for the second time in less than a week.

Thou old Adam's likeness, set to dress this garden.

—*Richard II iii.4.73*

CHAPTER 24

Wednesday, September 2

LESLIE UTILIZED HER FIRST-HOUR CLASS to clean up her room. Extra credit was given, of course. Emma sported five lovely black stitches in the back of her head, and a report was filed with Detective Niome, who came out to the school while grumbling about "those damn vandalous kids." Emma didn't think "vandalous" was a word, but correcting him probably wouldn't be useful either.

The teachers didn't bother sharing their speculations because, at this point, they didn't really have any, and Hunter had said anything they found out that related to sports and grades needed to be kept quiet. For now. Plus Carl was still hot on the mob trail, or whatever, of gambling mafiosi. No use smashing his Spencer Tracy fantasies.

Matter of fact, Emma was starting to wonder if they shouldn't be pursuing gangster leads and following some sort of money trail themselves. So far, the cigar box and love letters hadn't given them anything but head injuries and "vandalous" destruction.

"We need to go find those Adams," said Emma.

She and Leslie were sitting in her classroom for lunch, having a four-course meal that included veggie lasagna—Emma's favorite—courtesy of Mrs. Albert. Mrs. Albert had heard about Emma's injury and insisted upon healing with food. Emma didn't object.

"Yeah, let's go up and get their schedules," Leslie replied and punctuated her words with a satisfied belch. "Hopefully they have non-Hitleresque teachers who will allow them to leave class for a sec."

The teachers' lounge had a file cabinet beyond the mailboxes that contained student schedules. Hunter Wells was sitting at the back table, and he nodded at Emma and Leslie. Emma studiously ignored him but felt his eyes boring into the back of her head as they perused the files. It gave her a shiver of pleasure, knowing he was a part of their team instead of someone they had to be suspicious of. Of whom they had to be suspicious.

It turned out that Adam Evanovich was in American History with Martha Bonaventure.

"She loves me," said Leslie, "because I make Charlie look like such a fool. If I need to, she'll let me take her whole class."

Adam Butler was in PE. Well, that one might be tricky, so they went to the history class first. Martha was lecturing on the Revolutionary War, which made sense at the start of the school year. Her skirt and shoes were navy but otherwise identical to every other outfit Emma had seen.

Emma watched Martha for a minute and was surprised by what she saw. Martha's speaking style was everything but drab and ordinary. Her eyes sparkled as she paced, hands flying this way and that. She wasn't lecturing so much as storytelling, and the kids seemed completely taken in by the visual picture she drew. *Well, well. You learn something new every day.*

As soon as Martha paused to let kids check a reference, Leslie ran up and asked to borrow Adam Evanovich. A cowboy type stood and strutted up to Emma and Leslie amid numerous whistles. They even heard, "You go, dude!" when he left the room with the two women.

Adam Evanovich was typical of some of the farm kids Emma had seen in Pinewood, with a quick step and a ready smile and Wranglers that were just a *little* bit too tight. Some cowgirls had informed her, however, that that look, along with a button-up shirt and work boots, was about as sexy as one could possibly get. She took their word for it, as to her it only looked uncomfortable.

He smiled and tipped his head. "What can I do for you, ma'am and ma'am?

Emma looked around. *Is my mother here?* "Um, yes, Adam. We just have a quick question for you."

"I'd be glad to help you if'n I can." He had a black-and-white striped shirt on with his Wranglers, and his pants were secured—as if they'd fall off—with a belt that had a large round metal buckle. His blond hair was matted in the front. *Hat hair.* He seemed sweet.

"Did you know Melvin McManus?" asked Leslie. "Personally, I mean."

Adam looked confused for a moment. "Oh, you mean that janitor what was killed? No, ma'am. I never even heard of him until I saw his obituary in the paper. Didn't he work nights mostly?"

"Yes, mostly," replied Emma. "We thought maybe he was a family friend or something, or you might have seen him after school, I don't know—at sports practice or something?"

Adam ran a hand over the hair that was stuck to his forehead. "No, ma'am. I do rodeo, and that practice is at the fairgrounds. I'm sure sorry."

The two women exchanged a look, and Adam waited for them to speak.

Finally he said, "You want I should go back to class now?"

Leslie patted his shoulder. "You go ahead, Adam."

He loped back into the classroom.

"Well?" said Emma. "I guess we can try the other Adam and hope he knows more. Sweet kid though."

They walked toward the gym.

"Yeah, but don't ever fall in love with one, I hear—a cowboy, I mean," said Leslie. "They have that overwhelming charm and a heart that just won't stay put."

"Gee. I've never met anyone like that."

Emma coughed out the words "ex-husband," and Leslie followed suit with her own cough. They coughed words about cheating, charming men all the way down the hall.

Pretty soon they were both giggling, until they walked into the gym and Leslie got nailed in the head with a dodgeball. She stood there, stunned. A heavy kid was sniggering and pointing, but his glee was cut short when Leslie grabbed an incoming ball and, with deadly accuracy, pegged him right in the nose.

"You're out!" she exclaimed. "Go to jail, or wherever you go."

He watched them walk by, palm covering his nose and jaw dropping to the floor.

Emma smiled sweetly, lifted her hair to show off her stitches, and said, "You better not throw one my way. You should see the guy who did *this*."

The PE teacher was a woman, therefore not a Lounge Lizard, and she let Leslie and Emma borrow Adam Butler. The kid she called out of the game was about five feet tall, with pasty little legs and curly brown hair that Emma would kill for but that probably garnered him merciless torture. He looked like the kind of kid who got duct-taped on a regular basis. Her heart ached when his glance at her, followed by quickly downcast eyes, told her the whole story. *This is definitely not one of those kids for whom high school is the greatest time in life.*

He walked out with them. His thin legs shook all the way to the end of the gym hall, where they finally stopped wobbling.

He looked at Emma, then at Leslie, and with a tremulous voice, he asked, "Am I in trouble?" He had huge, round brown eyes that seemed to grow even larger with fear. His voice cracked on the last word.

Emma smiled at him reassuringly. "Of course not, honey. We just wanted to ask you a question."

He waited, obviously tense.

"Did you know Melvin McManus?" Leslie asked.

Adam's eyes took on that wet sheen that precedes tears, but he blinked them back. "Yeah, I knew him. We... well, he was my friend."

"How did you two get to be friends?" Emma asked.

He took a deep breath. "I... well, I was new here last year. I haven't met many people, and some of them are, well, they're not too nice. So I had this thing, see, with this kid at school last year and it... well, it made me pretty sad. So I didn't go home one day, just kinda sat in the corner of the boys' locker room for a long time."

Adam continued. "Melvin found me there, and instead of, I dunno, yelling at me to go home, he sat with me for a while. It kinda got to be, like, you know—like we were friends. He would meet me two or three times a week, and we'd just talk about, I dunno, things. He told me about some bad stuff that had happened to him when he was a kid, and how he, I dunno, had to leave home real young and all." His eyes got that sheen again. "I can't believe someone would kill him. He was, I dunno, the most harmless guy."

He shifted his weight from the balls of his feet to the heels and twisted the hem of his PE shirt. "So yeah, I knew him. I-I miss him."

I think maybe I could cry now. He was just so precious.

Leslie sighed. "'I count myself in nothing else so happy as in a soul remembering my good friends.'"

Emma wiped the corner of one eye. "I think that's from a Richard. Is that a Richard?"

Leslie smiled and nodded, looking like a sage impressed with her protégé.

Adam looked at them strangely. "Um, why do you need to know about Melvin?"

"Oh, yes." Emma unfolded the paper from Melvin's notepad, which she'd been holding. "Do you know what this means?"

Adam read it and nodded. "Yeah, it's something we were trying to fix. I overheard some jocks talking one day. You know, they pretty much don't realize I exist unless they're in the mood to give me some shit. Oops. 'Scuse me. Anyway, they were talking about changing their grades, you know, so they could be eligible for football. Someone was doing it for them. I didn't know who. And they're such assholes—'scuse me, but they are. I'm not some big snitch or anything, but I was having one of those 'life isn't fair' moments, ya know? And then a couple of them dumped me in a trash can, so…"

"Those assholes!" said Leslie.

Emma took her cue. "Yes, what total shitheads, right, Adam?"

Adam looked startled then pleased. "Yeah, total shitheads. Anyway, I thought maybe it was one of the coaches changing the grades, so I, like, asked Melvin if we could do anything about it. CHSSA stands for Colorado High School Sports Association, and I guess he was finding out what could happen if it was a coach or teacher changing grades."

"Wait a moment," Emma said. "That's an H?"

"Yeah. Melvin was getting better, but his handwriting was still kind of hard to read sometimes. I kept trying to get him to open up his Hs." He pointed at the middle of the sheet. "And this means criminal prosecution. I guess grades are a pretty big deal—I mean that they're all legally right, ya know—and we all know everyone here is bonkers over sports. So that's what that all says. He, like, wanted to ask me if

I'd heard any more about who was changing grades. He said he had to make up for some mistakes he'd made since he got here, and this might be a good way to do it."

Emma and Leslie exchanged knowing glances. So this note was about sports, too. Melvin was interested in the same thing Hunter was here for. Maybe Charlie Foreman was behind all of this? Granted, he was a total pig, and maybe involved with one of his golfers, but Emma wasn't sure he'd kill someone over sports. High school sports, for Pete's sake. Their faces conversed over Adam's head.

Emma's eyes said, *Do you really think someone would murder over high school sports?*

And Leslie's eyebrows roller coastered with a, *Honey, you have no idea.*

Emma knelt and held Adam's frail shoulder bones. "Adam, this is very important. Was it a coach or teacher changing the grades?"

He shrugged. "I saw it, I dunno, happening actually. This one kid who's an office aide alters the eligibility reports before he takes them in to the secretary. Or, you know, maybe he goes in and alters them when she's on her break if he isn't the one who picks them up. Not sure if it's a coach calling the shots or a player. Or maybe the secretary is letting him do it, I dunno." He ducked his head. "I didn't know who to tell now that Melvin's, like, gone. I'm really sorry." He expelled a huge breath, and his shoulders drooped even farther.

This time Leslie knelt and grasped Adam. "No, it's all right. We'll take care of it, okay? And you... well, you can come and talk to us any ol' time. We can just listen, or if you want, we have ways of dealing with asshole bullies." She winked and gestured toward the gym. "Just ask the guy with the nosebleed."

CHAPTER 25

"WELL, WHAT DO YOU THINK about that?" asked Emma. "The note couldn't have anything to do with Melvin's murder because—"

Leslie finished her sentence. "Because they hadn't gotten anyone in trouble yet. I mean, even if someone had found out Melvin was asking about CHSSA rules—"

"It probably wouldn't be that office aide kid." She thought for a minute. "What about Melvin needing to find the grade changers to fix a mistake he'd made? What kind of a mistake could he have been talking about? And do you think that could have gotten him killed?"

"Oh, aarrgghh." Leslie sighed. "'Why dost thou show to the apt hearts of men the things that are not?'"

"That's right. Not clues, not solutions, not killers." Emma felt discouraged.

Leslie said, "I'll tell you what. After fifth period, let's go talk to Hunter, tell him what we learned. Maybe he'll have some ideas."

"Sounds like a plan," Emma said. "Oh, listen to my plans for fifth period! After the silent reading I start all my classes with, we're going to work on improvisational speeches. It's this really great idea I found on the Internet—they pick topics from a cup of popsicle sticks and have to talk about the topic for one minute straight." She smiled. "I don't expect them all to be able to do it right away." Then she thought for a moment. "Hey, do you think I should talk to Kayla Quinlan during silent reading? I don't remember if I told you this, but Charlie pulled her out of my class yesterday. They have a coach/player relationship that looked sketchy, to say the least. Maybe she'll let something slip about him and his great plan to help her keep her grades up."

They arrived at Leslie's room.

"Why not?" Leslie said. "Melvin was involved in a little investigation of his own, and it was about sports and changing grades, and Charlie's all about sports and eligibility. If Kayla's involved with him though, she'll probably clam up. Just test the waters. If we find out they're involved, we're taking it to the police. Superintendent's son or no."

After wading through the three-fifteen flood of students, they arrived in front of Hunter's room in the social studies wing and entered. The room looked like a real teacher's room instead of an eligibility spy's, with one wall covered completely in map-of-the-world wallpaper.

"Halloo, Hunter!" called Leslie.

Emma just smiled at the handsome hunk sitting at his desk. She was so grateful he wasn't a killer.

He smiled back. "Hello, ladies. Are you here with news on the investigation? Not that you need a reason to visit, but..." He smiled wider and winked at Emma.

"Yes! We have some of the evidence you're searchin' for! For which you are searchin'." Emma winked back. "Just that there are grades being changed—no evidence yet that one or more of the coaches are involved."

Leslie explained their meeting with Adam. "Then Emma saw Charlie Foreman acting kinda sleazy with one of his golfers." She raised eyebrows at Emma. "Did you talk to her last hour?"

"I did. She was really forthcomin', said Charlie told her he could be really... convincing when it came to helping his athletes stay eligible. When I asked her how he did that, she said she had no idea but that she wasn't about to question someone who's helping her be a champion."

"My associate at CHSSA has actually spoken to both of the office aides from last year," said Hunter, "and we couldn't get them to say anything, nor could we connect them to a specific coach or teacher or even to a certain team. Maybe now that we have a witness, we can use that as leverage. As far as proving it's Charlie Foreman..." He shook his head. "He's so slimy. But that's not proof."

"He uses his father all the time," Leslie said. "There was a first-year teacher—oh, a few years ago, I guess—who had a background as a football coach. Former college player, really good. Nathan was looking to get him involved in the program, but everyone knew Charlie didn't see him as help, just competition. So he worked some kind of nepotistic magic and made sure the guy's provisional teaching contract didn't get renewed." She looked at Emma. "Did Kayla say anything else about that douche?"

Emma shook her head. "When I sort of hinted that she might have, you know, feelings for the man, you should've seen that girl's face! It instantly puckered up like she'd squeezed a whole box a'lemons in her mouth. 'Eeeewww, gross,' she said. 'Me and Charlie? He's totally old, like forty! And he's only got, like, one eyebrow, and his gut looks like he's pregnant.' Then she shivered and said eeewwww again, so I let her go back to silent reading." Emma grinned. "I really, really don't think she was pretending."

Hunter walked over to the map wall. Leslie took his chair, and Emma perched on the edge of his desk, doing some neck rolls. The wound to the back of her head was very sensitive, but she'd been doing neck rolls all day, which, instead of splitting her stitches, made her feel better, more relaxed.

"So where do we go from here?" Emma asked. "How can we find out if it's a teacher or student behind the grade changes?"

"I've been thinking about the break-ins in your classroom, Leslie," said Hunter.

"My poor classroom," Leslie replied. "Why, did you know that theater mask, the beautiful one on the bookshelf, was shattered into a million pieces? I got that mask on a student trip to London, for Pete's sake."

"You took students to London?" Emma asked.

"Yes, there are all sorts of companies doing student educational trips. This one was a theater-focused trip, and we saw eight Shakespeare plays in the actual Globe Theatre and the Royal Shakespeare Theatre in Stratford!"

"Fantastic," Emma breathed. "In the original place he invented them, no less."

"Well, not the *original* original Globe. That one burned down in

1613. Prop malfunction in *Henry the Eighth*. The students and I went to the new original Globe Theatre."

"That one was built in 1997, right?" Emma asked.

"Right, young Grasshoppah!" Leslie said, smiling. "They started with a performance of *Henry the Fifth*. You know, it's interesting to note—"

"Ladies! Ladies," Hunter interrupted as he walked back to the desk. "Much as I am enjoying this impromptu history-slash-English lesson, we were talking about your classroom."

"My poor maligned classroom."

"Your poor maligned classroom where your poor maligned friend was so grievously injured."

Emma touched her head. "Not grievously. My head hitting that desk was nothing compared to what happened to poor Melvin."

"Exactly!" Hunter said. "So despite the two break-ins to your room, Leslie, nothing was taken and we still don't know what they wanted. Right?"

"Right." Leslie looked at Emma. "Except we do know what they wanted."

Emma looked back at her friend. *Where is Leslie's personal hiding place? And what does she hide there?* "Of course we do! Why, we're the worst detectives ever. We should've figured this out after the first break-in."

"But how do we prove it?"

Emma thought. "We need to set a trap. We'll have to get the police involved."

Leslie's face mirrored Kayla Quinlan's. "Eeeewwwww. Are you sure? Carl the Clueless hasn't helped us so far at all."

"No, but Ah sure could've used him and his gun—or better yet, that gigantic sidekick of his with his gun—on the day I came back to retrieve Melvin's cigar box. Now that there's a real scandal connected to the school and we have witnesses, I think the police should be involved."

"Aw, snap. I suppose." Leslie huffed. "What kind of trap were you thinking?"

Hunter Wells stood in front of Leslie and Emma, watching their exchange as if he were viewing a tennis match. He put a hand on Emma's knee. "Stop. I'm getting dizzy. Excuse me if I'm being obtuse, but what, exactly, were you not able to figure out that is now becoming so clear?" He gazed beseechingly at Emma.

"Ah'm sorry, Hunter! That's right, you've only been out of the suspect pool for a little while, and I forgot to tell you this news."

"They were looking for my gradebook," Leslie said. "Whoever broke in wanted the backup gradebook I write grades in as well as the computer grading program."

A light broke in Hunter's eyes. "So if Charlie's getting grades changed in the school's program—"

"Leslie's book would have to match up. Anyone with a hard-copy gradebook would have to match up to the computer. So we just need to set a trap telling Charlie where the gradebooks are, then we…"

"Along with the police, apparently," Leslie said in her most put-upon voice, "can wait for him to appear and steal the hard copies. Which he's been trying to do since after he killed Melvin. Then we bust 'im. Hey, has anyone heard of another room being broken into? I can't be the only hard-copy dinosaur with players on the roll sheets."

Everybody shook their heads.

"Wow," Emma said. "We're really slow on the uptake. I think this will work though, don't you? Hey, and do you think Janice was involved too? Janice Tichner, the secretary? Remember that voice I heard out by the weight room? I'm sure it was talking to a woman. Maybe it was Janice."

"Yeah, that makes sense!" said Leslie. "Adam said he thought the aide would wait for a break to change the grades, but maybe she was in on it too."

"And Edward, you have to hear about Edward, who was a suspect like you." Emma said slyly, "Hm. School's out now, and after some grading at home, I'm sure I'll be famished."

Hunter grinned. "I have to hear about Edward the suspect. Can I pick you up for dinner at six?"

"Six sounds good," Emma breathed, and she lost herself in his melty gaze.

"Ahem," Leslie interrupted. "I'm so glad I have the perfect idea for a trap, as you two have rendered each other useless as detectives."

Emma shook herself free of Hunter's look. "Oh, good! What were you thinking?"

"First of all, Hunter, we'd have to let Martha Bonaventure in on the grade-changing scandal."

Hunter chuckled. "Oh yeah, Martha. Martha keeps herself way removed from anything having to do with sports or Lounge Lizards, especially Charlie Foreman."

"I think we can trust she's not involved," Leslie said. "But just in case, I'm not going to tell her this goes with our murder investigation. Just the grade-changing scandal." She looked satisfied.

"Oh, sure," said Emma. "If she's involved, then she obviously won't show up for our trap, and we can try something else."

"So, Emma, you go home and take care of your teaching duties. I'll find Martha, and we'll organize a special early edition of the newspaper. If we can do it tonight and distribute it tomorrow, then it will go to all the students and staff."

Emma said, "If everyone with hard-copy gradebooks has to turn them in at the end of the school day on Friday, then we could have the police at school on Friday night, and Charlie, or Janice, or Janice and Charlie, will have to try to come retrieve them."

"Excuse me," said Leslie. "*We* and the police. I'm sure you meant to say *we* and the police can be at the school on Friday night. But otherwise, I think that's perfect. All the teachers know that Nathan works all weekend. The teachers can turn them in directly to him on Friday, and he can lock them up until he comes back for them. They'll assume Nathan's going to check them on Saturday morning, so they'll have to try and steal them Friday night."

"Nathan the principal?" Emma asked. "He works on... weekends? I thought he didn't work at all."

Leslie shook her head. "That's what he wants students to think. He believes they won't relate to him if it looks like he takes his job too seriously, so he does the bare minimum all week and works his butt off when they're not here. It's actually impressive how much he can get done in two days. So the teachers will know better than to think he won't check their books, and they'll make sure to get them in on time. If the murderer is one of the secretaries, they won't try to open the lock box during the day, and if it's Charlie, he'll have to break into the lock box after hours. It's the perfect sting! I can't wait!"

"I don't know," Emma replied, setting aside her principal's guerrilla-like work ethic. She could learn to deal with his oddities when this was all over. "Despite your reliance on personal strength and those dodgeball-throwing biceps, I think we maybe should leave it to those big guys with guns I've wanted all along."

Hunter flexed his arms. "Hey. I'm a big guy with guns."

Emma giggled. "Gee, Popeye, thanks for the help, but I would feel more comfortable if we included the ones with bullets. Call me crazy, but this loon has already killed someone and maybe would have killed me if it weren't for Sir Toby."

He harrumphed. "Sir Toby? I'm pretty sure it was my timely interference that scared that ol' killer away."

"Sure," she said. They shared a goofy look. She had to restrain herself from smoothing the black hair curling above his brow.

Leslie rolled her eyes. "Oh, jeez, can we please get on to the business at hand? This lovey-dovey pseudo-PDA nonsense is going to make me puke."

Emma thought for a minute. "All right. We and the police. And our Terminators."

"All right, all joking aside," Hunter said, "you've already been in two dangerous situations, and this one is even more dangerous. Charlie will be getting desperate. Maybe we should just let the police take care of it."

Leslie jumped out of Hunter's chair. "Come on, Hunter! You could be there too, to protect us. I know you'd love to see this culmination of your investigation as it happens. 'Stand not upon the order of your going, but go at once.' *Macbeth*."

The two women moved around the desk. The more Emma thought about it, the more she wanted to be a part of it. *For Melvin.*

"Please, Hunter," Emma begged. "You can use your special investigator status to get us in good with Detective Niome."

Hunter crossed his arms and stepped back, eyeing the women suspiciously. "I'm pretty sure you two aren't looking for protection. Looking for partners in crime, maybe. Adrenaline rush, for sure. But you're right, I'd like to see this come to a solution. Leslie, go set up the newspaper edition, and I'll call the detective. No, I'll go see him actually. He might be mad about being left out of the CHSSA loop. Leslie, will you lock my room? I know you have keys for all of our classrooms." He winked and headed for the door. "Emma, see you tonight."

He left his room ahead of the two. Emma, of course, watched him go.

*This news, which is called true, is so like a tale
that the verity of it is in strong suspicion.*

—*The Winter's Tale V.2.27–9*

CHAPTER 26

Thursday, September 3

GPA GRENADE!!
Eligibility Scandal Explodes—Staff Members to Turn in Hard-Copy Gradebooks

FIRST THING THURSDAY MORNING, THE students and teachers were asked—loudly, over the PA—to show their pride in TJ High and share the paper with anyone they could.

Emma and Leslie met for lunch, sharing Mrs. Albert's dish of salmon over mixed greens. After the newspaper had gone out during first period, Emma gave her American Lit class some time to read it. Then she'd turned it into a literary history lesson.

"Really, the first newspaper was invented in 59 BC," Emma told Leslie, "but since this was American Literature, we talked about the first newspaper in the American colonies, circa 1690. Then they got to discuss which issues they think are most important, and they're bringin' their own headlines to class tomorrow." She smiled and chomped up lettuce like a hungry bunny.

"But that paper only had one issue, right?" Leslie asked, spooning up salmon. "Censorship and control issues have been around since people started communicating, it seems." She winked at Emma. "You have fantastically creative ideas, Ms. Lovett. I predict you will change the lives of many."

Emma blushed. "Ah sure hope Ah can." She picked up her edition of the school news. "Provided we can find Melvin's killer and bring him to justice without getting ourselves killed in the process."

"Hunter will get Carl Niome and his barrel-chested sidekick in the picture. Hunter will be in the picture. Plus, come on, *we* will be in the picture. Amazonians. Hear us roar."

Emma sighed. "Ah hope you're right."

Leslie took a swig of her iced tea. "Oh, stop worrying, silly goose." She struck a pose as though she was about to quote something. She was. "Worrying is like a rocking chair. It gives you something to do, but it doesn't take you anywhere."

"Worrying is like a... that doesn't sound like a Shakespeare quote."

"It's not. It's a Leslie quote. Not quite as poetic maybe, but it gets the point across, dontcha think? We're strong and able. And that new hunk of yours, the way he looks at you tells me he would do anything to protect his delicate Southern flower. How was dinner last night, by the way? Get any dessert?" She made smoochy noises at Emma.

"Yes, sure," Emma scoffed. "Now you're all for Hunter. Before, it was"—she adopted a nasally voice—"'No PDA! He's a suspect. He's a suspect!'" She grinned. "Dinner was fantastic. As for dessert, that's for me to know and me to know."

"Excuse me, lady! I don't sound that way. I—"

The two women were interrupted when Abigail Patterson tottered in. "Hello, dears."

They both stopped eating, afraid that chewing would interfere with their ability to hear her.

"Have you heard from Janice?" she asked.

"Janice Tichner?" asked Leslie.

Emma looked at her questioningly. *Maybe Janice took one look at today's edition and fled the scene.* "No, we haven't. Personally, I've never talked to her outside the office."

Abigail wrung her hands. "She never leaves. It seems like she lives there. Sometimes I think she does. Since her divorce, she's been very lonely. She keeps to herself though. I barely know anything about her, and she's been here over a year. But she hasn't been in since Monday."

"Is she sick?" Leslie asked.

Abigail looked around them as if she was afraid of being overheard. "Well, she *said* she's sick, but I don't believe it. She sent me an email on

Sunday night saying that she'd eaten some bad salmon and would be out for a couple of days due to food poisoning."

Emma nodded. "Why don't you believe that?"

"She's allergic to fish," Abigail said. "I made seafood stew once last year and offered to bring her some. She freaked out like I was trying to kill her."

"Have you called her house?" said Emma.

"Oh, yes, dear. I've called all week. And the vice principal called as well. He's very annoyed—she was supposed to be collating a demographics list of all student suspensions." She shrugged. "I don't understand that. Isn't the point to teach them? Who really cares about... well, never mind. Janice isn't here, and that has *never* happened. I'm very concerned."

Emma thought for a minute. "Have you called the hospital? Maybe she got so sick she had to be admitted?"

"Oh, of course, dear," whispered Abigail. "I'm not a complete helpless ninny. I've called the hospital and the police. No one has heard from her."

"Maybe a family member would know something?" asked Leslie.

Abigail shook her head. "No, she doesn't have any family. She said once, 'Even if my parents weren't dead, I've been dead to them for a long time.'" She tsked. "So sad. I asked in the teachers' lounge, and no one knows anything. Then I asked Edward in the library and thought I'd peek in here to see if you had any ideas. She's been gone for more than forty-eight hours, but when I called the police again, they said that they had no reason to believe anything was wrong. They said she had emailed me saying she wouldn't be in for a few days and she probably meant to say she'd had an allergic reaction rather than food poisoning. I don't know—it's just not normal for her."

"Well, Abigail," said Emma, "we have a planning period right now. We'd be glad to go to her house and check on her. Maybe she's sick and not answering her phone."

"'Sick now? Droop now? This sickness doth infect the very lifeblood of our enterprise.'" Leslie quipped. "*Henry the Fourth Part One*. Of course, something tells me ol' Henry's enterprise had nothing to do with demographic collation."

"Oh, girls, that would be wonderful!" Abigail's voice rose on the last syllable to an almost eavesdroppable level. "Are you sure? I wouldn't want to interfere with your lesson planning."

As if our murder investigation hasn't already accomplished that. "We're happy to go check on Janice for you. We'll just get her address on the way out."

"Oh, thank you. Please call me if you find anything, or if there's anything I can do to help her if she needs it." She bustled out, obviously feeling better.

Emma and Leslie cleared their plates and stacked them to be dropped off in the kitchen. They were on their way out when they were accosted by Edward Dixon.

"Hello, ladies! It's so wonderful to have the pleasure of your company on this fine Thursday afternoon."

A student walked toward the beeper gates. Edward stopped him, reached into the pocket of the kid's backpack, pulled out a book, thumped the kid on the head with it, and sent him on his way.

Leslie and Emma looked on in astonishment.

"Edward!" said Leslie. "That kid just tried to steal a book, and you didn't even almost pop an artery. What's the deal with that?"

Edward waved toward the gate. "Oh, you know, ladies, since the death of my friend Melvin, I've had somewhat of a... a revelation, you could say. Life is too short to almost pop *anything* over some library books. Don't you agree?"

Emma said, "Oh, Edward, we agree very much. We're so glad to hear you're feeling less stressed."

"Thank you, Emma. So any news on our murder investigation?" He looked around. "Sorry," he whispered, then he spoke in a goofy stage whisper that was louder than his original voice. "Any news on our murder investigation? Where are you going now?"

"Oh, it's not related," said Leslie. "We're going to collect a demographic collator." She ignored his perplexed look as she and Emma trotted through the gates.

Janice Tichner lived in a cheerless apartment house about three miles south of the school. The building was sad brown brick, and no plants grew on the few grass medians that surrounded carports and parking lots. Many of the cars in the lot looked like Emma's old green Honda, only dirtier. And dentier. *I don't think that's a word. I think I'll use my English teacher status to make up my own words.*

"There are a lot of cars here on a work day."

"Yeah, well," Leslie said, "I've observed that sometimes apartment houses that are a little lower on the rent scale are sometimes a little lower on the employment scale. Or many of the tenants work nights. Waiting or bartending or something that keeps you up until all hours."

"Well, Ah think it's sad that someone who works full time in a school can't afford to live in a better place."

They walked toward the lobby of the sad brown building.

"Have you *noticed* your pay stub?" said Leslie. "If it weren't for Tim the bastard's divorce proceeds, I'd be living in one of these buildings. I don't know how you found the little house you're in."

Emma smiled. "Delilah Thornberry. She saw me walking around the very day the previous owner put up a For Sale by Owner sign. She decided on the spot that I looked like someone she should have as a neighbor, and she even helped me barter my way into an affordable price."

Leslie smiled with a merry twinkle in her eye. "Delilah Thornberry, eh? That's very interesting..."

"Why is it so interesting? You know her. She makes me cobbler."

"Let's see: J. Tichner. Apartment 231." Leslie rolled right over Emma's question and headed up the stairs to the second floor.

"No, really, why is that interesting? I haven't let her bake me brownies, I promise." Emma's eyebrows rose, but her voice went quiet. "Hey, Janice is decently tall. Maybe she killed Melvin."

They arrived at the door of 231 just as Leslie said, "Never you mind. I—" She stopped and knocked on the door. No answer. "Janice? Janice Tichner? Halloo?"

Emma and Leslie looked at each other.

"Well, try the door," said Emma.

The doorknob turned easily. Leslie knocked cautiously and entered, calling, "Janice? Janice, are you all right?"

The door opened wider at her touch. They were both hit by a blast of cold air—the air conditioner was going at full speed apparently, even though it was only in the seventies outside.

"Janice?" She looked back at Emma.

Emma whispered, "Do you think we should go in? We don't have our Terminators."

Leslie shrugged and whispered, "Two of us, one of her." She pushed the door all the way open.

"Janice?" called Emma. "Abigail's very worried about you. Are you sick?"

No answer.

They walked in, calling Janice's name. The door opened into a postage stamp–sized kitchen with an archway that looked directly into the living room. Emma took another step into the kitchen, which could only be described as spartan. A small ivory refrigerator squatted next to a bare counter and a sink. A hot plate and a dish rack rested on top of the fridge, and there was a two-person wooden table with no tablecloth and no chairs. On the table was Janice's laptop, open to her email program.

Looks like Melvin McManus's house in terms of isolation. Seems as though we've come into contact with a parade of lonely people, and not a colorful, happy parade, like the one Macy's has with giant floating Tweety Birds. "There isn't anything in here. Not even dirty dishes."

Leslie went into the living room, inspecting the navy couch and flipping through the magazine rack across from a nineteen-inch television. "Hm. *Entertainment Weekly. US* magazine. *Cosmopolitan.* Nothing that a single woman wouldn't have in her magazine rack… wait. There are two magazines here about computers and electronics."

"So?" Emma came into the room. "Maybe she was interested in computers. She does work with one all day."

"Look here." Leslie pulled a piece of paper from a magazine called *Self Help*. "It's a stray piece of paper in the midst of this paperless, joyless environment." She opened the note. "Look, it's typed." She handed the note to Emma.

Janice: Dont do this. Yur better then this. Remember, sooner or later everyone sits down to a banquet of consequences. Robert Louis Stevenson. –M–

Emma gasped. "This note is from Melvin. Remember, that quote was in his little notebook!"

Leslie stared at the lettering. "A banquet of consequences. Consequences for taking part in the grade changing? You said the voice was talking to a woman, right? That woman's voice must have been Janice." Leslie stared at the note. "So there must've been two people in the office when Melvin was killed. Janice changing the grades…"

"And Charlie hit Melvin over the head when he showed up and tried to stop her," Emma said.

"I'll bet Janice is gone, skedaddled," Leslie said. "If Janice is on the run, going through with our trap might be the only way. We've got to catch the coach who's responsible for this mess. I think we should go back to school and do teacher things until Friday night."

Emma sniffed the air. "Okay, let's go. But don't you think it smells weird in here? Not like cold air conditioning, but like something spoiled. Like spoiled food."

Leslie pulled up the couch cushions. "No food in here." She gestured to the closed door opposite the couch. "Maybe she eats in bed, and this clean, bare front of the apartment is a façade for all the takeout food she eats in bed late at night."

"Why didn't you check the bedroom when you came in here?" asked Emma.

Leslie attempted indignation. "I was going to, but there was an article in *Cosmo* about older women and younger men, so I just… never mind. I was going to." She walked over to the door and knocked. "Janice? Are you awake?"

She pushed the door open, and the spoiled smell fluttered through the air. It landed in Emma's nose at the same time Leslie looked through the doorway, then she twisted around with both hands over her mouth.

"Oh God," Leslie whimpered through the hands. "Oh my God." Then she threw up.

CHAPTER 27

ESLIE'S EYES GLAZED OVER, AND she collapsed in the doorway, her body barely missing her pile of vomit.

Emma rushed to her side. "Leslie, what is it? What's..."

Then she glanced over Leslie's head into the room beyond. She somehow registered the same spartan environment that pervaded the rest of the house before her scan landed on the bed. Janice Tichner was sprawled across the plain green bedcover, arms splayed, legs hanging off the edges. One foot touched the floor, and her face was turned toward the side wall, so Emma couldn't see her expression.

What she could see was the small hole underneath Janice's right ear and the blood that turned the right half of the green bedspread black.

She couldn't take her eyes off of Janice. *I thought a gunshot wound would have a bigger hole. I thought we knew more than we did. I guess I figured this whole thing would be exciting and simple. Wrapped up by the end of the episode. I guess not.* She glanced at Leslie and found she was patting her friend's head.

"Is this how you felt when you first found Melvin?" Leslie asked. "I mean, I know it smelled bad, and I know he looked bad when I got there, but..." She looked back into the room and turned away again. "I don't know, it's just... I don't know. I don't know. I don't know." She buried her face in her hands. "I can't believe this is happening. Two dead people? Why did we start this stupid investigation? I didn't sign up for this. I don't know, I don't..."

Emma shushed her friend. "Shhhhh. We'll call the police right now."

"But that's *two* murders we've discovered. They're going to think we did it. We can't, we have to get out of here." She twisted her legs out from under her and tried to stand, but she plopped back down.

"We have to escape. 'This blow could be the end of it. If only we could escape the consequences of our actions hereon.' *Macbeth*. 'Who chants a doleful hymn to his own death?' *King John*." She took a deep breath. "'By some vile forfeit of untimely death, Death lies upon her like an untimely frost.' *Romeo and Juliet*. 'Life is a tale told by an idiot, full of sound and fury, signifying'"—her head drooped low—"'nothing.' That's *Macbeth* again. And then there's *Hamlet*. 'Murder most foul, as in the best this is. But murder most foul, strange and unnatural.' Oh, Hamlet *knows* foul, and this is it. This is foul. Foul to the highest power."

Emma placed her hands on Leslie's shoulders and shook them. "Stop! Stop it right now! You can't solve this with a Shakespeare quote! We have to call the police now."

Leslie kept mumbling.

"Stop it! Settle yerself down. Pull out the perfect, unstoppable Leslie. Do it or Ah'll, Ah'll, Ah'll slap you!" She shook her friend again. "Ah can't do this without you. Without the real you."

Leslie's glazed eyes cleared. She looked upward. "Did you just say 'I'll slap you'?"

Emma pulled Leslie to her feet, ignoring her question. "I would say we should check Janice and make sure she's not still breathing, but I think the smell answers the question."

She pulled Leslie toward the wall phone in the kitchen. Leslie was silent while Emma called the police.

When Carl Niome, Detective not-so-Extraordinaire, arrived with the giant in the blue uniform—*isn't his name Ted?*—the first thing Carl did was turn a boiling glare on the two women. Emma thought maybe he should first examine the crime scene before scolding them or perhaps accusing them of murder, but she prepared for the onslaught anyway.

Leslie stood at Emma's side, this time without the in-your-face confidence. She remained silent.

"Well, well, well. How is it, exactly, that we haven't had a murder in this town since 1989, and now we have two in two weeks? And you're discovering bodies at both crime scenes? How is that happening, hmm? Hmm?" He looked as if he was restraining himself from wagging his finger in front of their faces or tsking.

"Ah don't know, detective, Ah'm sure." *I don't know if the Southern violet thing will get us out of anything, but it's worth a try.* "Abigail Patterson? The school secretary? Well, she told us that Janice was out sick, and Janice wasn't answering her phone, so Abigail asked us to please go to Janice's house and check up on her."

"Did Ms. Patterson call the police when she couldn't reach Janice? Check the hospitals? Why wouldn't she think Janice was staying with family?"

"No offense, Officer Niome—"

"Detective."

"Detective Niome, but Ms. Patterson isn't a complete ninny." Emma tried a girlish giggle, so as not to make the detective feel like a complete ninny. *Making him aware of his incompetence will definitely not help us get out of this.* "She did all o' that, and Janice doesn't have any family that we know of."

The detective put his hands on his hips, struck a pose, and said, "Well, she might not have family, but she sure has enemies."

Emma waited for the *bom-bom Bommmm* that should follow a statement such as that, and she tried hard to stifle a smile. "I'm sure she has an enemy, Detective, but Leslie and I aren't her enemies. Are we, Les?"

Leslie, who still stared vacantly, came briefly out of her trance. "Huh? No, no, we're not her enemies. We were just looking for her. We only touched the phone and the doors when we opened them."

"Yes," Emma said, nodding. "Check for our fingerprints. You won't find them anywhere..." She suddenly remembered the magazines. Surreptitiously, she felt in her skirt pocket. The note from Melvin was there. "Else. Oh, except for some of the magazines."

The detective raised an eyebrow. "You were looking at magazines? In the home of a murder victim, which by the way, *smells* like there's a murder victim in it?"

"Or some spoiled steaks," Ted said, who until that moment had been, as much as was possible for a huge person, invisible. He was just coming out of Janice's bedroom. "Looks like a gunshot wound."

Emma put her hands on her hips, although she didn't wait for sound effects before she spoke. "It didn't smell like that when we first got here.

The air conditioning was all the way up, and the bedroom door was closed. Since she was supposed to be so sick and she didn't answer when we called for her, we looked for clues as to where she might be."

He sniggered. "You two were looking for *clues*? What, you think you're going to solve this murder in the ten minutes you've been here? Oh, ladies, ladies. Let me tell you something about our line of work. It's hard. Not any ol' Sally and Jane can do our work."

"Yeah!" said Ted.

"We have training," said the detective. "*Mucho* training."

"Yeah!" Ted said.

"Training in sentencing or speaking or… or spelling don't qualify— *doesn't* qualify you to solve murders."

"For sure!" said Ted.

"Now," Detective Niome said, "I did speak to Hunter Wells, a very important CHSSA special investigator, and he has some evidence of a sports scandal. It looks like you *maybe* had something to do with finding that evidence."

Emma smashed her lips into a thin line and tried not to smile. *This isn't funny, anyway. There's a dead person not fifteen feet from us, and if we can't find a way to grow even a combined brain in these two…* "Officers. Detectives. We just got lucky talking to a student, and we'd like to follow through on finding the grade changer. Ah wouldn't dream of tryin' to do your job for you. We were just looking for Janice. We were worried."

The detective stroked an invisible beard. "Well, you found her, didn't you? My forensics team will be looking for your fingerprints as they gather information. In someplace other than those places you've said. Maybe we'll find some on the gun."

That galvanized Leslie back into speech. "You found the gun?"

The two men looked at each other. Big Ted shook his head.

"No," said Detective Carl. "But that's just because we haven't looked for it yet!"

"Yeah," said Ted. "We were just on our way to do that."

Detective Niome shook himself. "Yes, our forensics team will start looking for it immediately. You two can go for now. Don't go far."

Leslie, who seemed to be recovering, looked at Emma.

Emma said, "How about back to school?"

"Yeah!" said Leslie, and the two really couldn't hide their grins.

"This isn't funny!" snapped the chief detective, and he struck the pose again. "This is murder! Get out and let us solve it. But don't go back to the school—you don't want to create pandemonium. Call in a substitute or call Nathan Farrar or whatever you have to do, and go have breakfast like you did the last time."

Pretending it wasn't one o'clock in the afternoon, Leslie and Emma promised to do that and to not create pandemonium at Durango Bagels.

"So are you feeling all right now?" asked Emma. They sat at a back table in the bagel shop, drinking tea since they'd already had lunch and weren't in the mood to eat anyway. "You had me worried there for a while."

Leslie dipped her tea bag in and out of the mug. "Yeah, I'm sorry. I don't know what came over me. It was like I've been treating this whole investigation like some grand adventure, like it's not even real, ya know? Even when I found you at the scene of Melvin's death, it seemed like Melvin wasn't a *real* dead body but something out of a television crime show. And then when I saw Janice…"

Emma nodded. "I know, I know. I guess there's something about being first on the scene."

"Well, let's not get any more practice on that, okay? We don't need to be graded on our ability to be first on the murder scene. And judging by our ability so far to solve murders, we don't need to be graded on that either."

"Agreed. We pretty much stink at both."

"I'm very good at teaching," Leslie said, "and I love it so much. You're already very good at teaching, and looking to get better and better as you go along. Let's go home and rest tonight, so we can do what we do best tomorrow."

"But it wouldn't hurt us to expose a grade-changing murderer tomorrow night, would it?" Emma grinned. "Then we'll have time to lesson plan for the rest of the weekend."

"And maybe plan some time with Mr. Wells?" Leslie said.

"Agreed. Master teaching with a little side hobby of dating."

Open, locks, whoever knocks.

—Macbeth IV i.146

CHAPTER 28

Friday, September 4

AFTER A HORRIBLE NIGHTMARE STARRING that green-turned-black-with-blood bedspread, Emma came to school feeling disoriented. She decided to turn first period into a silent reading session just so she could get her thoughts straightened out and be ready to face the rest of the day. She had a few students give previews of their news headlines though, and that helped her outlook. She looked forward to Monday's presentation. *Hopefully we'll have this whole grade-changing craziness figured out by then too.*

Her second-period Sophomore Lit class went okay, but Emma discovered that having them read the scenes and pose questions for later discussion worked better. There were so many nerves involved in reading Shakespeare that it was better to let them get through it then ponder it after.

In her third-period class, Tammy Kramer and Nick Luchyky were at the head of the classroom, reading the balcony scene from *Romeo and Juliet*. Emma had shown them the scene on the projector, since it was easier to decipher when it was performed, then they'd talked about whether or not someone could really be in love at such a young age. Most of them felt a person could, like, totally be in love at any age, but maybe not so intensely.

"'Sweet, so would I,'" Tammy said, blushing furiously.

Two sophomore boys snickered at the endearment. A stern gaze from Emma stifled them, and she nodded for Tammy to continue.

"'Yet I should kill thee with much cher-cherishing.' Cherishing?" She looked, questioning, at Emma.

"That's right, Tammy, cherishing," Emma confirmed. "If you cherish something, you love it. To kill Romeo with cherishing, she must love him so, *so* much. That's a lotta cherishing!" She welcomed the giggles. "Continue, Tammy. These last lines of yours are some of the best known in all of Shakespeare's plays."

"'Good night, good night! Parting is such sweet sorrow that I should say good night til it be morrow.'" Tammy let her paper rest in front of her, looking grateful to be finished.

"And how do you answer her, Romeo?" Emma asked. "She just told you she loves you to death." As she nodded for Nick to finish his line, her comment made her pause. *How can you love someone to death?* She thought of Marlena. *Maybe when we figure out her story, we'll know.*

Emma had already figured out Nick was one of those kids who never blushed or got embarrassed. He barreled into situations with bluster and bravado she couldn't imagine were real but were so fun to watch.

"'Sleep dwell in thine eyes, peace in thy breast!'" he shouted and held a warning hand to his friends to forestall their reaction at his use of the word "breast." "'Would I were sleep, and peace,'" he drawled, obviously anything but sleepy and peaceful, "'so sweet to rest! Hence will I to my ghostly friar's close cell, his help to crave and my dear hap to tell.'" With that, he bowed deeply to the class's applause. "Hey, Ms. Lovett, what's the haps?"

Emma clapped enthusiastically with the rest of the class. "Ah think the 'haps' are that we have Shakespearean stars in the making, you two! Very well done. Class, I'd like you to think about that when we have our discussions at the conclusion of all these readings. You know that Romeo and Juliet do die at the end. So can people love each other to death? Do you think their age and immaturity caused their deaths, or something else? Think about it." *And I'll think about it too.*

"Ms. Lovett, can Arnold and I go next?" Julia Ramsay raised her hand. "We're doing the scene with Portia and Bassanio from *Merchant of Venice*. Where Bassanio is trying to pick the right casket to win Portia's heart?"

"Yes, fantastic scene!" Emma said. "Lay it on me."

Julia Ramsay and Arnold Ortiz were unlikely partners for the scene reading, but they had chosen to do the scene together. As they walked to the front of the room, Emma was struck by their differences. She was tall, thin, and demanding, sweeping into rooms and overly confident. He was beefy and benevolent, trundling from here to there and sweeping the classroom with kindly eyes. He had black hair with a streak of white that made him look vaguely like a skunk—Emma assumed he thought that made him look cool. They began the scene, and it was obvious that they'd practiced, probably due to a combination of her exacting nature and his desire to please.

The scene was a long one, with Portia leading a song to persuade Bassanio to choose the right casket. To Emma's astonishment, Julia actually sang the song. There were no titters or giggles from the class, as Julia inspired their respect. Or maybe their fear?

Bassanio, a.k.a. Arnold, delivered a line that stopped Emma in her tracks. "'So may the onward shows be least themselves. The world is still deceived with ornament: In law, what plea so tainted and corrupt, but being seasoned with a gracious voice obscures the show of evil? In r—'"

"Stop, stop there for a second, Arnold," Emma said. "What do you think that means?"

Arnold thought. "Evil is bad, gracious is good. That's all I know."

Julia raised her hand. "He's talking about the law and how a lawyer fools everyone with smooth talk. But I think he's trying to choose the right casket, and the fancy schmancy one isn't going to be the right one, even though it looks so beautiful."

"Yeah, yeah!" Arnold said. "Just because it looks good doesn't mean it's the winner. The winner is, like, a plain lead box, isn't it?"

"And just because something looks a certain way doesn't mean that's the way it is, right, Ms. Lovett?" Julia peered at Emma, entreating her agreement.

"You're so right, Julia," Emma said. "What something looks like and what it really is can be completely different." She lost herself in an invisible point on the white board. *Shakespeare was such an expert on human behavior, I can hardly get over it. But I already knew that. Why do I keep locking in on these two ideas?* "Continue, Arnold."

But Emma kept staring at the invisible spot on the board throughout the rest of his speech, grateful she knew the play well enough to pose the right questions to the class when it was finished.

The thoughts that kept fusing in her brain twirled and combined with her worries about their evening crime-busting plans, and it was a real wonder she got to the end of the scene. Unable to concentrate on Shakespeare anymore, she tabled the remaining scenes for Monday and told her sophomores to read silently for the last half hour.

She sat at her desk, twirling the bust of Shakespeare by the top of his head. The class looked up only when she failed to catch her makeshift top and it landed on its side with a thump. *I really can't believe Charlie would kill two people over grades. And Melvin was so sweet, so great. Although it sounds like he made a bad choice as far as this grade thing goes. I wish I knew more about what would cause him to make that kind of choice. Must be the alcohol. Mixed with his lost love for Marlena?*

Melvin's cigar box was in her corner desk drawer, so she took it out and stared at it, trying some deep, calming breaths. She turned it over and shook it, which gleaned a few more stares from her students. She opened the box, took out the letters, and reread them. That didn't calm her—it just made her sad. She took out the little notebook and reread the quotes. One of them by Thoreau looked familiar: "'The question is not what you look at, but what you see.' Page 285."

Where did I hear that before? Oh, yes, Melvin said a version of that in Leslie's room when he was lookin' at that pretty bookmark, but I swear I've heard the exact Thoreau quote. Hmm.

She turned the page. The quote about a banquet of consequences was on that page, and Emma had to concentrate again on her calming breaths. But there was one strange thing. This quote looked like all the others, listed with a page number, but the number was circled several times. Page 723.

Then she opened the box again and took out the little Master key. *Maybe...*

Emma drew in a sharp breath. *I have an idea, maybe a crazy idea, but...* "Ahem. Class, keep reading for five minutes while I run to the ladies' room. You're doing great! Best students ever!"

She practically ran out the door. She skipped the hallway where her own classroom was; she knew those lockers went from the one hundreds to three-something. Her skirt whooshed as she turned the corner into what was commonly known as the senior hallway, where seventeen- and eighteen-year-olds too full of their own teenagerness packed in clusters, making it impossible to navigate the hall on any normal day. But all seniors were in class right now—or maybe not—so the hallway was empty. She ran down the left side—nope, all 400s.

She trotted across the commons, past the gymnasium doors, and into the freshman hall, tearing down one side then up the other, looking like an uncorked jog-walker. At the end of the freshman hallway, she saw it—number 723. It stood tall and proud on the end of the row, its door unscratched and shining a brilliant royal blue from a summer paint job.

And from its hasp hung a gleaming brass Master padlock.

Skipping back to class, Emma plopped back into her chair and tried not to tap her fingers on the desk for the whole remaining five minutes. The bell launched her out of the room, cigar box in hand, before the students even stood, and she flew through the emerging crowds like a formless spirit.

She flung open Leslie's door and stood there, panting.

Leslie was replacing her hard-copy gradebook in the secret desk drawer. "What's up? You look like a marathon runner. Don't puke in my classroom, 'kay? I just got it all cleaned up after you bled on it the other day."

Emma smiled and held up the padlock key. "Did you, oh, I don't know, want to see what this opens?"

Leslie's jaw dropped. "Are you kidding?"

"No, Ah found it. Locker 723, freshman hallway."

"How do you know that's it? Did you open it? What's in it? Holy crap!"

"I'm pretty sure this is it because this is the number circled in the quote list in his notebook, and also because I sneaked out to check—there's a padlock on the locker," Emma explained. "No, I don't know what's in it because I wanted you to be there when I opened it, partner." She curtseyed. "And I agree—holy crap!" She came in and closed the door. "If we wait a little while, I know most of the kids will clear out. We should be able to open it alone."

Leslie took the key and held it up to the light, then she danced around the room—not Fred-and-Ginger–type dancing, more like Riverdance.

"We found the ke-ey," she sang. "And then we found the lock-er. We are ter-rif-ic. Ooh ooh oohooh-ooh. We deserve a me-dal."

Emma stopped her. "Maybe we should wait and see what's in it first."

"Oh, come on. It has to be something cool, even if it doesn't tell us who killed Melvin. It's like a treasure hunt. Hey, maybe it's a treasure! How amazing would that be?"

"Oh yes, that's just what you need, Miss I-cleaned-out-my-ex-husband-and-now-I'm-independently-wealthy."

Leslie rolled her eyes. "Oh, I'd give it to you of course. It's the thrill of the chase that I enjoy."

Emma grinned. "Did you give that pertinent information to your drooling puppy boy toy?"

They waited until enough time had passed and the school was, for the most part, at lunch. They sneaked out of the room—although no sneaking was really necessary; it was the middle of the day, and they did work there, after all. Sneaking just felt more exhilarating. They tiptoed through the hallway, past the gym, and into the freshman hall.

Leslie made a beeline straight for the dazzling brass lock. "Ooohhh. Here it is." She wrapped her hand around it. "You ready?"

Emma nodded, inhaled, and inserted the key. It turned easily, and the latch dropped away. Leslie removed the lock, and they both held their breath as she pulled up the handle.

The inside of the locker was a shrine to the circus. No pun intended.

CHAPTER 29

THE THREE WALLS OF THE locker and the inside of its door were swathed in color. Vibrant flyers covered the back walls, with animals prancing and people contorting and clowns making faces that had big painted-on frowns but were designed to make children laugh. Circus flyers, of course. ***Ripple & Rand's Glorious Traveling Fun Show!*** screamed the headings. ***Come one, come all to Riveting Ripple & Rand's!***

Isn't that "come one, come all" thing trademarked or something?

The flyers were rigid and stiff with age, some yellowing at the corners but still a riot of color and appeal. Elephants with velvet capes lumbered across the bottom of some that were dated 1968, and some with a 1972 show boasted a family of trapeze artists in shiny gold Spandex leotards tumbling into a lion's giant mouth. Each flyer had a different clown face bordering the corner.

The locker door had the same characters, only as photos rather than flyers. There were three or four of clowns piling in to little bitty cars, and a few close-ups of the tamer inserting his head in the lion's mouth. Most of the photos were of the trapeze artists, though, a group clad in gold or silver or ruby outfits, flying through the air as though they had wings. One young woman was featured in many of the photos, her brilliant red hair in contrast with whatever bejeweled outfit she was wearing. The camera had picked up a sheen of sweat on her face; she looked breathless and happy.

Leslie ripped one of the photos from the door. "Marlena! This has to be her."

"Of course!" said Emma. "Remember her letter—it talked about whirling lights and twirling music. Reminders of the circus! And look!"

She pointed at the sequined bookmark Leslie had given him last week. "Reminders of his old life and his old love. I wonder what Melvin did there?"

"Well," surmised Leslie, "he was way too big to be shot out of a cannon. Lion tamer?"

There was one full-body shot of the lion tamer, and while he was big enough to be Melvin, he looked about forty years old, which would put Melvin in his late seventies upon his death. Emma figured him for fifty-five, sixty-something at the oldest.

"No, look at this." Emma pulled off another picture. "This clown."

One of the funnymen piling into the car was wearing a jumpsuit covered with geometric shapes in every color of the rainbow.

"He's definitely taller than the others. It could be Melvin." She peered at the picture, but the clown makeup and the angle made it impossible to tell.

"So this is the torrid affair—lovable circus clown and lovely air gymnast," said Leslie. "It's total movie-of-the-week material. But we're back to the original question—who is she? And would she have a reason to kill him forty years later?"

"Hmm..." Emma mused. "Maybe her husband is the president of PETA, and if he found out she was a part of the circus..."

"Maybe she's a senator and is afraid those questionable pictures of her and her one-night stand with the Unbelievable Stretching Man will surface." Leslie contorted her arms behind her head and made a lewd face.

Emma felt her face dawn like the breaking day. "Maybe she's a teacher, and she wants to put those circus rumors to rest once and for all."

Leslie's eyebrows shot up. "You think...?"

"Sure, Martha... Marlena. And she does have red hair. He was searching for his lost love to write her the letter he couldn't write back then. I mean, it makes sense he'd have found her here and was simply waiting for the right time."

"*And* he only worked after school, which means he could have hidden himself very effectively until he was ready." Leslie grabbed one of the flyers from the inside of the locker. "Of course! I'm so dumb!

Look—the Flying Bonnies. Martha Bonaventure—Marlena Bonnie. It's got to be. She's the right age too, probably late fifties or early sixties."

Emma sighed. "How sad. They're both living this solitary life—him drinking himself dizzy—and all because he was too proud to approach her or pick up a phone or have someone write a letter for him."

"Maybe he didn't have anyone," replied Leslie. "I remember Edward saying something about him leaving home really early. And Adam Butler said the same thing—that they had connected because of some things they had in common."

"Well, for Pete's sake," said Emma. "He could have had *Edward* write the silly old thing, once they got to be friends. Or Adam, for that matter. It's just such a waste. People who love each other should be together." Her mind flashed to Hunter, but she squelched it. *Stop it. You don't love him. You've only been on two dates.*

"So are we thinking that Martha is Marlena, and maybe she found out that Melvin was her old boyfriend, and she killed him because he never answered her letters?"

"No, I wasn't thinking that actually," Emma said. "I was just so excited to find out where the key fit. No, I don't think Martha killed Melvin. Why would she have done that in the main office? Or what, she killed him in her room and dragged his body to the main office? That's ridiculous. Plus we'd be able to see that. Ah'd have seen the blood trail." She frowned. *Poor, poor Melvin.* "I really think his death is about the grades."

"I'm sure you're right. But I'll bet once we confront her with what we've found, tell her we know the whole story, her reaction will tell us for sure."

Emma's fingers grazed the wound on her head. "How did she react when you got her to set up the newspaper? Did she say anything weird? I mean, couldn't we, oh, I don't know... set another trap or something?" She wished she had her phone with her so she could text Hunter, but in her excitement over the key, she'd left it in her desk. "Find really big guys with guns to back us up? I mean, I feel somewhat like that lion tamer sticking his head right down in the big ol'—"

Leslie waved her off. "Come on, ya wuss. I know Martha eats alone in her classroom. We can take 'er on." She flexed her biceps. "Check these puppies out. And you saw me take out that kid with the dodgeball, did you not?" She jumped around like Sugar Ray Leonard, popping her fists. "'What, shall we seek the lion in his den? And fright him there?'"

Slamming the locker door shut, Leslie started down the hallway on the balls of her feet, jabbing left and right. She hit a locker pretty hard, stopped for a minute and stuck her injured fist under her armpit, then she shook it off and continued jabbing and jumping.

Emma shook her head, made sure the padlock was secure, and sighed. "'Have you the lion's part written? Pray you, if it be, give it me; for I am slow of study.'"

Leslie stopped, turned around, her face aglow. "That's *Midsummer Night's Dream!* You are such a badass! Have I the lion's part written..." She chuckled. "Yeah, it is written that we kick its butt!"

She continued forward on the balls of her feet, careful when jabbing to avoid the metal lockers. Emma took a deep breath and trudged after her, worried that the only butt to be kicked was hers. *I wish Hunter were with us. Or Sir Toby. Or the Terminator.* Now might be a good time for any of that help to appear, but she saw no signs of life other than Leslie Ali. So she squared her shoulders, prepared for the task at hand, and followed her friend.

Social studies classrooms were on the other side of the commons. The brown tiles covering the wide expanse were dulled by the many feet that had traversed them during that day. Leslie's shoes made small squeaky noises and heel clicks as they hit the tiles with each jump and jab. As the two approached Martha's classroom, Leslie slowed to a sophisticated, worldly walk, which Emma tried in vain to adopt. Emma was pretty sure she looked more like a chicken with its neck stretched for chopping, but hey, points for effort.

Leslie rapped sharply on the door and heard Martha's muffled, "Enter."

They walked in, and Emma was immediately jealous of the many computers lining the walls of Martha's classroom. Martha did run the newspaper though—the computers were probably for her journalism classes. *English teachers have zero to one computer in their rooms. Shouldn't we have lots of computers too?* Otherwise, the room was about the same as hers in size and scope. She'd been too entranced by Martha's teaching style to notice her classroom when they ran in to get Adam Evanovich.

All the walls were covered in giant maps. They were rendered in bold Technicolor, and Emma wondered if this was Martha's way of reconstructing some of the vividness of her youth. She took a deep breath and exhaled slowly. *Guess we'll find out soon enough.*

"Hi, Martha!" said Leslie brightly. "How are you? Got a lot of work to do? You know, kids think we live here after school, and lookee here—guess we do! What are you doing? Any new headlines that make Charlie look like the douche he is? Your walls look great, by the way—where do you get these fantastic maps? They're all so pretty, pretty, pretty!"

Martha's and Emma's eyes got bigger and bigger as Leslie prattled on, launching into how great it was to have all those computers, all without taking a breath. She must be a little nervous about direct confrontation, after all. The thought made Emma feel a little more confident herself. *This is the second time I've seen SuperLeslie get rattled.*

Leslie finally stopped talking, if only to drag in a much-needed breath.

Martha hesitated, making sure Leslie was finished, before she spoke. "Goodness, Leslie, I'm not sure which of those questions to answer first—or if many of those were actual questions. Do you really want to know if I use wallpaper glue to put up the maps, or do you have another reason for being here? Until you came in for Adam, I'd never seen you on this side of the building. Then the special edition. Now here you are again. I'm not quite sure what to make of it." She arched her eyebrows and sat back in her seat.

Her red beehive hair was stacked tall, and Emma imagined it was quite long and pretty when unstacked. The color was brighter and less realistic than in the circus pictures, but maybe she used color from a bottle to cover up gray. In her dark-blue skirt and cardigan, and with those horrible oxford shoes, she really looked like a fifties relic. It was hard to reconcile this woman with the luminous acrobatic flyer from the photos. *But I did watch her teach. She was vibrant and luminous, remnants of Marlena.*

Leslie said, "We wanted to ask you about... we had some information about... uh, we needed to know..."

Martha cocked her head, puzzled. "Spit it out, dear."

Emma nudged Leslie, who turned glazed-over eyes her way. *Okay, never mind then.*

"Martha," said Emma. "Does the name 'Mickey' mean anything to you?"

What happened next was like dominoes falling. Martha's hairdo seemed to crumple, followed by her eyes, lips, chin, and shoulders. Even her chest bowed inward. Her lips trembled, and she turned glassy eyes toward the two women.

"Yes. It once meant very much to me actually." She sighed heavily, her gaze traveling to the corner of the room and back. Something flashed in her eyes. "Why do you ask? Who have you been talking to? Have you seen my father? I haven't seen Mickey since 1975; I keep telling Father that. My God in heaven, can't he let it go?"

Tears followed. She threw her elbows on the desk and buried her face in her hands. It was a disconcerting action coming from a woman who'd seemed equally as self-possessed as Leslie.

Well, Leslie was gibbering like an idiot, so who knew about self-possession? Emma came forward. "We haven't talked to your father. We found some letters written from you to him—well, from Marlena to Mickey. We didn't know it was you, though, until we found some pictures from Ripple and Rand's Glorious Traveling Fun Show."

Martha looked up and locked her bleak, moist eyes on Emma. "How did you know pictures from a circus were me? I don't look anything like I did then, and..." She stopped. "Oh. The bearded lady rumors. I started those, you know." A small smile built under the sadness. "Some people knew about the Flying Bonnies a long time ago. I thought, maybe, a red herring. Anyway, no one would ever believe I was Marlena Bonnie, darling of the circus circuit. People are more likely to disbelieve the bearded lady thing. Well, they love to spread the rumor, but still they don't believe it. No one goes looking into my past anyway."

She looked at Emma and Leslie. "No one except you, I guess. You said you had letters I wrote to Mickey? How did you get those? Did you..." She sucked in a breath. "Do you know Mickey? Is he here? I... oh God... is he in Pinewood? Where can I find him? What is he like? He kept my letters? I thought... oh God." Martha's eyes traveled back and forth between the two women, and her fingers patted at her cheekbones and traveled up to her forehead and down to her neck.

I think she's checking the firmness of her skin. Leslie's and Emma's eyes met over Martha's head.

What do you think? Emma asked with her expression.

I think she's either the greatest actress ever, or she doesn't know anything about Melvin, Leslie's replied.

Leslie came over and knelt on the other side of Martha's chair. "Mickey is Melvin McManus. I'm so sorry, Martha."

CHAPTER 30

MARTHA LOOKED CONFUSED. "MELVIN MC... oh God, you mean the custodian who was murdered? He *worked* here?" She started to cry again. "What was he doing here without telling me? Why would he come here and not tell me? I don't understand." Her hair listed to one side, and she hiccupped.

"He wanted to tell you," Emma said. "I don't think he got your letters for a long time—traveling with the circus and all that. He was learning to read and write so he could answer your letters first, then show himself. I'd guess he'd been searching for you for a long time."

"He didn't know how to read and write? Oh, I can't believe he was here and I didn't know it." The tears flowed down her cheeks. "Why would someone kill Mickey? He was the gentlest, sweetest man I know. Knew. Oh, this is horrible. How did you find out about him?"

"Martha, we have something to show you." Leslie stood and, along with Emma, helped Martha out the door. "We've been trying to find out who killed him. In the process, we've discovered some interesting things about his life. Maybe you could fill us in on your part in it."

Emma put an arm around Martha's waist to help her down the hall. The cardigan hid it, but she felt the tiny waist of Marlena Bonnie underneath. Ignoring some strange looks from student stragglers, the three headed up the left side of the commons and turned down the freshman hallway.

Leslie gently inserted the key in the padlock and opened the door. Martha stood before locker 723, her faltering hand reaching out to touch the photos inside. She pulled out the picture of the clowns and ran her fingers over the tallest funnyman they had tentatively identified as Melvin.

"His clown name was Mickey Manly," she said softly. "I never learned his real name—I didn't think he liked it. He was really quite private about his past, but the first time he came up to me, he pulled a flower from my ear and stuck it up his nose. I laughed so hard I thought I'd wet my leotard."

She sighed. "After a while, I was smitten. When he took off his makeup, that clinched it." She turned wistful eyes toward Emma. "There was no picture of Melvin McManus in the newspaper—just an obituary. Did he still have those beautiful blue eyes and that dimple? And that smile... oh my, Mickey had a smile that could melt ice."

Emma and Leslie looked at each other. How to handle this answer? Did they tell her he had been an alcoholic mess when he died? *Would that make it easier for her?*

Emma made the decision. "He looked just as you describe him, only older. A little gray at the temples, you know." She looked at Leslie and shrugged.

"Why did you two stop seeing each other?" asked Leslie. "Your letters seemed... well, here, you can read them again." She handed the packet to Martha. "And he, well, he was pursuing a whole new education in order to see you again. He probably had to search high and low to find 'Martha Bonaventure.' Is that your real name?"

Martha nodded. "'The Flying Bonaventures' has too many syllables—my father gave us our stage name. Mickey knew I loved Colorado though. I told him that once. We'd had a show in this little town called Grand Junction. It was beautiful, but I wanted to be at a higher altitude. So it's a little bit like flying every day, yes?" She smiled. "He knew I'd come live in Colorado someday, so from there, he probably had a long process of elimination. Reading phone books. I wonder who did that for him? The only Martha Bonaventure you can find on the Internet was born in 1926—found that one day on Ancestry.com." Two tears dropped off her chin and hit the floor. She gestured to the pictures. "Can I have some of these?"

Emma handed her the key. "You can have them all. Keep them like this, if you want, or clean out the locker and take them home."

Martha looked at the key, thought for a moment, and shut the door and padlock, leaving the shrine just as it was. They started back to her room.

"I grew up with the circus," Martha explained. "But my father was very opposed to the circus lifestyle. He kept us in our trailer as much as possible when we weren't practicing or performing, and we received extensive schooling behind those small walls. Alas"—she sighed—"not much schooling as to the world around us.

"My mother ran off with another performer, you see, and my father thought that our transient lifestyle, or some such nonsense, drove her to infidelity. So he never allowed us much contact with those outside our family."

"Do you think that was the cause of her infidelity?" That came from Leslie, who had some experience in this field.

Well, we've both had some experience there.

"No. I think my father was the cause, if you want to know the truth. He was a difficult man to live with—very arrogant, narrow minded. Plus I think, well, I think my mother fell in love. While I don't understand how she could have left me and my sisters, loving Mickey was a whole different plane of consciousness for me, and it helped me get in her head a bit."

"Why did your father stay with the circus, then?" asked Emma. "If he felt it caused him so much pain and created such worry?"

"I don't think he felt there was anything else he could do. He was self-educated—no degrees or pieces of paper to make him credible in business. Also, well... he was excellent at the trapeze, an artist in the real sense of the word. We all were very good—it was a natural way to make a living." She stopped for a minute, thoughtful. "I guess that sounds funny, doesn't it? It probably seems unnatural to most, but to us it was like breathing." Martha stopped in front of her classroom door. "I miss it sometimes, flying through the air, relying on someone else to catch me. I haven't relied on anyone that way for a long time."

The two women followed her inside.

"So what happened? I mean, why'd you leave?" asked Emma.

Leslie chimed in. "And what happened with Mickey?"

"My sister Alisa was paralyzed," said Martha. "She fell through the net. Oh, Ripple and Rand wasn't what you'd call a fleabag operation, but they did know how to cut corners. One of their money savers was to have the net repaired and re-repaired instead of buying a new one. So during one performance, my father missed a catch and she fell right through to the ground. She's here in Pinewood now, actually. She lives with me." She smiled wistfully. "We take pretty good care of each other.

"Anyway, I couldn't bring myself to go up the ladder again. My father and my other sister kept going until the mid-eighties, but I was finished after my sister's accident. I left the circus and went to Utah to get my teaching degree. Alisa and I have been here ever since. Hang on, I like to lock up when I'm not here. I think I should take a walk."

They stood quietly, and Emma pondered the forgotten life of the Bonnies and Mickey Manly.

Martha turned off computer monitors and straightened desks. She looked like a deflated balloon, red hairdo askew with a couple of strands coming loose and hanging down. Emma and Leslie remained silent. Emma knew Martha was preparing to tell them about Mickey and sensed she wasn't sure she was ready.

Martha went to her desk, sat, and took a deep breath. "After the meeting I told you about, the one where Mickey had me in stitches, we started meeting secretly. I would leave the trailer when my father was asleep, and Mickey and I would go behind the lion's cage. Rufus, the tamer you saw in the pictures, was a father figure to both of us and a hopeless romantic, so he had a place always laid out. Oh, we talked about everything: the other performers, my father, what we thought it was like out in the real world, even what we wanted to do when we left the circus. Together, of course." Her voice broke. "We were always going to do it together."

Emma couldn't stand it. "So what on earth happened? Why didn't you leave together after your sister's accident?"

Martha sighed heavily. "I think it was my father. He knew I was leaving with Alisa, and he… I guess he did something, had Mickey sent away for some reason or other. All I know is I couldn't find Mickey to tell him I was leaving. Since supposedly my father didn't even know we were together, I couldn't make a big fuss about it. I don't know. I look back and feel like such a fool; I don't know why I cared so much about what my father thought. He's a bitter old man now—we hardly talk. I should have stayed until I could find Mickey." Her eyes were bright with loss and unshed tears.

Leslie hugged her. "You were young and pretty sheltered, from what it sounds like. I would have done the same thing."

"You would?" She sniffed. "But now look at me. I'm an old spinster, and Mickey and I never had a chance. And now he's gone."

Leslie looked at a loss. "You're a great teacher, Martha. And look at what you've done for your sister. I guess all you can do is be thankful you had a great love for a while and take some comfort in the knowledge that someone loved you so much they spent a lifetime preparing to be with you again."

Martha snuffled and nodded.

Emma didn't nod. She straightened up and threw her shoulders back. "What a crock of utter baloney! It's better to have loved and lost? Come on, Leslie, spare me the platitudes. This sucks! Ah'd be furious if I were you, Martha! Vengeance on the world, Ah say!"

Leslie looked at Emma as if she had sprouted a second head. "My, my, the little Southern belle speaks up. You're right of course. It's completely unfair, and crappy, and there's not much we can do for it now except honor Melvin's memory and find his killer. Come on, Martha. At least we can spend the last ten minutes of lunchtime downing Mrs. Albert's latest gourmet creation. I don't know if that wreaks vengeance, but it sure feels righteous going down. You game?"

Martha gulped, straightened her beehive, and nodded.

"Plus we've still got two murders to solve," said Emma. "Maybe you could help us there as well."

The two friends helped Martha up from her desk and headed for the cafeteria.

O, that a man might know
The end of this day's business ere it come?
But it sufficeth that the day will end,
And then the end is known.

—*Julius Caesar V.i.122.5*

CHAPTER 31

Friday evening, September 4

AFTER SOME MORE HUFFING AND puffing about whether Hunter's special investigator status was really enough to bring himself and civilians to this dangerous operation, Detective Carl Niome ordered Emma, Leslie, and Hunter to stay in the back of the teachers' lounge, where they couldn't be seen by someone entering the office. He and the barrel-chested Hulk Hogan of an officer—otherwise known as Ted—took strategic positions closer to the action.

The three sat at the Lounge Lizard table in the back of the teachers' lounge, under a poster of Albert Einstein that said, "Great Spirits Often Encounter Violent Opposition from Mediocre Minds." It was nine o'clock, and the sun was setting over the long couch that backed up to the picture window. Emma watched the light hit names on the wooden mailbox holes as it went down: Bonaventure, Dixon, Lovett, Parker, Patterson, Wells.

She turned to look at Hunter, who was facing away from the sunset. His nose was larger than it looked from the front, which made Emma find his profile strong and made his long eyelashes anything but feminine. He and Leslie were deep in whispered conversation; she was pretty sure they were discussing how to save the day if Carl Niome turned out to be totally incompetent.

Leslie's voice was muted, but her hands shouted, darting and jabbing as she laid out the plan. Her blond hair bobbed in silent excitement. Emma gazed fondly at her two new friends, and when they turned toward her simultaneously and grinned, she felt as if she were in the happy glow of a toothpaste commercial. And not just any toothpaste commercial, but the super-whitening kind. She grinned back and scooted closer.

"So where are the detective and the big guy?" she whispered.

"I think Niome said something about hiding in a locker right by the office's entrance," said Hunter.

"Which his friend, of course, couldn't hide one little pinkie toe in," whispered Leslie. "So I'm not sure where he's hiding—possibly in the office itself, behind the far file cabinets."

"Wow, I sure hope we don't have to wait too long. Carl's probably getting unbelievable cramps from being stuffed in a locker."

"One can only hope," Leslie crooned.

By eleven, the three sat silent and bored. Emma was still turning over events of the day in her head. First, the strange reaction she'd had in her sophomore classes from some of those Shakespeare scenes, then the Martha Bonaventure/Melvin McManus love story that was never to be.

Hunter got up to fetch paper and a pen for hangman or tic-tac-toe, some real intellectual game that would keep them awake. He stopped at his mailbox, pulled out a magazine he must've stashed there, and idly flipped through the pages. Emma was strangely ecstatic to see it was the *New Yorker* and not *Sports Illustrated*.

He's so completely not what he appeared to be when we first met. What did Melvin say? "It ain't what it looks like, but what's really there." Hmmm. The question isn't what you look at, but what you see. She leaned over to Leslie. "Ah'm feeling somethin' pretty strongly right now, and I'd like your opinion."

Leslie's eyebrows rose. "What are you feeling, Grasshoppah? Enlighten me."

Emma thought. "I know you hate Charlie Foreman, and everything I've seen and heard about him says he's a total pig. But I just, I just can't see him killing another person. That angry voice I heard last week? Other than sounding pretty masculine, the voice didn't... didn't *elocute* like Charlie. It was much more formal and uptight sounding. What was the phrase I heard? 'Destiny is not a matter of chance, it's a matter of choice'? Have you ever heard anything like that come out of Charlie's mouth?"

"I'll admit, it does sound a little stuffy for Clown Charlie." She grinned. "So who are you thinking? None of the other coaches at this school are oratory superstars either, except maybe our friend Hunter here."

"Julia Ramsay and Arnold Ortiz did a scene from *The Merchant of Venice* today," Emma said, "and Bassanio had a line, something about beauty obscuring... obscuring..."

Leslie struck a pose on the chair. "'What plea so tainted and corrupt, but being seasoned with a gracious voice obscures the show of evil?' Yes, that's about shyster lawyers in thousand-dollar suits who—"

Emma held up a finger to stop her. "Yes, yes. Ah know what it means. But as for what it *means*... what if we're barking up the wrong tree? What if Melvin's death isn't about sports at all, but about something else?"

"Didn't the angry voice say it was about sports?" Leslie asked.

"That's just it! The voice only said that the person he was talking to— Janice, we think—had done it for sports before. Not that *this* demand was about sports." Her brain was racing, and she had to concentrate to keep her voice quiet. "Hang on, hang on." She pulled out her smart phone. "Oh, Ah know Ah'm a slave to technology, beholden twenty-four, seven, but Ah just need to Google this..." Her fingers tapped furiously on the little touch screen, and she stared at the results for a moment before looking at Leslie, triumphant. "Look at this! There are two parts to this adage by William Jennings Bryan: 'Destiny is not a matter of chance, it is a matter of choice. It is not a thing to be waited for, it is a thing to be achieved.'" Emma's face glowed. "Do you remember who said that second half last week? Someone who could easily be not waiting for destiny, but taking—"

"Taking no chances on how it gets achieved!" Leslie said. "You're so right. Why didn't we see this last week? I can't believe we missed it. How about another *Merchant of Venice* item? 'Truth will come to light; murder cannot be hid long.'"

Hunter wandered back to the table as the excitement built. "What, what have you figured out? I swear, you two, it's possible I could be 'twere'd' and 'thou'ed' to death by the end of this year, it's—"

He stopped short when they heard a muffled *thunk* from the office. All three froze to listen.

Suddenly—pandemonium. Yells muted by the small distance sounded as if they came through gauze, but whatever had crashed to the floor was loud and sharp. Emma gripped Hunter's arm; Leslie looked ready to charge down the short stairs.

"No, wait," hissed Hunter. "Listen for a minute."

A few more thuds and scuffles. Ted was yelling police-type things, like "Freeze" and "Hands over your head," and as the ambient noise faded, they heard an out-of-breath Niome reading someone their Miranda rights.

He needs to work out. He only ran from the locker to the office.

The detective came up the stairs, face flushed. "Come on in, you guys! We got him!"

Leslie and Emma exchanged puzzled glances as they followed. *Him? There's no way. I was so sure Charlie couldn't kill someone...*

The three went cautiously down the stairs. The main office was a mess. The crash they'd heard was Abigail's computer monitor, now in pieces on the floor. A disheveled Carl posed with his arms crossed while Ted held a little guy by the head. The little man was handcuffed, sweaty, and thoroughly miserable. He looked about as threatening as a five-year-old with his hand in the cookie jar and about as ready to cry.

Leslie walked up to him. "Lewis Fillmore! Your wife making you and Janice do all the dirty work? You're too short to have bonked Melvin over the top of his head, though. I bet Ophelia did that, didn't she?"

Carl held up Leslie's gradebook, its smooth red cover marred only by the name Parker. "Caught him red-handed. No pun intended. Didn't take too many of my awesome police skills to subdue him; he was sweaty and nervous already. Not much of a career criminal." He dropped into a chair, still breathing hard.

Ted nodded. "Yeah! We got 'im good."

Leslie marched over and took the gradebook from Carl. "I'll take that, thank you, and Camilla is really gonna have to keep that B-plus. Damned overreaching homicidal helicopter parenting."

Lewis opened his mouth but was interrupted by a banshee scream from the doorway. Ophelia Fillmore flew into the office, brown trench coat swinging behind her, holding her hands out in front of her. Holding a gun.

A gun! Emma twitched, fighting an urge to shout "Hit the deck!" and throw herself to the floor.

Ted reached for his weapon, but Ophelia stopped him with a warning look and threatening gesture. Detective Niome looked around in confusion, apparently missing his gun altogether. Leslie and Hunter held very still.

Ophelia Fillmore looked just as Emma remembered her, with the exception of a few hairs coming loose from the bun on the top of her head. She held the gun tight in both hands and kept pointing it in turns at all the people in the room, including her husband.

"I should have done this myself!" she spat at Lewis. "It seems I'm the only one able to aid in the perpetuation of my legacy. You"—she shook the gun at Leslie—"you have no idea what an incredible being you've met in my Camilla. She's going to do unheard-of things, and you tried to destroy it! A B-plus. Well, that's simply unacceptable for a legacy such as her. Anything less than an A is completely unacceptable. I had to fix it every time, don't you see? You couldn't possibly comprehend—"

As she babbled, Leslie took a small, careful step forward. "Legacy? Being? You're talking about your *daughter*, Ophelia. A person. A girl. Someone who's certainly capable of doing unheard-of things all on her own."

Ophelia stared at her.

"Or not. But killing someone over a grade? And a pretty good one, at that?" Leslie looked at her two friends for confirmation.

They nodded. A B-plus, pretty darn good, sure.

"There are many reasons one could be forced to kill," said Ophelia. She kept aiming between Leslie and the big police officer. "A successful legacy, that's a remarkably good reason, if you want to know. Better than many others. Passion or money, jealousy or anger; those pale in comparison, don't you think? Fashioning superiority in humanity, oh, that's an excellent reason."

Leslie said, "I see no real evidence of humanity here, killing Melvin because he showed up at the wrong time. And what about Janice? You roped Janice into your harebrained scheme by blackmailing her with some bad choices she'd already made. She was helping with the sports grade changing, wasn't she?"

Ophelia kept the gun trained on them and said nothing.

"I see no evidence of humanity anywhere," scolded Leslie, and she stood tall and angry.

Ophelia cocked the hammer and pointed it right at Leslie's chest. Leslie sucked in a breath but didn't budge. Emma was standing at Ophelia's right, almost behind her, and she noticed a gun behind the computer on the left desk—Detective Niome's gun. Emma was closest to it. *Oh, no. I'm closest!*

Leslie and Ophelia were engaged in a tense standoff, staring each other down, and the rest of the room held its breath. Emma inched slowly toward the desk, not sure what she'd do when she got there. Hunter stood next to Leslie, facing Ophelia, and he caught her subtle movement. His eyes widened; he shook his head slightly.

Hunter, what else can we do? This whacked-out woman has already killed twice for her daughter. What else can we do?

He shook his head again, then his shoulders slumped. Carl and Ted were right behind Leslie, directly in the line of fire. Emma was the only one. She lunged for the gun, seized it, and pointed it at Ophelia.

Then a few things happened at once.

Leslie's eyes got really big, and a screaming blur shot into the office, waving its hands and yelling "No!"

Ophelia swung around as the shape threw itself on her back. Emma heard a bang before she straightened and pointed the gun with shaking hands toward the small mess of bodies now on the floor—Ophelia, Hunter, and Edward Dixon, the blur.

Leslie whirled around, clearly shouting, but Emma couldn't hear her over the ringing in her ears. Emma stood over the squirming pile of people, but she was afraid to aim at the struggling group for fear she'd hit someone else. Her hand trembled. Hunter's arm came out with Ophelia's gun in it, although he couldn't get up since Edward's lanky body was sprawled over them, his hands and legs spread like a snow angel.

"Get off!" said Hunter. "Get off, I can't breathe."

Carl and Leslie bent to help Edward and Hunter, but Ophelia lay still on the floor.

Ted gently pried Emma's fingers from the gun, and she backed away.

"Is she shot?" Carl bent down and felt Ophelia's neck for a pulse.

Her eyes were open and she seemed to be breathing, but she was mute. No one looked to be shot. Carl stood her up and read her Miranda rights while he handcuffed her, and Ted held his gun trained on her until she was restrained. Lewis Fillmore watched from a chair in the back.

He must have decided enough was enough. I mean, look what happened to him when he was loyal to her.

Lewis, who had never talked much, was a real motormouth compared to his now-silent wife. "Remember how that car crashed into the school a few years ago? Nobody knew who did it, remember? Well, that was Melvin. I was his AA sponsor, and he told me all about it, and I told Ophelia even though I wasn't supposed to—I know. She used it against him. Used it to help Camilla. This didn't help Camilla though, did it? I see..."

He continued to babble as he and his razor-postured wife were escorted toward the doorway by Carl and Ted, who seemed incapable of even monosyllabic speech. Ophelia glared at them all on her way out.

Emma, Leslie, Hunter, and Edward shared a group hug.

"Edward, you third Musketeer, you," Leslie praised. "You and Emma saved the day!"

Edward beamed with pride. "I was in the library, doing work on a new program I've created: The Melvin McManus Adult Literacy Program."

Leslie threw an arm around Emma's shoulder. "Ah, Cromwell, I charge thee, fling away ambition: by that sin fell the angels.'"

"You're tellin' me," said Emma.

Fortune shall cull forth
Out of one side her happy minion
To whom in favour she shall give the day
And kiss him with a glorious victory.

—*King John, II.i.391–4*

CHAPTER 32

Monday, September 7

AFTER A BLISSFULLY UNEVENTFUL WEEKEND—LESLIE slept (or so she told Emma), while Emma, Martha, and Hunter helped Edward with plans for his new literacy program—Leslie and Emma took advantage of the Labor Day holiday and went out to breakfast on Monday. Cinnamon crunch bagels and honey cream cheese were the order of the day for Emma, and Leslie got a sundried tomato bagel with cream cheese and lox.

"*Lox?*" Emma asked. "*Yuck.*" They sat across from each other at the bagel shop, both quiet and introspective.

Leslie picked at the pink meat on her bagel. "What are you thinking about?"

Emma sucked some extra cream cheese off her fork. "Melvin. And Martha. And the Fillmores. It just seems so unfair, you know, that Melvin and Martha never got a chance to be together. And why? I'll tell you why. No good reason at all. I mean, we don't know why Melvin left home so early, but a questionable home situation probably factored in. Martha's father sounds like a narrow-minded prig, and Ophelia... well, she's a breed of her own. But Ophelia should just be a harmless, crazy breed, not a deadly one. I don't understand."

Leslie sighed. "Me neither, sweetie. I don't think it's accurate to cross it off with a 'life's not fair' platitude, but I'm not sure what else to do. Feel as vindicated as you can, I guess, by the work we did to solve the murders. And maybe now that Martha knows she wasn't some rejected loser, she can open up to the possibility of a love life."

Emma said, "Maybe we should set her up with Edward."

Leslie's hands flew up in horror. "Oh God. Or maybe we could just throw her into a blender and start pushing all the different buttons at once."

"You're right." Emma giggled. "He's doing better though, don't you think? But for now, we'll look outside of school to find someone for Martha." Checking the clock on the Durango Bagels wall, she smoothed her hair. "Hunter said he wanted us both at the school office by ten thirty, but he didn't say why."

Leslie collected their trash on a tray. "Okee dokee, artichokee. Let's go right now; there's something I wanna do there first."

When they got to the school, Leslie took Emma to the dusty closet located in the southernmost end of the school, between the library and the freshman hall. They loaded up on home economics books from 1953, staggering away with a full box apiece. Lumbering down the hallway, they took a left through the commons and out the door next to the gym, then they continued to the Dumpster. Leslie took obvious joy in pulling out the books, one by one, and flinging them into the garbage as Emma egged her on. When all the books were gone and the lid was slammed, Emma took the boxes and broke them down for recycling while Leslie wiped her hands in a gesture of satisfaction.

Emma looked at the space between the Dumpster and weight room, where she'd heard Ophelia and Janice conspiring. "Did I really hear them talking less than two weeks ago? I feel like so much has happened since then."

Leslie nodded. "So much *has* happened. Think about it: two murders solved, some teacher education-by-fire for you, Grasshoppah, plus a romance that'll go down in history."

Emma grinned. "Are you referring to Melvin and Martha, Hunter and me, or you and whoever this young guy is I still haven't met?"

Dodging the question once again, Leslie replied, "One thing we didn't see is Charlie Foreman getting any just desserts. What about the grade-changing scandal and the sports? Adam Butler did see that happening last year. Did Hunter tell you anything?"

The women opened the door and headed for the office. "He told me he had a late meeting with CHSSA on Saturday after we finished at the school. I don't know what happened."

The office was empty.

"Always strange being here when school's closed," said Leslie. "I'm used to Abigail bustling about and the phones ringing off the hook."

But the phone was silent, the room still as a ghost town. Leslie shrugged, leapt to hit the sign, and headed up the stairs. Emma took one more look around the now-clean-and-quiet crime scene then followed Leslie up the stairs.

"Surprise!"

The yell reverberated off the walls. The teachers' lounge was a circus. Literally. A rainbow of balloons covered the ceiling, and the announcements and posters that usually adorned the walls were covered by colorful cardboard clowns whose faces showed every emotion on the spectrum. Paper tablecloths covered with lumbering elephants and wide-mouthed lions and tigers petticoated the tables, and the coaches' table in the back had a long rectangular cake. Emma couldn't see what it said because of all the people. She beamed at Abigail, Nathan Farrar the principal, all the cooks, Hunter, Martha, Edward, and even her neighbor Delilah Thornberry.

Martha came forward to hug them both. "You two might've slept in this morning, but not everybody did!"

"This is so wonderful, Martha. Who did it?" said Emma.

Martha pushed forward a reluctant Abigail Patterson.

"We're so proud of you all," whispered Abigail. Emma and Leslie leaned forward to catch her words. "You and Hunter and Martha and Edward did the school a great service by catching Melvin's and Janice's killer. Thank you." She hugged them, her birdlike frame belied by her powerful embrace. Then she turned and cupped her mouth with her hands. "Let's have some cake! Come on, Bluelight Special on the cake!

Abigail brought her hands down, turned back to the duo with a smile as sweet as a kitten, and led them to the back of the room. Leslie gave Emma an I-told-you-it-was-her look.

The cake had white frosting almost hidden under a whirling circus tent. The striped tent started at the top of the cake and widened down around the sides. The tent opening revealed a miniature trapeze artist with bright-red hair flying off of a swing into a miniature clown car. The two white corners at the top of the cake had Emma's and Leslie's names, along with Martha's, Edward's, and Hunter's.

"I hope it's chocolate inside," whispered Leslie.

Nathan Farrar approached them, Delilah Thornberry trailing behind him. Her long skirt was a multicolored batik print, and her white crocheted vest almost reached her knees. Nathan wore his normal button-up, khakis, and crazy tie—this one had a circus motif. He was probably fifteen years younger than Delilah, but he was obviously taken with her.

Well, good for him. Social conventions be darned.

Delilah threaded her arm through his.

"Ladies," Nathan said, "you've done the school a great service, although if you talk to those policemen over there…" He nodded to the corner by the mailboxes, where Detective Niome and Officer Ted stood uncomfortably, sipping punch. Emma hadn't seen them when she came in. "You put yourselves in some unnecessary danger. Maybe—"

Delilah broke in. "Oh, quiet, you." She disentangled herself from his arm and gave the women hugs. "You are, like, the greatest gals ever. Nathan tried to tell me how you figured it out, but I'm afraid he didn't really explain it all that well."

"Emma figured it out," said Leslie. "She's Miss Marple and Nancy Drew all in one."

Emma blushed. "Well, it was just luck really. See, Ah was in Leslie's room when Ophelia Fillmore came to parent–teacher conferences and threw that hissy fit over her daughter's grade. Then Leslie was helping me learn the computer gradebook, and Ah saw her hard copy as well, which she kept hidden in her room. *Then*—" She smacked her lips, getting into it.

Delilah and Nathan were joined by a couple of secretaries, Mrs. Albert the cook, and a man with long curly hair Emma didn't quite recognize.

"I heard a meeting between Ophelia and Janice, though I didn't know it was Ophelia and Janice, where they planned to change her daughter's grade," Emma said.

"She'd had Melvin doing that for her daughter's whole high school career," Nathan said. "I guess he did something five years ago that made him vulnerable to blackmail." He nodded to the corner of the room. "Carl? Can you tell these lovely ladies what you told me?"

Carl glanced at Leslie, his posture rigid. "Ah, sure. Y'all know Melvin was a drinker? Well, one time he fell off the wagon big time. He wanted to go back to the school for some letters, I guess? And he was so drunk and disoriented, he stole a car from his elderly neighbor, Effie Fridley, and crashed it into the school. Remember that?"

All the people Emma assumed were long-time residents nodded.

"We knew it was Effie's car of course, because Melvin panicked and left it there and Effie reported it missing the next morning, but there was no evidence tracing it back to Melvin."

Emma knew Leslie called Carl clueless, and now she agreed. *Why wouldn't Carl have questioned everyone who worked at the school?*

"Anyway," Carl continued, "he told his AA sponsor, Lewis Fillmore."

Leslie leaned into Emma's side and whispered, "We know why *Lewis* was a drinker, anyway."

"And then he told Ophelia, even though that's a huge no-no for AA sponsors. So every time Camilla Fillmore got a B, she made Melvin change it."

"Until Melvin finally had had enough and started refusing," Emma said. "They found Janice to change her composition grade—"

"But Melvin was trying to get Janice to stop too," Leslie explained. She told the group about the note she'd discovered at Janice's house, then she spent five minutes describing how she'd found Janice's body. Instead of showing herself in the favorable light Emma thought most humans preferred, Leslie took glee in describing her vomitous reaction in Technicolor detail, concluding with, "And when Melvin showed up in the office that night, Ophelia must've decided to eliminate him as a problem."

"Then Janice had a change of heart as well," Emma added, "which is why Ophelia went to her house and killed her."

"That's right," Carl said, seeming eager to take over the story again. "Lewis has been a huge blabbermouth since we arrested the Fillmores. If Ophelia thought she might get away with this, she ain't thinkin' it now. Hey..." He paused as if he was just now remembering another aspect to the investigation. The former high school football star looked around the room in confusion. "But what about the sports grades? Hunter?"

Hunter winked at Emma. "Only students were involved. Thanks to Adam Butler's witness, we reapproached those office aides, and one of them confessed. They were part of a crowd of athletes, and two or three of them really, really wanted to stay eligible."

Nathan said, "I guess it's good we didn't win any championships last year, huh? Or none of those players got scholarships for college?" He chuckled. "Heh, heh, I never thought I'd be happy to say our football team stinks. That could've been a waaaay bigger mess than it is."

"And those students just wanted to play," Emma said. "Ophelia wanted much bigger things for her daughter that would require good grades. Ah just can't imagine what people will do over the prospect of a good college or professional sports."

"A lot, apparently," said someone in the back.

Emma loved having an audience. "Yes, sir, a lot. So between the break-ins in Leslie's room and the whole grade-mania thing that kept smackin' me right in the face"—her Southern accent got heavier with the storytelling—"Ah listened to some students quoting Shakespeare with two themes of killing for love and things being not what they seemed."

Leslie jumped in. "And we all thought it was Charlie until Emma figured it out. Oh, I don't know what this tells you about our resident Southern belle, but she's a genius at figuring out strange behavior. 'She swore, in faith 'twas strange, 'twas passing strange.'"

"Come on," said Emma. "That's not enough for anyone to identify the play. Give me some more."

"Fine, fine, young Grasshoppah. Here's some more: 'Twas pitiful, 'twas passing pitiful; she wished she had not heard it, yet she wished that heaven had made her such a man.'" Leslie raised her finger to the right side of her upper lip. "What do you think? How now, brown cow?"

"I think it's *Othello*, and you know I never could've figured it out until I learned all about strange behavior from you. Brown cow." Emma smiled at her friend.

Hunter shook his head at them. "Hey, thou amateur sleuths extraordinaire, let's have some cake. 'Twere the next stop on this magical mystery tour. Hunter Wells, Act One, Scene One." He'd been sitting at the cake table, listening with interest even though he already knew the story. "But while we eat, tell them how I was a suspect." He grinned. "Go ahead, tell them."

Emma shrugged. "Keep in mind, we had nothin' to work with. We were startin' from skee-ware one. But we went to the school and recreated the crime scene. Based on where Melvin's head injury was, we knew someone like me couldn't have reached his head."

Leslie chuckled. "So our only clue originally"—she gestured to herself, Edward, Martha, Hunter, even Nathan—"was that our killer was tall. Illuminating, eh?"

Everybody laughed.

Delilah joined in, ever the concerned granola lady. "What's going to happen to their daughter?"

"Camilla's not a bad kid, really," said Leslie. "A little full of herself, but you could say that about how many teenagers?"

Emma sighed. "Lewis has a sister who's going to take her in until she's eighteen. Anyway, we're so glad we could bring some closure to Melvin's death." She locked eyes with Martha. "He was a good guy. I'm so sad I only knew him in hindsight, as it were."

Martha nodded slightly, eyes misty but mouth smiling.

Leslie got her quoting look. "'Praising what is lost makes the remembrance dear.'" She shook her head and looked at the floor, a ham 'til the end.

The young man with curly brown hair materialized behind Leslie. "Well, call him hither. We are reconciled." He grinned.

"Emma and Hunter, everyone else, I'd like you to meet Rain Thornberry." Leslie grinned like the cat who ate the canary. "He owns the curbside recycling program but also dabbles in volunteerism at summer Shakespeare in the Park."

The man extended his hand. He had dark, flashing eyes and a crooked smile reminiscent of Kevin Costner. *The boy toy! The boy toy is Delilah's son!*

"Rainshadow!" Emma exclaimed. "I've seen pictures of you at your mom's house."

"I know; she's told me all about you," replied Rain. "It's so funny to hear my real name from someone other than my mom." He gestured toward Delilah, who was thick in whispered conversation with Nathan Farrar. "She thinks you guys are saving the world over here. In your classrooms, I mean."

Leslie squeezed his shoulder. He wasn't dressed like his mom. He looked more like a biker guy with his torn jeans and a leather vest over a white T-shirt.

"Anyway, I wanted to say congratulations. Everyone here's real proud of you." He stood. "I've gotta go to work—climate change waits for no man. Nice meeting you all."

Leslie waved at his retreating figure, then she dropped her head onto a yawning lion printed on the tablecloth. "My, my, my, he's cute. I think younger men are da bomb."

Emma laughed. "Well, I don't know if all's well that ends well exactly, but let's have some cake and make it so!"

Everyone clapped, and Abigail grabbed a cake knife.

Edward approached Emma and Leslie's table. "I wanted to tell you I'm so glad you're here." His toe twisted into the floor. "I miss Melvin, and I'll never understand the appeal of the *Twilight* teen series, but maybe I won't go work for the post office after all."

They grinned at each other, and Leslie gave them both cake.

Under the white frosting, it was chocolate.

There's a divinity that shapes our ends,
Rough-hew them how we will.

—*Hamlet V.2.10–11*

EPILOGUE

WHAT A WONDERFUL PLACE TO *live*. Emma crossed the glossy brown tiles of the commons after the party. *I wish Hannah could see this. I wish she could come visit our great town of Pinewood.* She shook off a sad memory before it could arise and retrieved her original train of thought. *I really think Pinewood's the place for me. Oh, yuck, that sounds like a bad bumper sticker.* She laughed.

She stopped in her room, since she'd left so quickly on Friday, and looked around. The flowery decor seemed homey and welcoming, and Shakespeare's bust smiled at her from the desk. Okay, it didn't smile exactly, but it certainly seemed happy to see her.

There was something else on her desk besides the clutter of papers she'd already accumulated. Emma got closer, curious.

On her desk was a giant Hershey bar. A note was attached, words penciled carefully on a piece of folded computer paper.

She unfolded the note.

Dear Miss Lovett,

Thank you for teaching us so much already, about Shakespeare and more.

You started on the first day with some advice for me and my goofball friends. I took your advice, and now Julia Ramsay is going to Homecoming with me!

Have an awesome long weekend!

—Arnold Ortiz

Emma grinned, folded the note, and sat down to prepare some lessons for Tuesday.

ACKNOWLEDGMENTS

To the Red Adept Publishing Acquisitions Team, thank you for seeing the potential in this book and the series and taking a chance I could reach it. Suzanne Warr, it was such a great experience having you as my content editor. I learned so much about the editing process—what a challenge you face! Cassie Cox, you definitely faced challenges in being *my* line editor. You showed great patience and panache. Thank you both for guiding me to a much better book than the one I started out with. Streetlight Graphics, what a great cover! You created an amazing visual for this series; I know it will draw in so many readers. I'd like to thank the other authors in the RAP house as well—you've given me much guidance, good ideas, feedback, and funny and/or inspiring posts about writing. To the entire RAP family: you are all rock stars!

Nancy Pickard, Frederick Ramsay, Matthew Pallamary, Michele Scott, and Michelle Gable: thank you so much for offering to use your stellar talents as writers to help promote or "blurb" this book. I hope to repay the favor.

Shawn Clingman, you are my superhuman superstar superhero. Your input and support began when I FIRST started writing this book clear back in 1999 and continued to the all-day Colorado powwow which helped shape that major rewrite near the end. Your help is beyond invaluable. You know I heart you so much, and I value our friendship like mad. Thank you thank you thank you.

To everyone who helped me with the minutiae of creating a novel: sentence structures, names, plot twists, and questions ad nauseam: Carol Bloch, Shawn Clingman, Sandy Haulman, Leslie Anderson, Lisa Burns, Erle Reid, Jim Gusich, Melissa Fischer, Joe Holmes, Larry Meredith, Kirby Richardson, Cindi Pierce, Kim Orozco, Jaxon Crow-

Mickle for the "Chalkboard Outlines" stroke of genius, and everyone who participated in the contest at the 2015 Southern California Writer's Conference. You all kept my brain turning and will keep it churning for future books in the series. Thank you!

Finally, to my husband, "Jim Darling" Jim Gusich. The outlook you have about our mission to support our family's dreams has allowed me to go after this achievement called "Writer" with all the passion I have, and I am so grateful. You may never know what a gift you've given to me and to our sons as they experience this support and encouragement. Thank you. I love you to infinity and beyond—to quote Buzz Lightyear—and because that is much further than to the moon and back. Speaking of our sons, I want to acknowledge them here, because I can't believe I get to do that! I waited so long for you, Grey and Griffen, and you guys were definitely worth the wait. How long will I love you? That's right, always. The fact that you are such wonderful little boys makes this writing job more rewarding, too. I hope you are half as proud of me as I am of you.

This book is dedicated to my father, Donald Wilson Bowles, who died in 2012 but whose influence is still so present in my life. His love for books and the language and culture of books exceeded that of anyone else I have ever known. I can only aspire. I'd like to acknowledge him and my mom, Shelley Rochelle "Rachel" Frick Bowles, for being THOSE parents. You know those parents—the ones for whom every achievement of their children, no matter how small, is placed on a stage and oohed and aahed over so much that those children will succeed no matter what. That kind of unconditional love and support is cherished by those children, every day. Thank you. I love you both so much.

To anyone who's reading this book, thank *you*. I'm so excited to share this story.

Kelley Kaye

ABOUT THE AUTHOR

Kelley Kaye taught high school English and drama for twenty years, but her love for storytelling dates back to creating captions for her high school yearbook. Maybe back to the tales she created around her Barbie and Ken—whatever the case, the love's been around for a long time.

Kelley is married to this amazing man who cooks for her, and they have two funny and wonderful sons. She lives in Southern California.

CPSIA information can be obtained
at www.ICGtesting.com
Printed in the USA
BVOW03s1836100717
488994BV00001B/57/P